Vonnegut 35502

Hocus pocus

HOCUS POCUS

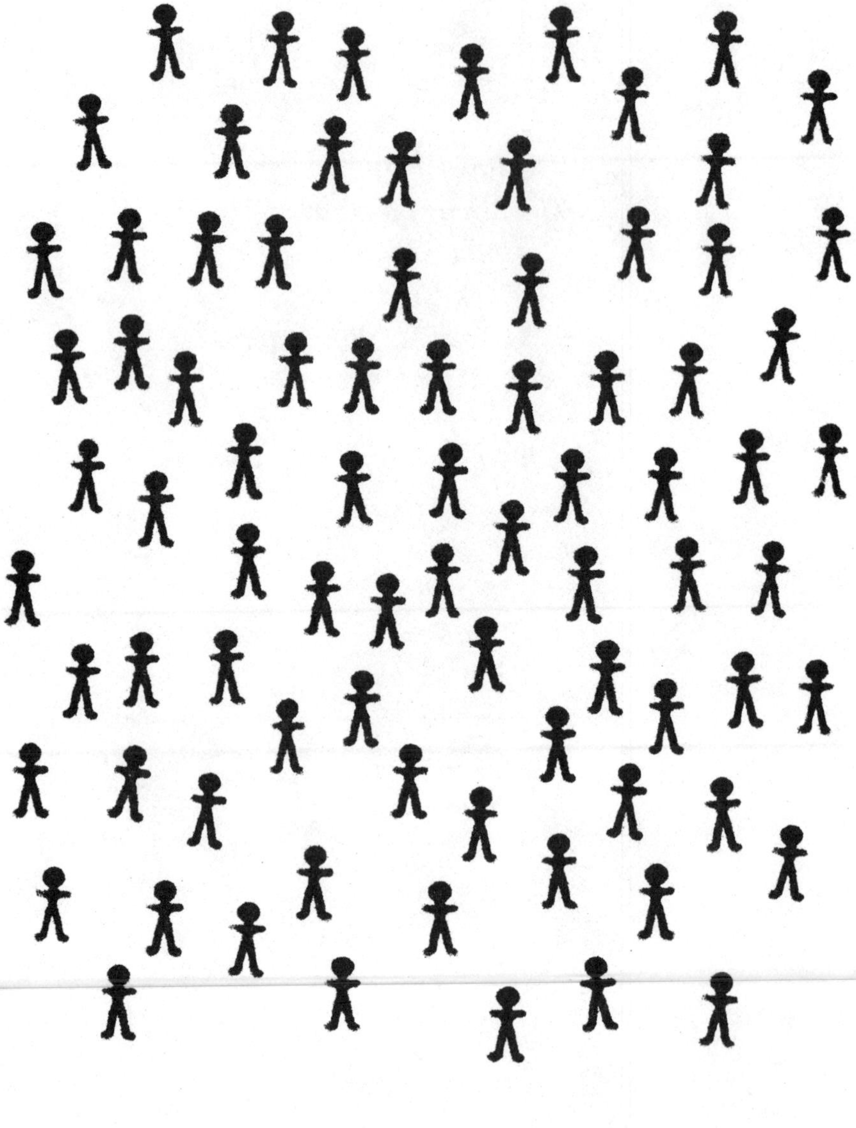

HOCUS POCUS

Kurt Vonnegut

G. P. PUTNAM'S SONS
New York

Published by G. P. Putnam's Sons,
200 Madison Avenue, New York, NY 10016
Published simultaneously in Canada

The text of this book is set in Gael.

Designed by MaryJane DiMassi

Library of Congress Cataloging-in-Publication Data

Vonnegut, Kurt
Hocus pocus / Kurt Vonnegut.
p.   cm.
ISBN 0-399-13524-3
ISBN 0-399-13549-9 (Limited Edition)
I. Title.
PS3572.05H6   1990   90-34535 CIP
813'.54—dc20

Printed in the United States of America
1   2   3   4   5   6   7   8   9   10

EDITOR'S NOTE

The author of this book did not have access to writing paper of uniform size and quality. He wrote in a library housing some eight hundred thousand volumes of interest to no one else. Most had never been read and probably never would be read, so there was nothing to stop him from tearing out their blank endpapers for stationery. This he did not do. Why he did not do this is not known. Whatever the reason, he wrote this book in pencil on everything from brown wrapping paper to the backs of business cards. The unconventional lines separating passages within chapters indicate where one scrap ended and the next began. The shorter the passage, the smaller the scrap.

One can speculate that the author, fishing through trash for anything to write on, may have hoped to establish a reputation for humility or insanity, since he was facing trial. It is equally likely, though, that he began this book impulsively, having no idea it would become a book, scribbling words on a scrap which happened to be right at hand. It could be that he found it congenial, then, to continue on from scrap to scrap, as though each were a bottle for him to fill. When he filled one up, possibly, no matter what its size, he could satisfy himself that he had written everything there was to write about this or that.

He numbered all the pages so there could be no doubt about their being sequential, nor about his hope that someone, undaunted by their disreputable appearance, would read them as a book. He in fact says here and there, with increasing confidence as he nears the end, that what he is doing is writing a book.

There are several drawings of a tombstone. The author made only one such drawing. The others are tracings of the original, probably made by superimposing translucent pieces of paper and pressing them against a sunlit library windowpane. He wrote words on the face of each burial marker, and in one case simply a question mark. These did not reproduce well on a printed page. So they have been set in type instead.

The author himself is responsible for the capitalization of certain words whose initial letters a meticulous editor might prefer to see in lowercase. So, too, did Eugene Debs Hartke choose for reasons unexplained to let numbers stand for themselves, except at the heads of sentences, rather than put them into words: for example, "2" instead of "two." He may have felt that numbers lost much of their potency when diluted by an alphabet.

To virtually all of his idiosyncrasies I, after much thought, have applied what another author once told me was the most sacred word in a great editor's vocabulary. That word is "stet."

K.V.

This work of pure fiction is dedicated to the memory of

EUGENE VICTOR DEBS
1855–1926

"While there is a lower class I am in it. While there is a criminal element I am of it. While there is a soul in prison I am not free."

HOCUS POCUS

1

My name is Eugene Debs Hartke, and I was born in 1940. I was named at the behest of my maternal grandfather, Benjamin Wills, who was a Socialist and an Atheist, and nothing but a groundskeeper at Butler University, in Indianapolis, Indiana, in honor of Eugene Debs of Terre Haute, Indiana. Debs was a Socialist and a Pacifist and a Labor Organizer who ran several times for the Presidency of the United States of America, and got more votes than has any other candidate nominated by a third party in the history of this country.

Debs died in 1926, when I was a negative 14 years of age. The year is 2001 now.

If all had gone the way a lot of people thought it would, Jesus Christ would have been among us again, and the American flag would have been planted on Venus and Mars.

No such luck!

At least the World will end, an event anticipated with great joy by many. It will end very soon, but not in the year 2000, which has come and gone. From that I conclude that God Almighty is not heavily into Numerology.

Grandfather Benjamin Wills died in 1948, when I was a plus 8 years of age, but not before he made sure that I knew by heart the most famous words uttered by Debs, which are:

"While there is a lower class I am in it. While there is a criminal element I am of it. While there is a soul in prison I am not free."

I, Debs' namesake, however, became anything but a bleeding heart. From the time I was 21 until I was 35 I was a professional soldier, a Commissioned Officer in the United States Army. During those 14 years I would have killed Jesus Christ Himself or Herself or Itself or Whatever, if ordered to do so by a superior officer. At the abrupt and humiliating and dishonorable end of the Vietnam War, I was a Lieutenant Colonel, with 1,000s and 1,000s of my own inferiors.

During that war, which was about nothing but the ammunition business, there was a microscopic possibility, I suppose, that I called in a white-phosphorus barrage or a napalm air strike on a returning Jesus Christ.

I never wanted to be a professional soldier, although I turned out to be a good one, if there can be such a thing. The idea that I should go to West Point came up as unexpectedly as the finale of the Vietnam War, near the end of my senior year in high school. I was all set to go to the University of Michigan, and take courses in English and History and Political Science, and work on the student daily paper there in preparation for a career as a journalist.

But all of a sudden my father, who was a chemical engineer involved in making plastics with a half-life of 50,000 years, and as full of excrement as a Christmas turkey, said I should go to West Point instead. He had never been in the military himself. During World War II, he was too valuable as a civilian deep-thinker about chemicals to be put in a soldier suit and turned into a suicidal, homicidal imbecile in 13 weeks.

14

I had already been accepted by the University of Michigan, when this offer to me of an appointment to the United States Military Academy came out of the blue. The offer arrived at a low point in my father's life, when he needed something to boast about which would impress our simpleminded neighbors. They would think an appointment to West Point was a great prize, like being picked for a professional baseball team.

So he said to me, as I used to say to infantry replacements fresh off the boat or plane in Vietnam, "This is a great opportunity."

What I would really like to have been, given a perfect world, is a jazz pianist. I mean jazz. I don't mean rock and roll. I mean the never-the-same-way-twice music the American black people gave the world. I played piano in my own all-white band in my all-white high school in Midland City, Ohio. We called ourselves "The Soul Merchants."

How good were we? We had to play white people's popular music, or nobody would have hired us. But every so often we would cut loose with jazz anyway. Nobody else seemed to notice the difference, but we sure did. We fell in love with ourselves. We were in ecstasy.

Father should never have made me go to West Point.

Never mind what he did to the environment with his nonbiodegradable plastics. Look what he did to me! What a boob he was! And my mother agreed with every decision he ever made, which makes *her* another blithering nincompoop.

They were both killed 20 years ago in a freak accident in a gift shop on the Canadian side of Niagara Falls, which the Indians in this valley used to call "Thunder Beaver," when the roof fell in.

There are no dirty words in this book, except for "hell" and "God," in case someone is fearing that an innocent child might see 1. The expression I will use here and there for the end of the Vietnam War, for example, will be: "when the excrement hit the air-conditioning."

Perhaps the only precept taught me by Grandfather Wills that I have honored all my adult life is that profanity and obscenity entitle people who don't want unpleasant information to close their ears and eyes to you.

The more alert soldiers who served under me in Vietnam would comment in some amazement that I never used profanity, which made me unlike anybody else they had ever met in the Army. They might ask if this was because I was religious.

I would reply that religion had nothing to do with it. I am in fact pretty much an Atheist like my mother's father, although I kept that to myself. Why argue somebody else out of the expectation of some sort of an Afterlife?

"I don't use profanity," I would say, "because your life and the lives of those around you may depend on your understanding what I tell you. OK? OK?"

I resigned my commission in 1975, after the excrement hit the air-conditioning, not failing, however, to father a son on my way home, unknowingly, during a brief stopover in the Philippines. I thought surely that the subsequent mother, a young female war correspondent for *The Des Moines Register,* was using foolproof birth control.

Wrong again!

Booby traps everywhere.

The biggest booby trap Fate set for me, though, was a pretty and personable young woman named Margaret Patton, who allowed me to woo and marry her soon after my graduation from West Point, and then had 2 children by me without telling me that there was a powerful strain of insanity on her mother's side of her family.

So then her mother, who was living with us, went insane, and then she herself went insane. Our children, moreover, had every reason to suspect that they, too, might go crazy in middle age.

Our children, full-grown now, can never forgive us for reproducing. What a mess.

I realize that my speaking of my first and only wife as something as inhuman as a booby trap risks my seeming to be yet another infernal device. But many other women have had no trouble relating to me as a person, and ardently, too, and my interest in them has gone well beyond the merely mechanical. Almost invariably, I have been as enchanted by their souls, their intellects, and the stories of their lives as by their amorous propensities.

But after I came home from the Vietnam War, and before either Margaret or her mother had shown me and the children and the neighbors great big symptoms of their inherited craziness, that mother-daughter team treated me like some sort of boring but necessary electrical appliance like a vacuum cleaner.

Good things have also happened unexpectedly, "manna from Heaven" you might want to call them, but not in such quantities as to make life a bowl of cherries or anything approaching that. Right after my war, when I had no idea what to do with the rest of my life, I ran into a former commanding officer of mine who had become President of Tarkington College, in Scipio, New York. I was then only 35, and my wife was still sane, and my mother-in-law was only slightly crazy. He offered me a teaching job, which I accepted.

I could accept that job with a clear conscience, despite my lack of academic credentials beyond a mere BS Degree from West Point, since all the students at Tarkington were learning-disabled in some way, or plain stupid or comatose or whatever. No matter what the subject, my old CO assured me, I would have little trouble keeping ahead of them.

The particular subject he wanted me to teach, what's more, was 1 in which I had excelled at the Academy, which was Physics.

The greatest stroke of luck for me, the biggest chunk of manna from Heaven, was that Tarkington had need of somebody to play the Lutz Carillon, the great family of bells at the top of the tower of the college library, where I am writing now.

I asked my old CO if the bells were swung by ropes.

He said they used to be, but that they had been electrified and were played by means of a keyboard now.

"What does the keyboard look like?" I said.

"Like a piano," he said.

I had never played bells. Very few people have that clanging opportunity. But I could play a piano. So I said, "Shake hands with your new carillonneur."

The happiest moments in my life, without question, were when I played the Lutz Carillon at the start and end of every day.

I went to work at Tarkington 25 years ago, and have lived in this beautiful valley ever since. This is home.

I have been a teacher here. I was a Warden for a little while, after Tarkington College officially became Tarkington State Reformatory in June of 1999, 20 months ago.

Now I myself am a prisoner here, but with pretty much the run of the place. I haven't been convicted of anything yet. I am awaiting trial, which I guess will take place in Rochester, for supposedly having masterminded the mass prison break at the New York State Maximum Security Adult Correctional Institution at Athena, across the lake from here.

It turns out that I also have tuberculosis, and my poor, addled wife Margaret and her mother have been put by court order into a lunatic asylum in Batavia, New York, something I had never had the guts to do.

I am so powerless and despised now that the man I am named after, Eugene Debs, if he were still alive, might at last be somewhat fond of me.

2

IN more optimistic times, when it was not widely understood that human beings were killing the planet with the by-products of their own ingenuity and that a new Ice Age had begun in any case, the generic name for the sort of horse-drawn covered wagon that carried freight and settlers across the prairies of what was to become the United States of America, and eventually across the Rocky Mountains to the Pacific Ocean, was "Conestoga"—since the first of these were built in the Conestoga Valley of Pennsylvania.

They kept the pioneers supplied with cigars, among other things, so that cigars nowadays, in the year 2001, are still called "stogies" sometimes, which is short for "Conestoga."

By 1830, the sturdiest and most popular of these wagons were in fact made by the Mohiga Wagon Company right here in Scipio, New York, at the pinched waist of Lake Mohiga, the deepest and coldest and westernmost of the long and narrow Finger Lakes. So sophisticated cigar-smokers might want to stop calling their stinkbombs "stogies" and call them "mogies" or "higgies" instead.

The founder of the Mohiga Wagon Company was Aaron Tarkington, a brilliant inventor and manufacturer who nevertheless could not read or write. He now would be identified as a blameless inheritor of the genetic defect known as dyslexia. He said of himself that he was like the Emperor Charlemagne, "too busy to learn to read and write." He was not too busy, however, to have his wife read to him for 2 hours every evening. He had an excellent memory, for he delivered weekly lectures to the workmen at the factory that were laced with lengthy quotations from Shakespeare and Homer and the Bible, and on and on.

He sired 4 children, a son and 3 daughters, all of whom could read and write. But they still carried the gene of dyslexia, which would disqualify several of their own descendants from getting very far in conventional schemes of education. Two of Aaron Tarkington's children were so far from being dyslexic, in fact, as to themselves write books, which I have read only now, and which nobody, probably, will ever read again. Aaron's only son, Elias, wrote a technical account of the construction of the Onondaga Canal, which connected the northern end of Lake Mohiga to the Erie Canal just south of Rochester. And the youngest daughter, Felicia, wrote a novel called *Carpathia,* about a headstrong, high-born young woman in the Mohiga Valley who fell in love with a half-Indian lock-tender on that same canal.

That canal is all filled in and paved over now, and is Route 53, which forks at the head of the lake, where the locks used to be. One fork leads southwest through farm country to Scipio. The other leads southeast through the perpetual gloom of the Iroquois National Forest to the bald hilltop crowned by the battlements of the New York State Maximum Security Adult Correctional Institution at Athena, a hamlet directly across the lake from Scipio.

Bear with me. This is history. I am trying to explain how this valley, this verdant cul-de-sac, got to be what it is today.

All 3 of Aaron Tarkington's daughters married into prosperous and enterprising families in Cleveland, New York, and Wilmington, Delaware—innocently making the threat of dyslexia pandemic in an emerging ruling class of bankers and industrialists, largely displaced in my time by Germans, Koreans, Italians, English, and, of course, Japanese.

The son of Aaron, Elias, remained in Scipio and took over his father's properties, adding to them a brewery and a steam-driven carpet factory, the first such in the state. There was no water power in Scipio, whose industrial prosperity until the introduction of steam was based not on cheap energy and locally available raw materials but on inventiveness and high standards of workmanship.

Elias Tarkington never married. He was severely wounded at the age of 54 while a civilian observer at the Battle of Gettysburg, top hat and all. He was there to see the debuts of 2 of his inventions, a mobile field kitchen and a pneumatic recoil mechanism for heavy artillery. The field kitchen, incidentally, with slight modifications, would later be adopted by the Barnum & Bailey Circus, and then by the German Army during World War I.

Elias Tarkington was a tall and skinny man with chin whiskers and a stovepipe hat. He was shot through the right chest at Gettysburg, but not fatally.

The man who shot him was 1 of the few Confederate soldiers to reach the Union lines during Pickett's Charge. That Johnny Reb died in ecstasy among his enemies, believing that he had shot Abraham Lincoln. A crumbling newspaper account I have found here in what used to be the college library, which is now the prison library, gives his last words as follows: "Go home, Bluebellies. Old Satan's daid."

During my 3 years in Vietnam, I certainly heard plenty of last words by dying American footsoldiers. Not 1 of them, however, had illusions that he had somehow accomplished something worthwhile in the process of making the Supreme Sacrifice.

One boy of only 18 said to me while he was dying and I was holding him in my arms, "Dirty joke, dirty joke."

3

Elias Tarkington, the severely wounded Abraham Lincoln look-alike, was brought home in 1 of his own wagons to Scipio, to his estate overlooking the town and lake.

He was not well educated, and was more a mechanic than a scientist, and so spent his last 3 years trying to invent what anyone familiar with Newton's Laws would have known was an impossibility, a perpetual-motion machine. He had no fewer than 27 contraptions built, which he foolishly expected to go on running, after he had given them an initial spin or whack, until Judgment Day.

I found 19 of those stubborn, mocking machines in the attic of what used to be their inventor's mansion, which in my time was the home of the College President, about a year after I came to work at Tarkington. I brought them back downstairs and into the 20th Century. Some of my students and I cleaned them up and restored any parts that had deteriorated during the intervening 100 years. At the least they were exquisite jewelry, with garnets and amethysts for bearings, with arms and legs of exotic woods, with tumbling balls of ivory, with chutes and counterweights of silver. It was as though dying Elias hoped to overwhelm science with the magic of precious materials.

The longest my students and I could get the best of them to run was 51 seconds. Some eternity!

To me, and I passed this on to my students, the restored devices demonstrated not only how quickly anything on Earth runs down without steady infusions of energy. They reminded us, too, of the craftsmanship no longer practiced in the town below. Nobody down there in our time could make things that cunning and beautiful.

Yes, and we took the 10 machines we agreed were the most beguiling, and we put them on permanent exhibit in the foyer of this library underneath a sign whose words can surely be applied to this whole ruined planet nowadays:

THE COMPLICATED FUTILITY OF IGNORANCE

I have discovered from reading old newspapers and letters and diaries from back then that the men who built the machines for Elias Tarkington knew from the first that they would never work, whatever the reason. Yet what love they lavished on the materials that comprised them! How is this for a definition of high art: "Making the most of the raw materials of futility"?

Still another perpetual-motion machine envisioned by Elias Tarkington was what his Last Will and Testament called "The Mohiga Valley Free Institute." Upon his death, this new school would take possession of his 3,000-hectare estate above Scipio, plus half the shares in the wagon company, the carpet company, and the brewery. The other half was already owned by his sisters far away. On his deathbed he predicted that Scipio would 1 day be a great metropolis and that its wealth would transform his little college into a university to rival Harvard and Oxford and Heidelberg.

It was to offer a free college education to persons of either

24

sex, and of any age or race or religion, living within 40 miles of Scipio. Those from farther away would pay a modest fee. In the beginning, it would have only 1 full-time employee, the President. The teachers would be recruited right here in Scipio. They would take a few hours off from work each week, to teach what they knew. The chief engineer at the wagon company, for example, whose name was André Lutz, was a native of Liège, Belgium, and had served as an apprentice to a bell founder there. He would teach Chemistry. His French wife would teach French and Watercolor Painting. The brewmaster at the brewery, Hermann Shultz, a native of Leipzig, would teach Botany and German and the flute. The Episcopalian priest, Dr. Alan Clewes, a graduate of Harvard, would teach Latin, Greek, Hebrew, and the Bible. The dying man's physician, Dalton Polk, would teach Biology and Shakespeare, and so on.

And it came to pass.

In 1869 the new college enrolled its first class, 9 students in all, and all from right here in Scipio. Four were of ordinary college age. One was a Union veteran who had lost his legs at Shiloh. One was a former black slave 40 years old. One was a spinster 82 years old.

The first President was only 26 years old, a schoolteacher from Athena, 2 kilometers by water from Scipio. There was no prison over there back then, but only a slate quarry and a sawmill and a few subsistence farms. His name was John Peck. He was a cousin of the Tarkingtons'. His branch of the family, however, was and remains unhampered by dyslexia. He has numerous descendants in the present day, 1 of whom, in fact, is a speech writer for the Vice-President of the United States.

Young John Peck and his wife and 2 children and his mother-in-law arrived at Scipio by rowboat, with Peck and his wife at the oars, their children seated in the stern, and their luggage and the mother-in-law in another boat they towed behind.

They took up residence on the third floor of what had been Elias Tarkington's mansion. The rooms on the first 2 floors would be classrooms, a library, which was already a library with 280 volumes collected by the Tarkingtons, study halls, and a dining room. Many treasures from the past were taken up to the attic to make room for the new activities. Among these were the failed perpetual-motion machines. They would gather dust and cobwebs until 1978, when I found them up there, and realized what they were, and brought them down the stairs again.

One week before the first class was held, which was in Latin, taught by the Episcopalian priest Alan Clewes, André Lutz the Belgian arrived at the mansion with 3 wagons carrying a very heavy cargo, a carillon consisting of 32 bells. He had cast them on his own time and at his own expense in the wagon factory's foundry. They were made from mingled Union and Confederate rifle barrels and cannonballs and bayonets gathered up after the Battle of Gettysburg. They were the first bells and surely the last bells ever to be cast in Scipio.

Nothing, in my opinion, will ever again be cast in Scipio. No industrial arts of any sort will ever again be practiced here.

André Lutz gave the new college all those bells, even though there was no place to hang them. He said he did it because he was so sure that it would 1 day be a great university with a bell tower and everything. He was dying of emphysema as a result of the fumes from molten metals that he had been breathing since he was 10 years old. He had no time to wait for a place to hang the most wonderful consequence of his having been alive for a little while, which was all those bells, bells, bells.

They were no surprise. They had been 18 months in the making. The founders whose work he supervised had shared his dreams of immortality as they made things as impractical and beautiful as bells, bells, bells.

So all the bells but 1 from a middle octave were slathered with grease to prevent their rusting and stored in 4 ranks in the estate's great barn, 200 meters from the mansion. The 1 bell that was going to get to sing at once was installed in the cupola of the mansion, with its rope running all the way down to the first floor. It would call people to classes and, if need be, also serve as a fire alarm.

The rest of the bells, it turned out, would slumber in the loft for 30 years, until 1899, when they were hanged as a family, the 1 from the cupola included, on axles in the belfry of the tower of a splendid library given to the school by the Moellenkamp family of Cleveland.

The Moellenkamps were also Tarkingtons, since the founder of their fortune had married a daughter of the illiterate Aaron Tarkington. Eleven of them so far had been dyslexic, and they had all gone to college in Scipio, since no other institution of higher learning would take them in.

The first Moellenkamp to graduate from here was Henry, who enrolled in 1875, when he was 19, and when the school was only 6 years old. It was at that time that its name was changed to Tarkington College. I have found the crumbling minutes of the Board of Trustees meeting at which that name change was made. Three of the 6 trustees were men who had married daughters of Aaron Tarkington, 1 of them the grandfather of Henry Moellenkamp. The other 3 trustees were the Mayor of Scipio, and a lawyer who looked after the Tarkington daughters' interests in the valley, and the area Congressman, who was surely the sisters' faithful servant, too, since they were partners with the college in his district's most important industries.

And according to the minutes, which fell apart in my

hands as I read them, it was the grandfather of young Henry Moellenkamp who proposed the name change, saying that "The Mohiga Valley Free Institute" sounded too much like a poorhouse or a hospital. It is my guess that he would not have minded having the place sound like a catchment for the poor, if only he had not suffered the misfortune of having his own grandson go there.

It was in that same year, 1875, that work began across the lake from Scipio, on a hilltop above Athena, on a prison camp for young criminals from big-city slums. It was believed that fresh air and the wonders of Nature would improve their souls and bodies to the point that they would find it natural to be good citizens.

When I came to work at Tarkington, there were only 300 students, a number that hadn't changed for 50 years. But the rustic work-camp across the lake had become a brutal fortress of iron and masonry on a naked hilltop, the New York State Maximum Security Adult Correctional Institution at Athena, keeping 5,000 of the state's worst criminals under lock and key.

Two years ago, Tarkington still had only 300 students, but the population of the prison, under hideously overcrowded conditions, had grown to 10,000. And then, 1 cold winter's night, it became the scene of the biggest prison break in American history. Until then, nobody had ever escaped from Athena.

Suddenly, everybody was free to leave, and to take a weapon from the prison armory, too, if he had use for 1. The lake between the prison and the little college was frozen solid, as easily traversed as the parking lot of a great shopping mall.

What next?

Yes, and by the time André Lutz's bells were at last made to sing as a carillon, Tarkington College had not only a new library but luxurious dormitories, a science building, an art building, a chapel, a theater, a dining hall, an administration building, 2 new buildings of classrooms, and athletic facilities that were the envy of the institutions with which it had begun to compete in track and fencing and swimming and baseball, which were Hobart, the University of Rochester, Cornell, Union, Amherst, and Bucknell.

These structures bore the names of wealthy families as grateful as the Moellenkamps for all the college had managed to do for offspring of theirs whom conventional colleges had deemed ineducable. Most were unrelated to the Moellenkamps or to anyone who carried the Tarkington gene of dyslexia. Nor were the young they sent to Tarkington necessarily troubled by dyslexia. All sorts of different things were wrong with them, including an inability to write legibly with pen and ink, although what they tried to write down made perfect sense, and stammering so severe as to prevent their saying a word in class, and petit mal, which caused their minds to go perfectly blank for seconds or minutes anywhere, anytime, and so on.

It was simply the Moellenkamps who first challenged the new little college to do what it could for a seemingly hopeless case of plutocratic juvenile incapacity, namely Henry. Not only would Henry graduate with honors from Tarkington. He would go on to Oxford, taking with him a male companion who read aloud to him and wrote down thoughts Henry could only express orally. Henry would become 1 of the most brilliant speakers in a golden age of American purple, bow-wow oratory, and serve as a Congressman and then a United States Senator from Ohio for 36 years.

That same Henry Moellenkamp was author of the lyrics to one of the most popular turn-of-the-century ballads, "Mary, Mary, Where Have You Gone?"

The melody of that ballad was composed by Henry's friend Paul Dresser, brother of the novelist Theodore Dreiser. This was 1 of the rare instances in which Dresser set another man's words to music instead of his own. And then Henry appropriated that tune and wrote, or rather dictated, new words which sentimentalized student life in this valley.

Thus was "Mary, Mary, Where Have You Gone?" transmogrified into the alma mater of this campus until it became a penitentiary 2 years ago.

History.

Accident after accident has made Tarkington what it is today. Who would dare to predict what it will be in 2021, only 20 years from now? The 2 prime movers in the Universe are Time and Luck.

As the tag line of my favorite dirty joke would have it: "Keep your hat on. We could wind up miles from here."

If Henry Moellenkamp had not come out of his mother's womb dyslexic, Tarkington College wouldn't even have been called Tarkington College. It would have gone on being The Mohiga Valley Free Institute, which would have died right along with the wagon factory and the carpet factory and the brewery when the railroads and highways connecting the East and West were built far to the north and south of Scipio—so as not to bridge the lake, so as not to have to penetrate the deep and dark virgin hardwood forest, now the Iroquois National Forest, to the east and south of here.

If Henry Moellenkamp hadn't come out of his mother's womb dyslexic, and if that mother hadn't been a Tarkington and so known about the little college on Lake Mohiga, this library would never have been built and filled with 800,000 bound volumes. When I was a professor here, that was 70,-000 more bound volumes than Swarthmore College had! Among small colleges, this library used to be second only to the 1 at Oberlin, which had 1,000,000 bound volumes.

So what is this structure in which I sit now, thanks to Time and Luck? It is nothing less, friends and neighbors, than the greatest prison library in the history of crime and punishment!

It is very lonely in here. Hello? Hello?

I might have said the same sort of thing back when this was an 800,000-bound-volume college library: "It is very lonely in here. Hello? Hello?"

I have just looked up Harvard University. It has 13,000,-000 bound volumes now. What a read!

And almost every book written for or about the ruling class.

If Henry Moellenkamp hadn't come out of his mother's womb dyslexic, there would never have been a tower in which to hang the Lutz Carillon.

Those bells might never have gotten to reverberate in the valley or anywhere. They probably would have been melted up and made back into weapons during World War I.

If Henry Moellenkamp had not come out of his mother's womb dyslexic, these heights above Scipio might have been all darkness on the cold winter night 2 years ago, with Lake Mohiga frozen hard as a parking lot, when 10,000 prisoners at Athena were suddenly set free.

Instead, there was a little galaxy of beckoning lights up here.

4

Regardless of whether Henry Moellenkamp came out of his mother's womb dyslexic or not, I was born in Wilmington, Delaware, 18 months before this country joined the fighting in World War II. I have not seen Wilmington since. That is where they keep my birth certificate. I was the only child of a housewife and, as I've said, a chemical engineer. My father was then employed by E. I. Du Pont de Nemours & Company, a manufacturer of high explosives, among other things.

When I was 2 years old, we moved to Midland City, Ohio, where a washing-machine company named Robo-Magic Corporation was beginning to make bomb-release mechanisms and swivel mounts for machine guns on B-17 bombers. The plastics industry was then in its infancy, and Father was sent to Robo-Magic to determine what synthetic materials from Du Pont could be used in the weapons systems in place of metal, in order to make them lighter.

By the time the war was over, the company had gotten out of the washing-machine business entirely, had changed its name to Barrytron, Limited, and was making weapon, airplane, and motor vehicle parts composed of plastics it had developed on its own. My father had become the company's Vice-President in Charge of Research and Development.

When I was about 17, Du Pont bought Barrytron in order to capture several of its patents. One of the plastics Father had helped to develop, I remember, had the ability to scatter radar signals, so that an airplane clad in it would look like a flock of geese to our enemies.

This material, which has since been used to make virtually indestructible skateboards and crash helmets and skis and motorcycle fenders and so on, was an excuse, when I was a boy, for increasing security precautions at Barrytron. To keep Communists from finding out how it was made, a single fence topped with barbed wire was no longer adequate. A second fence was put outside that one, and the space between them was patrolled around the clock by humorless, jackbooted armed guards with lean and hungry Dobermans.

When Du Pont took over Barrytron, the double fence, the Dobermans, my father and all, I was a high school senior, all set to go to the University of Michigan to learn how to be a journalist, to serve John Q. Public's right to know. Two members of my 6-piece band, The Soul Merchants, the clarinet and the string bass, were also going to Michigan.

We were going to stick together and go on making music at Ann Arbor. Who knows? We might have become so popular that we went on world tours and made great fortunes, and been superstars at peace rallies and love-ins when the Vietnam War came along.

Cadets at West Point did not make music. The musicians in the dance band and the marching band were Regular Army enlisted men, members of the servant class.

They were under orders to play music as written, note for note, and never mind how they felt about the music or about anything.

For that matter, there wasn't any student publication at West Point. So never mind how the cadets felt about anything. Not interesting.

I was fine, but all kinds of things were going wrong with my father's life. Du Pont was looking him over, as they were looking over everybody at Barrytron, deciding whether to keep him on or not. He was also having a love affair with a married woman whose husband caught him in the act and beat him up.

This was a sensitive subject with my parents, naturally, so I never discussed it with them. But the story was all over town, and Father had a black eye. He didn't play any sports, so he had to make up a story about falling down the basement stairs. Mother weighed about 90 kilograms by then, and berated him all the time about his having sold all his Barrytron stock 2 years too soon. If he had hung on to it until the Du Pont takeover, he would have had $1,000,000, back when it meant something to be a millionaire. If I had been learning-disabled, he could easily have afforded to send me to Tarkington.

Unlike me, he was the sort of man who had to be in extremis in order to commit adultery. According to a story I heard from enemies at high school, Father had done the jumping-out-the-window thing, hippity-hopping like Peter Cottontail across backyards with his pants around his ankles, and getting bitten by a dog, and getting tangled up in a clothesline, and all the rest of it. That could have been an exaggeration. I never asked.

I myself was deeply troubled by our little family's image problem, which was complicated when Mother broke her nose 2 days after Father got the black eye. To the outside world it looked as though she had said something to Father about the reason he had a black eye, and his reply had been to slug her. I didn't think he would ever slug her, no matter what.

There is a not quite remote possibility that he really did slug her, of course. Lesser men would have slugged her under similar circumstances. The real truth of the matter became unavailable to historians forever when the falling ceiling of a gift shop on the Canadian side of Niagara Falls killed both participants, as I've said, some 20 years ago. They were said to have died instantly. They never knew what hit them, which is the best way to go.

There was no argument about that in Vietnam or, I suppose, on any battlefield. One kid I remember stepped on an antipersonnel mine. The mine could have been one of our own. His best friend from Basic Training asked him what he could do for him, and the kid replied: "Turn me off like a light bulb, Sam."

The dying kid was white. The kid who wanted to help him was black, or a light tan, actually. His features were practically white, you would have to say.

A woman I was making love to a few years ago asked me if my parents were still alive. She wanted to know more about me, now that we had our clothes off.

I told her that they had suffered violent deaths in a foreign country, which was true. Canada is a foreign country.

But then I heard myself spinning this fantastic tale of their being on a safari in Tanganyika, a place about which I know almost nothing. I told that woman, and she believed me, that my parents and their guide were shot by poachers who were killing elephants for their ivory and mistook them for game wardens. I said that the poachers put their bodies on top of anthills, so that their skeletons were soon picked clean. They could be positively identified only by their dental work.

I used to find it easy and even exhilarating to lie that elaborately. I don't anymore. And I wonder now if I didn't develop that unwholesome habit very young, and because my parents were such an embarrassment, and especially my mother, who was fat enough to be a circus freak. I described much more attractive parents than I really had, in order to make people who knew nothing about them think well of me.

And during my final year in Vietnam, when I was in Public Information, I found it as natural as breathing to tell the press and replacements fresh off the boats or planes that we were clearly winning, and that the folks back home should be proud and happy about all the good things we were doing there.

I learned to lie like that in high school.

Another thing I learned in high school that was helpful in Vietnam: Alcohol and marijuana, if used in moderation, plus loud, usually low-class music, make stress and boredom infinitely more bearable. It was manna from Heaven that I came into this world with a gift for moderation in my intake of mood-modifying substances. During my last 2 years in high school, I don't think my parents even suspected that I was half in the bag a lot of the time. All they ever complained about was the music, when I played the radio or the phonograph or when The Soul Merchants rehearsed in our basement, which Mom and Dad said was jungle music, and much too loud.

In Vietnam, the music was always much too loud. Practically everybody was half in the bag, including Chaplains. Several of the most gruesome accidents I had to explain to the press during my last year over there were caused by people who had rendered themselves imbecilic or maniacal by ingesting too much of what, if taken in moderation, could be a helpful chemical. I ascribed all such accidents, of course, to human error. The press understood. Who on this Earth hasn't made a mistake or 2?

The assassination of an Austrian archduke led to World War I, and probably to World War II as well. Just as surely, my father's black eye brought me to the sorry state in which I find myself today. He was looking for some way, almost any way, to recapture the respect of the community, and to attract favorable attention from Barrytron's new owner, Du Pont. Du Pont, of course, has now been taken over by I. G. Farben of Germany, the same company that manufactured and packaged and labeled and addressed the cyanide gas used to kill civilians of all ages, including babes in arms, during the Holocaust.

What a planet.

So Father, his injured eye looking like a slit in a purple and yellow omelet, asked me if I was likely to receive any sort of honors at high school graduation. He didn't say so, but he was frantic for something to brag about at work. He was so desperate that he was trying to get blood out of the turnip of my nonparticipation in high school sports, student government, or school-sponsored extracurricular activities. My grade average was high enough to get me into the University of Michigan, and on the honor roll now and then, but not into the National Honor Society.

It was so pitiful! It made me mad, too, because he was trying to make me partly responsible for the family's image problem, which was all his fault. "I was always sorry you didn't go out for football," he said, as though a touchdown would have made everything all right again.

"Too late now," I said.

"You let those 4 years slip by without doing anything but making jungle music," he said.

It occurs to me now, a mere 43 years later, that I might

have said to him that at least I managed my sex life better than he had managed his. I was getting laid all the time, thanks to jungle music, and so were the other Soul Merchants. Certain sorts of not just girls but full-grown women, too, found us glamorous free spirits up on the bandstand, imitating black people and smoking marijuana, and loving ourselves when we made music, and laughing about God knows what just about anytime.

I guess my love life is over now. Even if I could get out of prison, I wouldn't want to give some trusting woman tuberculosis. She would be scared to death of getting AIDS, and I would give her TB instead. Wouldn't that be nice?

So now I will have to make do with memories. As a prosthesis for my memory, I have begun to list all the women, excluding my wife and prostitutes, with whom I have "gone all the way," as we used to say in high school. I find it impossible to remember any conquest I made as a teenager with clarity, to separate fact from fantasy. It was all a dream. So I begin my list with Shirley Kern, to whom I made love when I was 20. Shirley is my datum.

How many names will there be on the list? Too early to tell, but wouldn't that number, whatever it turns out to be, be as good a thing as any to put on my tombstone as an enigmatic epitaph?

I am certainly sorry if I ruined the lives of any of those women who believed me when I said I loved them. I can only hope against hope that Shirley Kern and all the rest of them are still OK.

If it is any consolation to those who may not be OK, my own life was ruined by a Science Fair.

Father asked me if there wasn't some school-sponsored extracurricular activity I could still try out for. This was only 8 weeks before my graduation! So I said, in a spirit of irony, since he knew science did not delight me as it delighted him, that my last opportunity to amount to anything was the County Science Fair. I got Bs in Physics and Chemistry, but you could stuff both those subjects up your fundament as far as I was concerned.

But Father rose from his chair in a state of sick excitement. "Let's go down in the basement," he said. "There's work to do."

"What kind of work?" I said. This was about midnight.

And he said, "You are going to enter and win the Science Fair."

Which I did. Or, rather, Father entered and won the Science Fair, requiring only that I sign an affidavit swearing that the exhibit was all my own work, and that I memorize his explanation of what it proved. It was about crystals and how they grew and why they grew.

His competition was weak. He was, after all, a 43-year-old chemical engineer with 20 years in industry, taking on teenagers in a community where few parents had higher educations. The main business in the county back then was still agriculture, corn and pigs and beef cattle. Barrytron was the sole sophisticated industry, and only a handful of people such as Father understood its processes and apparatus. Most of the company's employees were content to do what they were told and incurious as to how it was, exactly, that they had worked the miracles that somehow arrived all packaged and labeled and addressed on the loading docks.

I am reminded now of dead American soldiers, teenagers mostly, all packaged and labeled and addressed on loading docks in Vietnam. How many people knew or cared how these curious artifacts were actually manufactured?

A few.

Why Father and I were not branded as swindlers, why my exhibit was not thrown out of the Science Fair, why I am a prisoner awaiting trial now instead of a star reporter for the

39

Korean owners of *The New York Times* has to do with compassion, I now believe. The feeling was general in the community, I think, that our little family had suffered enough. Nobody in the county gave much of a darn about science anyway.

The other exhibits were so dumb and pitiful, too, that the best of them would make the county look stupid if it and its honest creator went on to the statewide competition in Cleveland. Our exhibit sure looked slick and tidy. Another big plus from the judges' point of view, maybe, when they thought about what the county's best was going to be up against in Cleveland: our exhibit was extremely hard for an ordinary person to understand or find at all interesting.

I remained philosophical, thanks to marijuana and alcohol, while the community decided whether to crucify me as a fraud or to crown me as a genius. Father may have had a buzz on, too. Sometimes it's hard to tell. I served under 2 Generals in Vietnam who drank a quart of whiskey a day, but it was hard to detect. They always looked serious and dignified.

So off Father and I went to Cleveland. His spirits were high. I knew we would go smash up there. I don't know why he didn't know we would go smash up there. The only advice he gave me was to keep my shoulders back when I was explaining my exhibit and not to smoke where the judges might see me doing it. He was talking about ordinary cigarettes. He didn't know I smoked the other kind.

I make no apologies for having been zapped during my darkest days in high school. Winston Churchill was bombed out of his skull on brandy and Cuban cigars during the darkest days of World War II.

Hitler, of course, thanks to the advanced technology of Germany, was among the first human beings to turn their brains to cobwebs with amphetamine. He actually chewed on carpets, they say. Yum yum.

Mother did not come to Cleveland with Father and me. She was ashamed to leave the house, she was so big and fat. So I had to do most of the marketing after school. I also had to do most of the housework, she had so much trouble getting around. My familiarity with housework was useful at West Point, and then again when my mother-in-law and then my wife went nuts. It was actually sort of relaxing, because I could see that I had accomplished something undeniably good, and I didn't have to think about my troubles while I was doing it. How my mother's eyes used to shine when she saw what I had cooked for her!

My mother's story is 1 of the few real success stories in this book. She joined Weight Watchers when she was 60, which is my age now. When the ceiling fell on her at Niagara Falls, she weighed only 52 kilograms!

This library is full of stories of supposed triumphs, which makes me very suspicious of it. It's misleading for people to read about great successes, since even for middle-class and upper-class white people, in my experience, failure is the norm. It is unfair to youngsters particularly to leave them wholly unprepared for monster screw-ups and starring roles in Keystone Kop comedies and much, much worse.

The Ohio Science Fair took place in Cleveland's beautiful Moellenkamp Auditorium. The theater seats had been removed and replaced with tables for all the exhibits. There was a hint of my then distant future in the auditorium's having been given to the city by the Moellenkamps, the same coal and shipping family that gave Tarkington College this library. This was long before they sold the boats and mines to a British and Omani consortium based in Luxembourg.

But the present was bad enough. Even as Father and I were setting up our exhibit, we were spotted by other contestants as a couple of comedians, as Laurel and Hardy, maybe, with Father as the fat and officious one and me as the dumb and skinny one. The thing was, Father was doing all the setting up, and I was standing around looking bored. All I wanted to do was go outside and hide behind a tree or something and smoke a cigarette. We were violating the most basic rule of the Fair, which was that the young exhibitors were supposed to do all the work, from start to finish. Parents or teachers or whatever were forbidden in writing to help at all.

It was as though I had entered the Soapbox Derby over in Akron, Ohio, in a car for coasting down hills that I had supposedly built myself but was actually my dad's Ferrari Gran Turismo.

We hadn't made any of the exhibit in the basement. When, at the very beginning, Father said that we should go down in the basement and get to work, we had actually gone down in the basement. But we stayed down there for only about 10 minutes while he thought and thought, growing ever more excited. I didn't say anything.

Actually, I *did* say one thing. "Mind if I smoke?" I said.

"Go right ahead," he said.

That was a breakthrough for me. It meant I could smoke in the house whenever I pleased, and he wouldn't say anything.

Then he led the way back up to the living room. He sat down at Mother's desk and made a list of things that should go into the exhibit.

"What are you doing, Dad?" I said.

"Shh," he said. "I'm busy. Don't bother me."

So I didn't bother him. I had more than enough to think about as it was. I was pretty sure I had gonorrhea. It was some sort of urethral infection, which was making me very uncomfortable. But I hadn't seen a doctor about it, because the doctor, by law, would have had to report me to the Department of Health, and my parents would have been told about it, as though they hadn't had enough heartaches already.

Whatever the infection was, it cleared itself up without my doing anything about it. It couldn't have been gonorrhea, which never stops eating you up of its own accord. Why should it ever stop of its own accord? It's having such a nice time. Why call off the party? Look how healthy and happy the kids are.

Twice in later life I would contract what was unambiguously gonorrhea, once in Tegucigalpa, Honduras, and then again in Saigon, now Ho Chi Minh City, in Vietnam. In both instances I told the doctors about the self-healing infection I had had in high school.

It might have been yeast, they said. I should have opened a bakery.

So Father started coming home from work with pieces of the exhibit, which had been made to his order at Barrytron: pedestals and display cases, and explanatory signs and labels made by the print shop that did a lot of work for Barrytron. The crystals themselves came from a Pittsburgh chemical supply house that did a lot of business with Barrytron. One crystal, I remember, came all the way from Burma.

The chemical supply house must have gone to some trouble to get together a remarkable collection of crystals for us, since what they sent us couldn't have come from their regular stock. In order to please a big customer like Barrytron, they may have gone to somebody who collected and sold crystals for their beauty and rarity, not as chemicals but as jewelry.

At any rate, the crystals, which were of museum quality,

caused Father to utter these famous last words after he spread them out on the coffee table in our living room, gloatingly: "Son, there is no way we can lose."

Well, as Jean-Paul Sartre says in Bartlett's *Familiar Quotations,* "Hell is other people." Other people made short work of Father's and my invincible contest entry in Cleveland 43 years ago.

Generals George Armstrong Custer at the Little Bighorn, and Robert E. Lee at Gettysburg, and William Westmoreland in Vietnam all come to mind.

Somebody said 1 time, I remember, that General Custer's famous last words were, "Where are all these blankety-blank Injuns comin' from?"

Father and I, and not our pretty crystals, were for a little while the most fascinating exhibit in Moellenkamp Auditorium. We were a demonstration of abnormal psychology. Other contestants and their mentors gathered around us and put us through our paces. They certainly knew which buttons to push, so to speak, to make us change color or twist and turn or grin horribly or whatever.

One contestant asked Father how old he was and what high school he was attending.

That was when we should have packed up our things and gotten out of there. The judges hadn't had a look at us yet, and neither had any reporters. We hadn't yet put up the sign that said what my name was and what school system I represented. We hadn't yet said anything worth remembering.

If we had folded up and vanished quietly right then and there, leaving nothing but an empty table, we might have entered the history of American science as no-shows who got sick or something. There was already an empty table,

44

which would stay empty, only 5 meters away from ours. Father and I had heard that it was going to stay empty and why. The would-be exhibitor and his mother and father were all in the hospital in Lima, Ohio, not Lima, Peru. That was their hometown. They had scarcely backed out of their driveway the day before, headed for Cleveland, they thought, with the exhibit in the trunk, when they were rear-ended by a drunk driver.

The accident wouldn't have been half as serious as it turned out to be if the exhibit hadn't included several bottles of different acids which broke and touched off the gasoline. Both vehicles were immediately engulfed in flames.

The exhibit was, I think, meant to show several important services that acids, which most people were afraid of and didn't like to think much about, were performing every day for Humanity.

The people who looked us over and asked us questions, and did not like what they saw and heard, sent for a judge. They wanted us disqualified. We were worse than dishonest. We were ridiculous!

I wanted to throw up. I said to Father, "Dad, honest to God, I think we better get out of here. We made a mistake."

But he said we had nothing to be ashamed of, and that we certainly weren't going to go home with our tails between our legs.

Vietnam!

So a judge did come over, and easily determined that I had no understanding whatsoever of the exhibit. He then took Father aside and negotiated a political settlement, man to man. He did not want to stir up bad feelings in our home county, which had sent me to Cleveland as its champion. Nor did he want to humiliate Father, who was an upstanding member of his community who obviously had not read the rules carefully. He would not humiliate us with a formal disqualification, which might attract unfavorable publicity, if Father in turn would not insist on having my entry put in serious competition with the rest as though it were legitimate.

When the time came, he said, he and the other judges would simply pass us by without comment. It would be their secret that we couldn't possibly win anything.

That was the deal.

History.

5

THE person who won that year was a girl from Cincinnati. As it happened, she too had an exhibit about crystallography. She, however, had either grown her own or gathered specimens herself from creek beds and caves and coal mines within 100 kilometers of her home. Her name was Mary Alice French, I remember, and she would go on to place very close to the bottom in the National Finals in Washington, D.C.

When she set off for the Finals, I heard, Cincinnati was so proud of her and so sure she would win, or at least place very high with her crystals, that the Mayor declared "Mary Alice French Day."

I have to wonder now, with so much time in which to think about people I've hurt, if Father and I didn't indirectly help set up Mary Alice French for her terrible disappointment in Washington. There is a good chance that the judges in Cleveland gave her First Prize because of the moral contrast between her exhibit and ours.

Perhaps, during the judging, science was given a backseat, and because of our ill fame, she represented a golden opportunity to teach a rule superior to any law of science: that honesty was the best policy.

But who knows?

Many, many years after Mary Alice French had her heart broken in Washington, and I had become a teacher at Tarkington, I had a male student from Cincinnati, Mary Alice French's hometown. His mother's side of the family had just sold Cincinnati's sole remaining daily paper and its leading TV station, and a lot of radio stations and weekly papers, too, to the Sultan of Brunei, reputedly the richest individual on Earth.

This student looked about 12 when he came to us. He was actually 21, but his voice had never changed, and he was only 150 centimeters tall. As a result of the sale to the Sultan, he personally was said to be worth $30,000,000, but he was scared to death of his own shadow.

He could read and write and do math all the way up through algebra and trigonometry, which he had taught himself. He was also probably the best chess player in the history of the college. But he had no social graces, and probably never would have any, because he found everything about life so frightening.

I asked him if he had ever heard of a woman about my age in Cincinnati whose name was Mary Alice French.

He replied: "I don't know anybody or anything. Please don't ever talk to me again. Tell everybody to stop talking to me."

I never did find out what he did with all his money, if anything. Somebody said he got married. Hard to believe!

Some fortune hunter must have got him.

Smart girl. She must be on Easy Street.

But to get back to the Science Fair in Cleveland: I headed for the nearest exit after Father and the judge made their deal. I needed fresh air. I needed a whole new planet or death. Anything would be better than what I had.

The exit was blocked by a spectacularly dressed man. He

was wholly unlike anyone else in the auditorium. He was, incredibly, what I myself would become: a Lieutenant Colonel in the Regular Army, with many rows of ribbons on his chest. He was in full-dress uniform, with a gold citation cord and paratrooper's wings and boots. We were not then at war anywhere, so the sight of a military man all dolled up like that among civilians, especially so early in the day, was startling. He had been sent there to recruit budding young scientists for his alma mater, the United States Military Academy at West Point.

The Academy had been founded soon after the Revolutionary War because the country had so few military officers with mathematical and engineering skills essential to victories in what was modern warfare way back then, mainly mapmaking and cannonballs. Now, with radar and rockets and airplanes and nuclear weapons and all the rest of it, the same problem had come up again.

And there I was in Cleveland, with a great big round badge pinned over my heart like a target, which said:

EXHIBITOR.

This Lieutenant Colonel, whose name was Sam Wakefield, would not only get me into West Point. In Vietnam, where he was a Major General, he would award me a Silver Star for extraordinary valor and gallantry. He would retire from the Army when the war still had a year to go, and become President of Tarkington College, now Tarkington Prison. And when I myself got out of the Army, he would hire me to teach Physics and play the bells, bells, bells.

Here are the first words Sam Wakefield ever spoke to me, when I was 18 and he was 36:

"What's the hurry, Son?"

6

"WHAT'S the hurry, Son?" he said. And then, "If you've got a minute, I'd like to talk to you."

So I stopped. That was the biggest mistake of my life. There were plenty of other exits, and I should have headed for 1 of those. At that moment, every other exit led to the University of Michigan and journalism and music-making, and a lifetime of saying and wearing what I goshdarned pleased. Any other exit, in all probability, would have led me to a wife who wouldn't go insane on me, and kids who gave me love and respect.

Any other exit would have led to a certain amount of misery, I know, life being what it is. But I don't think it would have led me to Vietnam, and then to teaching the unteachable at Tarkington College, and then getting fired by Tarkington, and then teaching the unteachable at the penitentiary across the lake until the biggest prison break in American history. And now I myself am a prisoner.

But I stopped before the 1 exit blocked by Sam Wakefield. There went the ball game.

Sam Wakefield asked me if I had ever considered the advantages of a career in the military. This was a man who had been wounded in World War II, the 1 war I would have liked to fight in, and then in Korea. He would eventually resign from the Army with the Vietnam War still going on, and then become President of Tarkington College, and then blow his brains out.

I said I had already been accepted by the University of Michigan and had no interest in soldiering. He wasn't having any luck at all. The sort of kid who had reached a state-level Science Fair honestly wanted to go to Cal Tech or MIT, or someplace a lot friendlier to freestyle thinking than West Point. So he was desperate. He was going around the country recruiting the dregs of Science Fairs. He didn't ask me about my exhibit. He didn't ask about my grades. He wanted my body, no matter what it was.

And then Father came along, looking for me. The next thing I knew, Father and Sam Wakefield were laughing and shaking hands.

Father was happier than I had seen him in years. He said to me, "The folks back home will think that's better than any prize at a Science Fair."

"What's better?" I said.

"You have just won an appointment to the United States Military Academy," he said. "I've got a son I can be proud of now."

Seventeen years later, in 1975, I was a Lieutenant Colonel on the roof of the American Embassy in Saigon, keeping everybody but Americans off helicopters that were ferrying badly rattled people out to ships offshore. We had lost a war!

Losers!

I wasn't the worst young scientist Sam Wakefield persuaded to come to West Point. One classmate of mine, from a little high school in Wyoming, had shown early promise by making an electric chair for rats, with little straps and a little black hood and all.

51

That was Jack Patton. He was no relation to "Old Blood and Guts" Patton, the famous General in World War II. He became my brother-in-law. I married his sister Margaret. She came with her folks from Wyoming to see him graduate, and I fell in love with her. We sure could dance.

Jack Patton was killed by a sniper in Hué—pronounced "whay." He was a Lieutenant Colonel in the Combat Engineers. I wasn't there, but they say he got it right between the eyes. Talk about marksmanship! Whoever shot him was a real winner.

The sniper didn't stay a winner very long, though, I heard. Hardly anybody does. Some of our people figured out where he was. I heard he couldn't have been more than 15 years old. He was a boy, not a man, but if he was going to play men's games he was going to have to pay men's penalties. After they killed him, I heard, they put his little testicles and penis in his mouth as a warning to anybody else who might choose to be a sniper.

Law and order. Justice swift and justice sure.

Let me hasten to say that no unit under my command was encouraged to engage in the mutilation of bodies of enemies, nor would I have winked at it if I had heard about it. One platoon in a battalion I led, on its own initiative, took to leaving aces of spades on the bodies of enemies, as sort of calling cards, I guess. This wasn't mutilation, strictly speaking, but still I put a stop to it.

What a footsoldier can do to a body with his pipsqueak technology is nothing, of course, when compared with the ordinary, unavoidable, perfectly routine effects of aerial bombing and artillery. One time I saw the severed head of a bearded old man resting on the guts of an eviscerated water buffalo, covered with flies in a bomb crater by a paddy in Cambodia. The plane whose bomb made the crater was so high when it dropped it that it couldn't even be seen from the ground. But what its bomb did, I would have to say, sure beat the ace of spades for a calling card.

I don't think Jack Patton would have wanted the sniper who killed him mutilated, but you never know. When he was alive he was like a dead man in 1 respect: everything was pretty much all right with him.

Everything, and I mean everything, was a joke to him, or so he said. His favorite expression right up to the end was, "I had to laugh like hell." If Lieutenant Colonel Patton is in Heaven, and I don't think many truly professional soldiers have ever expected to wind up there, at least not recently, he might at this very moment be telling about how his life suddenly stopped in Hué, and then adding, without even smiling, "I had to laugh like hell." That was the thing: Patton would tell about some supposedly serious or beautiful or dangerous or holy event during which he had had to laugh like hell, but he hadn't really laughed. He kept a straight face, too, when he told about it afterward. In all his life, I don't think anybody ever heard him do what he said he had to do all the time, which was laugh like hell.

He said he had to laugh like hell when he won a science prize in high school for making an electric chair for rats, but he hadn't. A lot of people wanted him to stage a public demonstration of the chair with a tranquilized rat, wanted him to shave the head of a groggy rat and strap it to the chair, and, according to Jack, ask it if it had any last words to say, maybe wanted to express remorse for the life of crime it had led.

The execution never took place. There was enough common sense in Patton's high school, although not in the Science Department, apparently, to have such an event denounced as cruelty to dumb animals. Again, Jack Patton said without smiling, "I had to laugh like hell."

He said he had to laugh like hell when I married his sister Margaret. He said Margaret and I shouldn't take offense at that. He said he had to laugh like hell when anybody got married.

I am absolutely sure that Jack did not know that there was inheritable insanity on his mother's side of the family, and neither did his sister, who would become my bride. When I married Margaret, their mother seemed perfectly OK still, except for a mania for dancing, which was a little scary sometimes, but harmless. Dancing until she dropped wasn't nearly as loony as wanting to bomb North Vietnam back to the Stone Age, or bombing anyplace back to the Stone Age.

My mother-in-law Mildred grew up in Peru, Indiana, but never talked about Peru, even after she went crazy, except to say that Cole Porter, a composer of ultrasophisticated popular songs during the first half of the last century, was also born in Peru.

My mother-in-law ran away from Peru when she was 18, and never went back again. She worked her way through the University of Wyoming, in Laramie, of all places, which I guess was about as far away from Peru as she could get without leaving the Milky Way. That was where she met her husband, who was then a student in the university's School of Veterinary Science.

Only after the Vietnam War, with Jack long dead, did Margaret and I realize that she wanted nothing more to do with Peru because so many people there knew she came from a family famous for spawning lunatics. And then she got married, keeping her family's terrifying history to herself, and she reproduced.

My own wife married and reproduced in all innocence of the danger she herself was in, and the risk she would pass on to our children.

Our own children, having grown up with a notoriously insane grandmother in the house, fled this valley as soon as

they could, just as she had fled Peru. But they haven't reproduced, and with their knowing what they do about their
booby-trapped genes, I doubt that they ever will.

Jack Patton never married. He never said he wanted kids.
That could be a clue that he did know about his crazy relatives in Peru, after all. But I don't believe that. He was
against everybody's reproducing, since human beings were,
in his own words, "about 1,000 times dumber and meaner
than they think they are."

I myself, obviously, have finally come around to his point
of view.

During our plebe year, I remember, Jack all of a sudden
decided that he was going to be a cartoonist, although he
had never thought of being that before. He was compulsive.
I could imagine him back in high school in Wyoming, all of
a sudden deciding to build an electric chair for rats.

The first cartoon he ever drew, and the last one, was of 2
rhinoceroses getting married. A regular human preacher in
a church was saying to the congregation that anybody who
knew any reason these 2 should not be joined together in
holy matrimony should speak now or forever hold his peace.

This was long before I had even met his sister Margaret.

We were roommates, and would be for all 4 years. So he
showed me the cartoon and said he bet he could sell it to
Playboy.

I asked him what was funny about it. He couldn't draw for
sour apples. He had to tell me that the bride and groom
were rhinoceroses. I thought they were a couple of sofas
maybe, or maybe a couple of smashed-up sedans. That
would have been fairly funny, come to think of it: 2
smashed-up sedans taking wedding vows. They were going
to settle down.

"What's funny about it?" said Jack incredulously.
"Where's your sense of humor? If somebody doesn't stop the
wedding, those two will mate and have a baby rhinoceros."

"Of course," I said.

"For Pete's sake," he said, "what could be uglier and dumber than a rhinoceros? Just because something can reproduce, that doesn't mean it should reproduce."

I pointed out that to a rhinoceros another rhinoceros was wonderful.

"That's the point," he said. "Every kind of animal thinks its own kind of animal is wonderful. So people getting married think they're wonderful, and that they're going to have a baby that's wonderful, when actually they're as ugly as rhinoceroses. Just because we think we're so wonderful doesn't mean we really are. We could be really terrible animals and just never admit it because it would hurt so much."

During Jack's and my cow year at the Point, I remember, which would have been our junior year at a regular college, we were ordered to walk a tour for 3 hours on the Quadrangle, in a military manner, as though on serious guard duty, in full uniform and carrying rifles. This was punishment for our having failed to report another cadet who had cheated on a final examination in Electrical Engineering. The Honor Code required not only that we never lie or cheat but that we snitch on anybody who had done those things.

We hadn't seen the cadet cheat. We hadn't even been in the same class with him. But we were with him, along with one other cadet, when he got drunk in Philadelphia after the Army–Navy game. He got so drunk he confessed that he had cheated on the exam the previous June. Jack and I told him to shut up, that we didn't want to hear about it, and that we were going to forget about it, since it probably wasn't true anyway.

But the other cadet, who would later be fragged in Vietnam, turned all of us in. We were as corrupt as the cheater, supposedly, for trying to cover up for him. "Fragging," incidentally, was a new word in the English language that came out of the Vietnam War. It meant pitching a fizzing frag-mentation grenade into the sleeping quarters of an unpopu-lar officer. I don't mean to boast, but the whole time I was in Vietnam nobody offered to frag me.

The cheater was thrown out, even though he was a firstie, which meant he would graduate in only 6 more months. And Jack and I had to walk a 3-hour tour at night and in an ice-cold rain. We weren't supposed to talk to each other or to anyone. But the nonsensical posts he and I had to march intersected at 1 point. Jack muttered to me at one such meeting, "What would you do if you heard somebody had just dropped an atom bomb on New York City?"

It would be 10 minutes before we passed again. I thought of a few answers that were obvious, such as that I would be horrified, I would want to cry, and so on. But I understood that he didn't want to hear my answer. Jack wanted me to hear his answer.

So here he came with his answer. He looked me in the eye, and he said without a flicker of a smile, "I'd laugh like hell."

The last time I heard him say that he had to laugh like hell was in Saigon, where I ran into him in a bar. He told me that he had just been awarded a Silver Star, which made him my equal, since I already had one. He had been with a platoon from his company, which was planting mines on paths lead-ing to a village believed to be sympathetic with the enemy, when a firefight broke out. So he called for air support, and the planes dropped napalm, which is jellied gasoline devel-oped by Harvard University, on the village, killing Viet-namese of both sexes and all ages. Afterward, he was ordered to count the bodies, and to assume that they had all been enemies, so that the number of bodies could be in the news that day. That engagement was what he got the Silver Star for. "I had to laugh like hell," he said, but he didn't crack a smile.

He would have wanted to laugh like hell if he had seen me on the roof of our embassy in Saigon with my pistol drawn. I had won my Silver Star for finding and personally killing 5 enemy soldiers who were hiding in a tunnel underground. Now I was on a rooftop, while regiments of the enemy were right out in the open, with no need to hide from anybody, taking possession without opposition of the streets below. There they were down there, in case I wanted to kill lots more of them. *Pow! Pow! Pow!*

I was up there to keep Vietnamese who had been on our side from getting onto helicopters that were ferrying Americans only, civilian employees at the embassy and their dependents, to our Navy ships offshore. The enemy could have shot down the helicopters and come up and captured or killed us, if they had wanted. But all they had ever wanted from us was that we go home. They certainly captured or killed the Vietnamese I kept off the helicopter after the very last of the Americans, who was Lieutenant Colonel Eugene Debs Hartke, was out of there.

The rest of that day:

The helicopter carrying the last American to leave Vietnam joined a swarm of helicopters over the South China Sea, driven from their roosts on land and running out of gasoline. How was that for Natural History in the 20th Century: the sky filled with chattering, manmade pterodactyls, suddenly homeless, unable to swim a stroke, about to drown or starve to death.

Below us, deployed as far as the eye could see, was the most heavily armed armada in history, in no danger whatsoever from anyone. We could have all the deep blue sea we wanted, as far as the enemy was concerned. Enjoy! Enjoy!

My own helicopter was told by radio to hover with 2 others over a minesweeper, which had a landing platform for 1 pterodactyl, its own, which took off so ours could land.

Down we came, and we got out, and sailors pushed our big, dumb, clumsy bird overboard. That process was repeated twice, and then the ship's own improbable creature claimed its roost again. I had a look inside it later on. It was loaded with electronic gear that could detect mines and submarines under the water, and incoming missiles and planes in the sky above.

And then the Sun itself followed the last American helicopter to leave Saigon to the bottom of the deep blue sea.

At the age of 35, Eugene Debs Hartke was again as dissolute with respect to alcohol and marijuana and loose women as he had been during his last 2 years in high school. And he had lost all respect for himself and the leadership of his country, just as, 17 years earlier, he had lost all respect for himself and his father at the Cleveland, Ohio, Science Fair.

His mentor Sam Wakefield, the man who recruited him for West Point, had quit the Army a year earlier in order to speak out against the war. He had become President of Tarkington College through powerful family connections.

Three years after that, Sam Wakefield would commit suicide. So there is another loser for you, even though he had been a Major General and then a College President. I think exhaustion got him. I say that not only because he seemed very tired all the time to me, but because his suicide note wasn't even original and didn't seem to have that much to do with him personally. It was word for word the same suicide note left way back in 1932, when I was a negative 8 years old, by another loser, George Eastman, inventor of the Kodak camera and founder of Eastman Kodak, now defunct, only 75 kilometers north of here.

Both notes said this and nothing more: "My work is done."

In Sam Wakefield's case, that completed work, if he didn't want to count the Vietnam War, consisted of 3 new buildings, which probably would have been built anyway, no matter who was Tarkington's President.

I am not writing this book for people below the age of 18, but I see no harm in telling young people to prepare for failure rather than success, since failure is the main thing that is going to happen to them.

In terms of basketball alone, almost everybody has to lose. A high percentage of the convicts in Athena, and now in this much smaller institution, devoted their childhood and youth to nothing but basketball and still got their brains knocked out in the early rounds of some darn fool tournament.

Let me say further to the chance young reader that I would probably have wrecked my body and been thrown out of the University of Michigan and died on Skid Row somewhere if I had not been subjected to the discipline of West Point. I am talking about my body now, and not my mind, and there is no better way for a young person to learn respect for his or now her bones and nerves and muscles than to accept an appointment to any one of the 3 major service academies.

I entered the Point a young punk with bad posture and a sunken chest, and no history of sports participation, save for a few fights after dances where our band had played. When I graduated and received my commission as a Second Lieutenant in the Regular Army, and tossed my hat in the air, and bought a red Corvette with the back pay the Academy had put aside for me, my spine was as straight as a ramrod, my lungs were as capacious as the bellows of the forge of Vulcan, I was captain of the judo and wrestling teams, and I had not smoked any sort of cigarette or swallowed a drop of alcohol for 4 whole years! Nor was I sexually promiscuous anymore. I never felt better in my life.

I can remember saying to my mother and father at graduation, "Can this be me?"

They were so proud of me, and I was so proud of me.

I turned to Jack Patton, who was there with his booby-trapped sister and mother and his normal father, and I asked him, "What do you think of us now, Lieutenant Patton?" He was the goat of our class, meaning he had the lowest grade average. So had General George Patton been, again no relative of Jack's, who had been such a great leader in World War II.

What Jack replied, of course, unsmilingly, was that he had to laugh like hell.

7

I have been reading issues of the Tarkington College alumni magazine, *The Musketeer,* going all the way back to its first issue, which came out in 1910. It was so named in honor of Musket Mountain, a high hill not a mountain, on the western edge of the campus, at whose foot, next to the stable, so many victims of the escaped convicts are buried now.

Every proposed physical improvement of the college plant triggered a storm of protest. When Tarkington graduates came back here, they wanted it to be exactly as they remembered it. And 1 thing at least never did change, which was the size of the student body, stabilized at 300 since 1925. Meanwhile, of course, the growth of the prison population on the other side of the lake, invisible behind walls, was as irresistible as Thunder Beaver, as Niagara Falls.

Judging from letters to *The Musketeer,* I think the change that generated the most passionate resistance was the modernization of the Lutz Carillon soon after World War II, a memorial to Ernest Hubble Hiscock. He was a Tarkington graduate who at the age of 21 was a nose-gunner on a Navy bomber whose pilot crashed his plane with a full load of bombs onto the flight deck of a Japanese aircraft carrier in the Battle of Midway during World War II.

I would have given anything to die in a war that meaningful.

Me? I was in show business, trying to get a big audience for the Government on TV by killing real people with live ammunition, something the other advertisers were not free to do.

The other advertisers had to fake everything.

Oddly enough, the actors always turned out to be a lot more believable on the little screen than we were. Real people in real trouble don't come across, somehow.

There is still so much we have to learn about TV!

Hiscock's parents, who were divorced and remarried but still friends, chipped in to have the bells mechanized, so that one person could play them by means of a keyboard. Before that, many people had to haul away on ropes, and once a bell was set swinging, it stopped swinging in its own sweet time. There was no way of damping it.

In the old days 4 of the bells were famously off-key, but beloved, and were known as "Pickle" and "Lemon" and "Big Cracked John" and "Beelzebub." The Hiscocks had them sent to Belgium, to the same bell foundry where André Lutz had been an apprentice so long ago. There they were machined and weighted to perfect pitch, their condition when I got to play them.

It can't have been music the carillon made in the old days. Those who used to make whatever it was described it in their letters to *The Musketeer* with the same sort of batty love and berserk gratitude I hear from convicts when they tell me what it was like to take heroin laced with amphetamine, and angel dust laced with LSD, and crack alone, and on and on. I think of all those learning-disabled kids in the old days, hauling away on ropes with the bells clanging sweet and sour and as loud as thunder directly overhead, and I am sure they were finding the same undeserved happiness so many of the convicts found in chemicals.

63

And haven't I myself said that the happiest parts of my life were when I played the bells? With absolutely no basis in reality, I felt like many an addict that I'd won, I'd won, I'd won!

When I was made carillonneur, I taped this sign on the door of the chamber containing the keyboard: "Thor." That's who I felt like when I played, sending thunderbolts down the hillside and through the industrial ruins of Scipio, and out over the lake, and up to the walls of the prison on the other side.

There were echoes when I played—bouncing off the empty factories and the prison walls, and arguing with notes just leaving the bells overhead. When Lake Mohiga was frozen, their argument was so loud that people who had never been in the area before thought the prison had its own set of bells, and that their carillonneur was mocking me.

And I would yell into the mad clashing of bells and echoes, "Laugh, Jack, laugh!"

After the prison break, the College President would shoot convicts down below from the belfry. The acoustics of the valley would cause the escapees to make many wrong guesses as to where the shots were coming from.

8

I N my day, the bells no longer swung. They were welded to rigid shafts. Their clappers had been removed. They were struck instead by bolts thrust by electricity from Niagara Falls. Their singing could be stopped in an instant by brakes lined with neoprene.

The room in which a dozen or more learning-disabled bell-pullers used to be zonked out of their skulls by hellishly loud cacophony contained a 3-octave keyboard against 1 wall. The holes for the ropes in the ceiling had been plugged and plastered over.

Nothing works up there anymore. The room with the keyboard and the belfry above were riddled by bullets and also bazooka shells fired by escaped convicts down below after a sniper up among the bells shot and killed 11 of them, and wounded 15 more. The sniper was the President of Tarkington College. Even though he was dead when the convicts got to him, they were so outraged that they cruci-fied him in the loft of the stable where the students used to keep their horses, at the foot of Musket Mountain.

So a President of Tarkington, my mentor Sam Wakefield, blew his brains out with a Colt .45. And his successor, al-though he couldn't feel anything, was crucified.

One would have to say that that was extra-heavy history.

As for light history: The no longer useful clappers of the bells were hung in order of size, but unlabeled, on the wall of the foyer of this library, above the perpetual-motion machines. So it became a college tradition for upperclasspersons to tell incoming freshmen that the clappers were the petrified penises of different mammals. The biggest clapper, which had once belonged to Beelzebub, the biggest bell, was said to be the penis of none other than Moby Dick, the Great White Whale.

Many of the freshmen believed it, and were watched to see how long they went on believing it, just as they had been watched when they were little, no doubt, to see how long they would go on believing in the Tooth Fairy, the Easter Bunny, and Santa Claus.

Vietnam.

Most of the letters to *The Musketeer* protesting the modernization of the Lutz Carillon are from people who had somehow hung on to the wealth and power they had been born to. One, though, is from a man who admitted that he was in prison for fraud, and that he had ruined his life and that of his family with his twin addictions to alcohol and gambling. His letter was like this book, a gallows speech.

One thing he had still looked forward to, he said, after he had paid his debt to society, was returning to Scipio to ring the bells with ropes again.

"Now you take that away from me," he said.

One letter is from an old bell-puller, very likely dead by now, a member of the Class of 1924 who had married a man named Marthinus de Wet, the owner of a gold mine in Krugersdorp, South Africa. She knew the history of the bells, that they had been made from weapons gathered up after

66

the Battle of Gettysburg. She did not mind that the bells would soon be played electrically. The bad idea, as far as she was concerned, was that the sour bells, Pickle and Lemon and Big Cracked John and Beelzebub, were going to be turned on lathes in Belgium until they were either in tune or on the scrap heap.

"Are Tarkington students no longer to be humanized and humbled as I was day after day," she asked, "by the cries from the bell tower of the dying on the sacred, blood-soaked grounds of Gettysburg?"

The bells controversy inspired a lot of purple prose like that, much of it dictated to a secretary or a machine, no doubt. It is quite possible that Mrs. de Wet graduated from Tarkington without being able to write any better than most of the ill-educated prisoners across the lake.

If my Socialist grandfather, nothing but a gardener at Butler University, could read the letter from Mrs. de Wet and note its South African return address, he would be grimly gratified. There was a clear-as-crystal demonstration of a woman living high on profits from the labor of black miners, overworked and underpaid.

He would have seen exploitation of the poor and powerless in the growth of the prison across the lake as well. The prison to him would have been a scheme for depriving the lower social orders of leadership in the Class Struggle and for providing them with a horrible alternative to accepting whatever their greedy paymasters would give them in the way of working conditions and subsistence.

By the time I got to Tarkington College, though, he would have been wrong about the meaning of the prison across the lake, since poor and powerless people, no matter how docile, were no longer of use to canny investors. What they used to do was now being done by heroic and uncomplaining machinery.

67

So an appropriate sign to put over the gate to Athena might have been, instead of "Work Makes Free," for example: "Too bad you were born. Nobody has any use for you," or maybe: "Come in and stay in, all you burdens on Society."

9

A former roommate of Ernest Hubble Hiscock, the dead war hero, who had also been in the war, who had lost an arm as a Marine on Iwo Jima, wrote that the memorial Hiscock himself would have wanted most was a promise by the Board of Trustees at the start of each academic year to keep the enrollment the same size it had been in his time.

So if Ernest Hubble Hiscock is looking down from Heaven now, or wherever it is that war heroes go after dying, he would be dismayed to see his beloved campus surrounded by barbed wire and watchtowers. The bells are shot to hell. The number of students, if you can call convicts that, is about 2,000 now.

When there were only 300 "students" here, each one had a bedroom and a bathroom and plenty of closets all his or her own. Each bedroom was part of a 2-bedroom, 2-bathroom suite with a common living room for 2. Each living room had couches and easy chairs and a working fireplace, and state-of-the-art sound-reproduction equipment and a big-screen TV.

At the Athena state prison, as I would discover when I went to work over there, there were 6 men to each cell and each cell had been built for 2. Each 50 cells had a recreation room with one Ping-Pong table and one TV. The TV, moreover, showed only tapes of programs, including news, at least 10 years old. The idea was to keep the prisoners from becoming distressed about anything going on in the outside world that hadn't been all taken care of one way or the other, presumably, in the long-ago.

They could feast their eyes on whatever they liked, just so long as it wasn't relevant.

How those letter-writers loved not just the college but the whole Mohiga Valley—the seasons, the lake, the forest primeval on the other side. And there were few differences between student pleasures in their times and my own. In my time, students didn't skate on the lake anymore, but on an indoor rink given in 1971 by the Israel Cohen Family. But they still had sailboat races and canoe races on the lake. They still had picnics by the ruins of the locks at the head of the lake. Many students still brought their own horses to school with them. In my time, several students brought not just 1 horse but 3, since polo was a major sport. In 1976 and again in 1980, Tarkington College had an undefeated polo team.

There are no horses in the stable now, of course. The escaped convicts, surrounded and starving a mere 4 days after the prison break, calling themselves "Freedom Fighters" and flying an American flag from the top of the bell tower of this library, ate the horses and the campus dogs, too, and fed pieces of them to their hostages, who were the Trustees of the college.

The most successful athlete ever to come from Tarkington, arguably, was a horseman from my own time, Lowell Chung. He won a Bronze Medal as a member of the United States Equestrian Team in Seoul, South Korea, back in 1988.

70

His mother owned half of Honolulu, but he couldn't read or write or do math worth a darn. He could sure do Physics, though. He could tell me how levers and lenses and electricity and heat and all sorts of power plants worked, and predict correctly what an experiment would prove before I'd performed it—just as long as I didn't insist that he quantify anything, that he tell me what the numbers were.

He earned his Associate in the Arts and Sciences Degree in 1984. That was the only degree we awarded, fair warning to other institutions and future employers, and to the students themselves, that our graduates' intellectual achievements, while respectable, were unconventional.

Lowell Chung got me on a horse for the first time in my life when I was 43 years old. He dared me. I told him I certainly wasn't going to commit suicide on the back of one of his firecracker polo ponies, since I had a wife and a mother-in-law and 2 children to support. So he borrowed a gentle, patient old mare from his girlfriend at the time, who was Claudia Roosevelt.

Comically enough, Lowell's then girlfriend was a whiz at arithmetic, but otherwise a nitwit. You could ask her, "What is 5,111 times 10,022 divided by 97?" Claudia would reply, "That's 528,066.4. So what? So what?"

So what indeed! The lesson I myself learned over and over again when teaching at the college and then the prison was the uselessness of information to most people, except as entertainment. If facts weren't funny or scary, or couldn't make you rich, the heck with them.

When I later went to work at the prison, I encountered a mass murderer named Alton Darwin who also could do arithmetic in his head. He was Black. Unlike Claudia Roosevelt, he was highly intelligent in the verbal area. The people he had murdered were rivals or deadbeats or police informers or cases of mistaken identity or innocent bystanders in the illegal drug industry. His manner of speaking was elegant and thought-provoking.

He hadn't killed nearly as many people as I had. But then again, he hadn't had my advantage, which was the full cooperation of our Government.

Also, he had done all his killing for reasons of money. I had never stooped to that.

When I found out that he could do arithmetic in his head, I said to him, "That's a remarkable gift you have."

"Doesn't seem fair, does it," he said, "that somebody should come into the world with such a great advantage over the common folk? When I get out of here, I'm going to buy me a pretty striped tent and put up a sign saying 'One dollar. Come on in and see the Nigger do arithmetic.' " He wasn't ever going to get out of there. He was serving a life sentence without hope of parole.

Darwin's fantasy about starring in a mental-arithmetic show when he got out, incidentally, was inspired by something 1 of his great-grandfathers did in South Carolina after World War I. All the airplane pilots back then were white, and some of them did stunt flying at country fairs. They were called "barnstormers."

And 1 of these barnstormers with a 2-cockpit plane strapped Darwin's great-grandfather in the front cockpit, even though the great-grandfather couldn't even drive an automobile. The barnstormer crouched down in the rear cockpit, so people couldn't see him but he could still work the controls. And people came from far and wide, according to Darwin, "to see the Nigger fly the airplane."

He was only 25 years old when we first met, the same age as Lowell Chung when Lowell won the Bronze Medal for horseback riding in Seoul, South Korea. When I was 25, I hadn't killed anybody yet, and hadn't had nearly as many women as Darwin had. When he was only 20, he told me, he paid cash for a Ferrari. I didn't have a car of my own, which was a good car, all right, a Chevrolet Corvette, but nowhere near as good as a Ferrari, until I was 21.

At least I, too, had paid cash.

When we talked at the prison, he had a running joke that was the assumption that we came from different planets. The prison was all there was to his planet, and I had come in a flying saucer from one that was much bigger and wiser.

This enabled him to comment ironically on the only sexual activities possible inside the walls. "You have little babies on your planet?" he asked.

"Yes, we have little babies," I said.

"We got people here trying to have babies every which way," he said, "but they never get babies. What do you think they're doing wrong?"

He was the first convict I heard use the expression "the PB." He told me that sometimes he wished he had "the PB." I thought he meant "TB," short for "tuberculosis," another common affliction at the prison—common enough that I have it now.

It turned out that "PB" was short for "Parole Board," which is what the convicts called AIDS.

That was when we first met, back in 1991, when he said that sometimes he wished he had the PB, and long before I myself contracted TB.

Alphabet soup!

He was hungry for descriptions of this valley, to which he had been sentenced for the rest of his life and where he could expect to be buried, but which he had never seen. Not only the convicts but their visitors, too, were kept as ignorant as possible of the precise geographical situation of the

73

prison, so that anybody escaping would have no clear idea of what to watch out for or which way to go.

Visitors were brought into the cul-de-sac of the valley from Rochester in buses with blacked-out windows. Convicts themselves were delivered in windowless steel boxes capable of holding 10 of them wearing leg irons and handcuffs, mounted on the beds of trucks. The buses and the steel boxes were never opened until they were well inside the prison walls.

These were exceedingly dangerous and resourceful criminals, after all. While the Japanese had taken over the operation of Athena by the time I got there, hoping to operate it at a profit, the blacked-out buses and steel boxes had been in use long before they got there. Those morbid forms of transportation became a common sight on the road to and from Rochester in maybe 1977, about 2 years after I and my little family took up residence in Scipio.

The only change the Japanese made in the vehicles, which was under way when I went to work over there in 1991, was to remount the old steel boxes on new Japanese trucks.

So it was in violation of long-standing prison policy that I told Alton Darwin and other lifers all they wanted to know about the valley. I thought they were entitled to know about the great forest, which was their forest now, and the beautiful lake, which was their lake now, and the beautiful little college, which was where the music from the bells was coming from.

And of course, this enriched their dreams of escaping, but what were those but what we could call in any other context the virtue hope? I never thought they would ever really get out of here and make use of the knowledge I had given them of the countryside, and neither did they.

I used to do the same sort of thing in Vietnam, too, helping mortally wounded soldiers dream that they would soon be well and home again.

Why not?

I am as sorry as anybody that Darwin and all the rest really tasted freedom. They were horrible news for themselves and everyone. A lot of them were real homicidal maniacs. Darwin wasn't 1 of those, but even as the convicts were crossing the ice to Scipio, he was giving orders as if he were an Emperor, as if the break were his idea, although he had had nothing to do with it. He hadn't known it was coming.

Those who had actually breached the walls and opened the cells had come down from Rochester to free only 1 convict. They got him, and they were headed out of the valley and had no interest in conquering Scipio and its little army of 6 regular policemen and 3 unarmed campus cops, and an unknown number of firearms in private hands.

Alton Darwin was the first example I had ever seen of leadership in the raw. He was a man without any badges of rank, and with no previously existing organization or widely understood plan of action. He had been a modest, unremarkable man in prison. The moment he got out, though, sudden delusions of grandeur made him the only man who knew what to do next, which was to attack Scipio, where glory and riches awaited all who dared to follow him.

"Follow me!" he cried, and some did. He was a sociopath, I think, in love with himself and no one else, craving action for its own sake, and indifferent to any long-term consequences, a classic Man of Destiny.

Most did not even follow him down the slope and out onto the ice. They returned to the prison, where they had beds of their own, and shelter from the weather, and food and

75

water, although no heat or electricity. They chose to be good boys, concluding correctly that bad boys roaming free in the valley, but completely surrounded by the forces of law and order, would be shot on sight in a day or 2, or maybe even sooner. They were color-coded, after all.

In the Mohiga Valley, their skin alone sufficed as a prison uniform.

About half of those who followed Darwin out onto the ice turned back before they reached Scipio. This was before they were fired upon and suffered their first casualty. One of those who went back to the prison told me that he was sickened when he realized how much murder and rape there would be when they reached the other side in just a few minutes.

"I thought about all the little children fast asleep in their beds," he said. He had handed over the gun he had stolen from the prison armory to the man next to him, there in the middle of beautiful Lake Mohiga. "He didn't have a gun," he said, "until I gave him 1."

"Did you wish each other good luck or anything like that?" I asked him.

"We didn't say anything," he told me. "Nobody was saying anything but the man in front."

"And what was he saying?" I asked.

He replied with terrible emptiness, " 'Follow me, follow me, follow me.' "

"Life's a bad dream," he said. "Do you know that?"

Alton Darwin's charismatic delusions of grandeur went on and on. He declared himself to be President of a new country. He set up his headquarters in the Board of Trustees Room of Samoza Hall, with the big long table for his desk.

I visited him there at high noon on the second day after

the great escape. He told me that this new country of his was going to cut down the virgin forest on the other side of the lake and sell the wood to the Japanese. He would use the money to refurbish the abandoned industrial buildings in Scipio down below. He didn't know yet what they would manufacture, but he was thinking hard about that. He would welcome any suggestions I might have.

Nobody would dare attack him, he said, for fear he would harm his hostages. He held the entire Board of Trustees captive, but not the College President, Henry "Tex" Johnson, nor his wife, Zuzu. I had come to ask Darwin if he had any idea what had become of Tex and Zuzu. He didn't know.

Zuzu, it would turn out, had been killed by a person or persons unknown, possibly raped, possibly not. We will never know. It was not an ideal time for Forensic Medicine. Tex, meanwhile, was ascending the tower of the library here with a rifle and ammunition. He was going clear to the top, to turn the belfry itself into a sniper's nest.

Alton Darwin was never worried, no matter how bad things got. He laughed when he heard that paratroops, advancing on foot, had surrounded the prison across the lake and, on our side, were digging in to the west and south of Scipio. State Police and vigilantes had already set up a roadblock at the head of the lake. Alton Darwin laughed as though he had achieved a great victory.

I knew people like that in Vietnam. Jack Patton had that sort of courage. I could be as brave as Jack over there. In fact, I am pretty sure that I was shot at more and killed more people. But I was worried sick most of the time. Jack never worried. He told me so.

I asked him how he could be that way. He said, "I think I must have a screw loose. I can't care about what might happen next to me or anyone."

Alton Darwin had the same untightened screw. He was a

convicted mass murderer, but never showed any remorse that I could see.

During my last year in Vietnam, I, too, reacted at press briefings as though our defeats were victories. But I was under orders to do that. That wasn't my natural disposition.

Alton Darwin, and this was true of Jack Patton, too, spoke of trivial and serious matters in the same tone of voice, with the same gestures and facial expressions. Nothing mattered more or less than anything else.

Alton Darwin, I remember, was talking to me with seemingly deep concern about how many of the convicts who had crossed the ice with him to Scipio were deserting, were going back across the ice to the prison, or turning themselves in at the roadblock at the head of the lake in hopes of amnesty. The deserters were worriers. They didn't want to die, and they didn't want to be held responsible, even though many of them were responsible, for the murders and rapes in Scipio.

So I was pondering the desertion problem when Alton Darwin said with exactly the same intensity, "I can skate on ice. Do you believe that?"

"I beg your pardon?" I said.

"I could always roller-skate," he said. "But I never got a chance to ice-skate till this morning."

That morning, with the phones dead and the electricity cut off, with unburied bodies everywhere, and with all the food in Scipio already consumed as though by a locust plague, he had gone up to Cohen Rink and put on ice skates for the first time in his life. After a few tottering steps, he had found himself gliding around and around, and around and around.

"Roller-skating and ice-skating are just about the very same thing!" he told me triumphantly, as though he had made a scientific discovery that was going to throw an entirely new light on what had seemed a hopeless situation. "Same muscles!" he said importantly.

That's what he was doing when he was fatally shot about an hour later. He was out on the rink, gliding around and around, and around and around. I'd left him in his office, and I assumed that he was still up there. But there he was on the rink instead, going around and around, and around and around.

A shot rang out, and he fell down.

Several of his followers went to him, and he said something to them, and then he died.

It was a beautiful shot, if Darwin was really the man the College President was shooting at. He could have been shooting at me, since he knew I used to make love to his wife Zuzu when he was out of the house.

If he was shooting at Darwin instead of me, he solved one of the most difficult problems in marksmanship, the same problem solved by Lee Harvey Oswald when he shot President Kennedy, which is where to aim when you are high above your target.

As I say, "Beautiful shot."

I asked later what Alton Darwin's last words had been, and was told that they made no sense. His last words had been, "See the Nigger fly the airplane."

10

SOMETIMES Alton Darwin would talk to me about the planet he was on before he was transported in a steel box to Athena. "Drugs were food," he said. "I was in the food business. Just because people on one planet eat a certain kind of food they're hungry for, that makes them feel better after they eat it, that doesn't mean people on other planets shouldn't eat something else. On some planets I'm sure there are people who eat stones, and then feel wonderful for a little while afterwards. Then it's time to eat stones again."

I thought very little about the prison during the 15 years I was a teacher at Tarkington, as big and brutal as it was across the lake, and growing all the time. When we went picnicking at the head of the lake, or went up to Rochester on some errand or other, I saw plenty of blacked-out buses and steel boxes on the backs of trucks. Alton Darwin might have been in one of those boxes. Then again, since the steel boxes were also used to carry freight, there might have been nothing but Diet Pepsi and toilet paper in there.

Whatever was in there was none of my business until Tarkington fired me.

Sometimes when I was playing the bells and getting particularly loud echoes from the prison walls, usually in the dead of the wintertime, I would have the feeling that I was shelling the prison. In Vietnam, conversely, if I happened to be back with the artillery, and the guns were lobbing shells at who knows what in some jungle, it seemed very much like music, interesting noises for the sake of interesting noises, and nothing more.

During a summer field exercise when Jack Patton and I were still cadets, I remember, we were asleep in a tent and the artillery opened up nearby.

We awoke. Jack said to me, "They're playing our tune, Gene. They're playing our tune."

Before I went to work at Athena, I had seen only 3 convicts anywhere in the valley. Most people in Scipio hadn't seen even 1. I wouldn't have seen even 1, either, if a truck with a steel box in back hadn't broken down at the head of the lake. I was picnicking there, near the water, with Margaret, my wife, and Mildred, my mother-in-law. Mildred was crazy as a bedbug by then, but Margaret was still sane, and there seemed a good chance that she always would be.

I was only 45, foolishly confident that I would go on teaching here until I reached the mandatory retirement age of 70 in 2010, 9 years from now. What in fact will happen to me in 9 more years? That is like worrying about a cheese spoiling if you don't put it in the refrigerator. What can happen to a pricelessly stinky cheese that hasn't already happened to it?

My mother-in-law, no danger to herself or anyone else, adored fishing. I had put a worm on her hook for her and pitched it out to a spot that looked promising. She gripped the rod with both hands, sure as always that something miraculous was about to happen.

She was right this time.

I looked up at the top of the bank, and there was a prison truck with smoke pouring out of its engine compartment. There were only 2 guards on board, and 1 of them was the driver. They bailed out. They had already radioed the prison for help. They were both white. This was before the Japanese took over Athena as a business proposition, before the road signs all the way from Rochester were in both English and Japanese.

It looked as though the truck might catch fire, so the 2 guards unlocked the little door in the back of the steel box and told the prisoners to come out. And then they backed off and waited with sawed-off automatic shotguns leveled at the little door.

Out the prisoners came. There were only 3 of them, clumsy in leg irons, and their handcuffs were shackled to chains around their waists. Two were black and 1 was white, or possibly a light Hispanic. This was before the Supreme Court confirmed that it was indeed cruel and inhuman punishment to confine a person in a place where his or her race was greatly outnumbered by another 1.

The races were still mixed in prisons throughout the country. When I later went to work at Athena, though, there was nothing but people who had been classified as Black in there.

My mother-in-law did not turn around to see the smoking van and all. She was obsessed by what might happen at any moment at the other end of her fishline. But Margaret and I gawked. For us back then, prisoners were like pornography, common things nice people shouldn't want to see, even though the biggest industry by far in this valley was punishment.

When Margaret and I talked about it later, she didn't say

it was like pornography. She said it was like seeing animals on their way to a slaughterhouse.

We, in turn, must have looked to those convicts like people in Paradise. It was a balmy day in the springtime. A sailboat race was going on to the south of us. The college had just been given 30 little sloops by a grateful parent who had cleaned out the biggest savings and loan bank in California.

Our brand-new Mercedes sedan was parked on the beach nearby. It cost more than my annual salary at Tarkington. The car was a gift from the mother of a student of mine named Pierre LeGrand. His maternal grandfather had been dictator of Haiti, and had taken the treasury of that country with him when he was overthrown. That was why Pierre's mother was so rich. He was very unpopular. He tried to win friends by making expensive gifts to them, but that didn't work, so he tried to hang himself from a girder of the water tower on top of Musket Mountain. I happened to be up there, in the bushes with the wife of the coach of the Tennis Team.

So I cut him down with my Swiss Army knife. That was how I got the Mercedes.

Pierre would have better luck 2 years later, jumping off the Golden Gate Bridge, and a campus joke was that now I had to give the Mercedes back.

So there were plenty of heartaches in what, as I've said, must have looked to those 3 convicts like Paradise. There was no way they could tell that my mother-in-law was as crazy as a bedbug, as long as she kept her back to them. They could not know, and neither could I, of course, that hereditary insanity would hit my pretty wife like a ton of bricks in about 6 months' time and turn her into a hag as scary as her mother.

If we had had our 2 kids with us on the beach, that would have completed the illusion that we lived in Paradise. They could have depicted another generation that found life as comfortable as we did. Both sexes would have been represented. We had a girl named Melanie and a boy named Eugene Debs Hartke, Jr. But they weren't kids anymore. Melanie was 21, and studying mathematics at Cambridge University in England. Eugene Jr. was completing his senior year at Deerfield Academy in Massachusetts, and was 18, and had his own rock-and-roll band, and had composed maybe 100 songs by then.

But Melanie would have spoiled our tableau on the beach. Like my mother until she went to Weight Watchers, she was very heavy. That must be hereditary. If she had kept her back to the convicts, she might at least have concealed the fact that she had a bulbous nose like the late, great, alcoholic comedian W. C. Fields. Melanie, thank goodness, was not also an alcoholic.

But her brother was.

And I could kill myself now for having boasted to him that on my side of the family the men had no fear of alcohol, since they knew how to drink in moderation. We were not weak and foolish where drugs were concerned.

At least Eugene Jr. was beautiful, having inherited the features of his mother. When he was growing up in this valley, people could not resist saying to me, with him right there to hear it, that he was the most beautiful child they'd ever seen.

I have no idea where he is now. He stopped communicating with me or anybody in this valley years ago.

He hates me.

So does Melanie, although she wrote to me as recently as 2 years ago. She was living in Paris with another woman. They were both teaching English and math in an American high school over there.

My kids will never forgive me for not putting my mother-in-law into a mental hospital instead of keeping her at home, where she was a great embarrassment to them. They couldn't bring friends home. If I had put Mildred into a nuthouse, though, I couldn't have afforded to send Melanie and Eugene Jr. to such expensive schools. I got a free house at Tarkington, but my salary was small.

Also, I didn't think Mildred's craziness was as unbearable as they did. In the Army I had grown used to people who talked nonsense all day long. Vietnam was 1 big hallucination. After adjusting to that, I could adjust to anything.

What my children most dislike me for, though, is my reproducing in conjunction with their mother. They live in constant dread of suddenly going as batty as Mildred and Margaret. Unfortunately, there is a good chance of that.

Ironically enough, I happen to have an illegitimate son about whom I learned only recently. Since he had a different mother, he need not expect to go insane someday. Some of his kids, if he ever has any, could inherit my own mother's tendency to fatness, though.

But they could join Weight Watchers as Mother did.

Heredity is obviously much on my mind these days, and should be. So I have been reading up on it some in a book that also deals with embryology. And I tell you: People who are wary of what they might find in a book if they opened 1 are right to be. I have just had my mind blown by an essay on the embryology of the human eye.

No combination of Time and Luck could have produced a camera that excellent, not even if the quantity of time had been 1,000,000,000,000 years! How is that for an unsolved mystery?

When I went to work at Athena, I hoped to find at least 1 of the 3 convicts who had seen Mildred and Margaret and me having a picnic so long ago. As I've said, I took 1 of them to be a White, or possibly Hispanic. So he would have been transferred to a White or Hispanic prison before I ever got there. The other 2 were clearly black, but I never found either of them. I would have liked to hear what we looked like to them, how contented we seemed to be.

They were probably dead. AIDS could have got them, or murder or suicide, or maybe tuberculosis. Every year, 30 inmates at Athena died for every student who was awarded an Associate in the Arts and Sciences Degree by Tarkington.

Parole.

If I had found a convict who had witnessed our picnic, we might have talked about the fish my mother-in-law hooked while he was watching. He saw her rod bend double, heard the reel scream like a little siren. But he never got to see the monster who had taken her bait and was headed south for Scipio. Before he could see it, he was back in darkness in another van.

It was heavy test line I had put on the reel. This was deep-sea stuff made for tuna and shark, although, as far as we knew, there was nothing in Lake Mohiga but eels and perch and little catfish. That was all Mildred had ever caught before.

One time, I remember, she caught a perch too little to keep. So I turned it loose, even though the barb of the hook had come out through one eye. A few minutes later she hooked that same perch again. We could tell by the mangled eye. Think about that. Miraculous eyes, and no brains whatsoever.

I put such heavy test line on Mildred's reel so that nothing could ever get away from her. In Honduras 1 time I did the same thing for a 3-star General, whose aide I was.

Mildred's fish couldn't snap the line, and Mildred wouldn't let go of the rod. She didn't weigh anything, and the fish weighed a lot for a fish. Mildred went down on her knees in the water, laughing and crying.

I'll never forget what she was saying: "It's God! It's God!"

I waded out to help her. She wouldn't let go of the rod, so I grasped the line and began to haul it in, hand over hand.

How the water swirled and boiled out there!

When I got the fish into shallow water, it suddenly quit fighting. I guess it had used up every bit of its energy. That was that.

This fish, which I picked up by the gills and flung up on the bank, was an enormous pickerel. Margaret looked down at it in horror and said, "It's a crocodile!"

I looked at the top of the bank to see what the convicts and guards thought of a fish that big. They were gone. There was nothing but the broken-down van up there. The little door to its steel box was wide open. Anybody was free to climb inside and close the door, in case he or she wondered what it felt like to be a prisoner.

To those fascinated by Forensic Medicine: The pickerel had not bitten on the worm on the hook. It had bitten on a perch which had bitten on the worm on the hook.

I thought that would be interesting to my mother-in-law during our trip back home in the new Mercedes. But she didn't want to talk about the fish at all. It had scared the daylights out of her, and she wanted to forget it.

As the years went by, I would mention the fish from time to time without getting anything back from her but a stony silence. I concluded that she really had purged it from her memory.

But then, on the night of the prison break, when the 3 of us were living in an old house in the hamlet of Athena, down below the prison walls, there was this terrific explosion that woke us up.

If Jack Patton had been there with us, he might have said to me, "Gene! Gene! They're playing our tune again."

The explosion was in fact the demolition of Athena's main gate from the outside, not the inside. The purported head of the Jamaican drug cartel, Jeffrey Turner, had been brought down to Athena in a steel box 6 months before, after a televised trial lasting a year and a half. He was given 25 consecutive life sentences, said to be a new record. Now a well-rehearsed force of his employees, variously estimated as being anything from a platoon to a company, had arrived outside the prison with explosives, a tank, and several half-tracks taken from the National Guard Armory about 10 kilometers south of Rochester, across the highway from the Meadowdale Cinema Complex. One of their number, it has since come out, moved to Rochester and joined the National Guard, swearing to defend the Constitution and all that, with the sole purpose of stealing the keys to the Armory.

The Japanese guards were wholly unprepared and unmotivated to resist such a force, especially since the attackers were all dressed in American Army uniforms and waving American flags. So they hid or put their hands up or ran off into the virgin forest. This wasn't their country, and guarding prisoners wasn't a sacred mission or anything like that. It was just a business.

The telephone and power lines were cut, so they couldn't even call for help or blow the siren.

The assault lasted half an hour. When it was over, Jeffrey Turner was gone, and he hasn't been seen since. The attackers also disappeared. Their uniforms and military vehicles were subsequently found at an abandoned dairy farm owned by German land speculators a kilometer north of the end of the lake. There were tire tracks of many automobiles, which led police to conclude that it was by means of unremarkable civilian vehicles, seemingly unrelated, and no doubt leaving the farm at timed intervals, that the lawless force had made its 100-percent-successful getaway.

Meanwhile, back at the prison, anyone who didn't want to stay inside the walls anymore was free to walk out of there, first taking, if he was so inclined and got there early, a rifle or a shotgun or a pistol or a tear-gas grenade from the wide-open prison armory.

The police said, too, that the attackers of the prison obviously had had first-class military training somewhere, possibly at a private survival school somewhere in this country, or maybe in Bolivia or Colombia or Peru.

Anyway: Margaret and Mildred and I were awakened by the explosion, which demolished the main gate of the prison. There was no way we could have imagined what was really going on.

The 3 of us were sleeping in separate bedrooms. Margaret was on the first floor, Mildred and I were on the second floor. No sooner had I sat up, my ears ringing, than Mildred came into my room stark naked, her eyes open wide.

She spoke first. She used a slang word for hugeness I had never heard her speak before. It wasn't slang of her generation or even mine. It was slang of my children's generation. I guess she had heard it and liked it, and then held it in reserve for some really important occasion.

Here is what she said, as sporadic small-arms fire broke out at the prison: "Do you remember that *humongous* fish I caught?"

11

AT one time I fully expected to spend the rest of my life in this valley, but not in jail. I envisioned my mandatory retirement from Tarkington College in 2010. I would be modestly well-off with Social Security and a pension from the College. My mother-in-law would surely be dead by then, I thought, so I would have only Margaret to care for. I would rent a little house in the town below. There were plenty of empty ones.

But that dream would have been blasted even if there hadn't been a prison break, even if the Social Security system hadn't gone bust and the College Treasurer hadn't run off with the pension funds and so on. For, as I've said before, in 1991 Tarkington College fired me.

There I was in late middle age, cut loose in a thoroughly looted, bankrupt nation whose assets had been sold off to foreigners, a nation swamped by unchecked plagues and superstition and illiteracy and hypnotic TV, with virtually no health services for the poor. Where to go? What to do?

The man who got me fired was Jason Wilder, the celebrated Conservative newspaper columnist, lecturer, and television talk-show host. He saved my life by doing that. If it weren't for him, I would have been on the Scipio side of the lake instead of the Athena side during the prison break.

I would have been facing all those convicts as they crossed the ice to Scipio in the moonlight, instead of watching them in mute wonderment from the rear, like Robert E. Lee during Pickett's Charge at the Battle of Gettysburg. They wouldn't have known me, and I would still have seen only 3 Athena convicts in all my time.

I would have tried to fight in some way, although, unlike the College President, I would have had no guns. I would have been killed and buried along with the College President and his wife Zuzu, and Alton Darwin and all the rest of them. I would have been buried next to the stable, in the shadow of Musket Mountain when the Sun went down.

The first time I saw Jason Wilder in person was at the Board meeting when they fired me. He was then only an outraged parent. He would later join the Board and become by far the most valuable of the convicts' hostages after the prison break. Their threat to kill him immobilized units of the 82nd Airborne Division, which had been brought in by school bus from the South Bronx. The paratroops sealed off the valley at the head of the lake and occupied the shoreline across from Scipio and to the south of Scipio, and dug in on the western slope of Musket Mountain. But they dared not come any closer, for fear of causing the death of Jason Wilder.

There were other hostages, to be sure, including the rest of the Trustees, but he was the only famous one. I myself was not strictly a hostage, although I would probably have been killed if I had tried to leave. I was a sort of floating, noncombatant wise man, wandering wherever I pleased in Scipio under siege. As at Athena Prison, I tried to give the most honest answer I could to any question anyone might care to put to me. Otherwise I stayed silent. I volunteered no advice

91

at Athena, and none in Scipio under siege. I simply described the truth of the inquirer's situation in the context of
the world outside as best I could. What he did next was up
to him.

I call that being a teacher. I don't call that being a mastermind of a treasonous enterprise. All I ever wanted to over-
throw was ignorance and self-serving fantasies.

I was fired without warning on Graduation Day. I was
playing the bells at high noon when a girl who had just
completed her freshman year brought the news that the
Board of Trustees, then meeting in Samoza Hall, the administration building, wanted to talk to me. She was Kimberley
Wilder, Jason Wilder's learning-disabled daughter. She was
stupid. I thought it was odd but not menacing that the Trustees would have used her for a messenger. I couldn't imagine
what business she might have had that would bring her
anywhere near their meeting. She had in fact been testify-
ing before them about my supposed lack of patriotism, and
had then asked for the honor of fetching me to my liquida-
tion.

She was one of the few underclasspersons still on the campus. The rest had gone home, and relatives of those about
to get their Associate in the Arts and Sciences certificates
had taken over their suites. No relative of Kimberley's was
about to graduate. She had stayed around for the Trustees'
meeting. And her famous father had come by helicopter to
back her up. The soccer field was being used as a heliport.
It looked like a rookery for pterodactyls.

Others had arrived in conventional aircraft at Rochester,
where they had been met by rented limousines provided by
the college. One senior's stepmother said, I remember, that
she thought she had landed in Yokohama instead of Rochester because there were so many Japanese. The thing was
that the changing of the guard at Athena had coincided with
Graduation Day. New guards, mostly country boys from

Hokkaido, who spoke no English and had never seen the United States, were flown directly to Rochester from Tokyo every 6 months, and taken to Athena by bus. And then those who had served 6 months at the gates, and on the walls and catwalks over the mess halls, and in the watchtowers, and so on, were flown straight home.

"How come you haven't gone home, Kimberley?" I said.

She said that she and her father wanted to hear the graduation address, which was to be delivered by her father's close friend and fellow Rhodes Scholar, Dr. Martin Peale Blankenship, the University of Chicago economist who would later become a quadriplegic as a result of a skiing accident in Switzerland.

Dr. Blankenship had a niece in the graduating class. That was what brought him to Scipio. His niece was Hortense Mellon. I have no idea what became of Hortense. She could play the harp. I remember that, and her upper teeth were false. The real teeth were knocked out by a mugger as she left a friend's coming-out party at the Waldorf-Astoria, which has since burned down. There is nothing but a vacant lot there now, which was bought by the Japanese.

I heard that her father, like so many other Tarkington parents, lost an awful lot of money in the biggest swindle in the history of Wall Street, stock in a company called Microsecond Arbitrage.

I had spotted Kimberley as a snoop, all right, but not as a walking recording studio. All through the academic year now ending, our paths had crossed with puzzling frequency. Again and again I would be talking to somebody, almost anywhere on the campus, and realize that Kimberley was lurking close by. I assumed that she was slightly cracked, and was eavesdropping on everyone, avid for gossip. She wasn't even taking a course of mine for credit, although she did audit both Physics for Nonscientists and Music Appreciation for Nonmusicians. So what could I possibly be to her or she to me? We had never had a conversation about anything.

One time, I remember, I was shooting pool in the new recreation center, the Pahlavi Pavilion, and she was so close that I was having trouble working my cuestick, and I said to her, "Do you like my perfume?"

"What?" she said.

"I find you so close to me so often," I said, "I thought maybe you liked my perfume. I'm very flattered, if that's the case, because that's nothing but my natural body odor. I don't use perfume."

I can quote myself exactly, since those words were on one of the tapes the Trustees would play back for me.

She shrugged as though she didn't know what I was talking about. She didn't leave the Pavilion in great embarrassment. On the contrary! She gave me a little more room for my cuestick but was still practically on top of me.

I was playing 8-ball head to head with the novelist Paul Slazinger, that year's Writer in Residence. He was dead broke and out of print, which is the only reason anybody ever became Writer in Residence at Tarkington. He was so old that he had actually been in World War II. He had won a Silver Star like me when I was only 3 years old!

He asked me who Kimberley was, and I said, and she got this on tape, too, "Pay no attention. She's just another member of the Ruling Class."

So the Board of Trustees would want to know what it was, exactly, that I had against the Ruling Class.

I didn't say so back then, but I am perfectly happy to say now that the trouble with the Ruling Class was that too many of its members were nitwits like Kimberley.

One theory I had about her snooping was that she was titillated by my reputation as the campus John F. Kennedy as far as sex outside of marriage was concerned.

If President Kennedy up in Heaven ever made a list of all the women he had made love to, I am sure it would be 2 or 3 times as long as the one I am making down here in jail. Then again, he had the glamour of his office, and the full cooperation of the Secret Service and the White House Staff. None of the names on my list would mean anything to the general public, whereas many on his would belong to movie stars. He made love to Marilyn Monroe. I sure never did. She evidently expected to marry him and become First Lady, which was a joke to everybody but her.

She eventually committed suicide. She finally found life too embarrassing.

I still hardly knew Kimberley when she appeared in the bell tower on Graduation Day. But she was chatty, as though we were old, old pals. She was still recording me, although what she already had on tape was enough to do me in.

She asked me if I thought the speech Paul Slazinger, the Writer in Residence, gave in Chapel had been a good one. This was probably the most anti-American speech I had ever heard. He gave it right before Christmas vacation, and was never again seen in Scipio. He had just won a so-called Genius Grant from the MacArthur Foundation, $50,000 a year for 5 years. On the same night of his speech he bugged out for Key West, Florida.

He predicted, I remember, that human slavery would come back, that it had in fact never gone away. He said that so many people wanted to come here because it was so easy to rob the poor people, who got absolutely no protection from the Government. He talked about bridges falling down and water mains breaking because of no maintenance. He talked about oil spills and radioactive waste and poisoned aquifers and looted banks and liquidated corporations. "And nobody ever gets punished for anything," he said. "Being an American means never having to say you're sorry."

On and on he went. No matter what he said, he was still going to get $50,000 a year for 5 years.

I said to Kimberley that I thought Slazinger had said some things which were worth considering, but that, on the whole, he had made the country sound a lot worse than it really was, and that ours was still far and away the best one on the planet.

She could not have gotten much satisfaction from that reply.

What do I myself make of that reply nowadays? It was an inane reply.

She asked me about my own lecture in Chapel only a month earlier. She hadn't attended and so hadn't taped it. She was seeking confirmation of things other people had said I said. My lecture had been humorous recollections of my maternal grandfather, Benjamin Wills, the old-time Socialist.

She accused me of saying that all rich people were drunks and lunatics. This was a garbling of Grandfather's saying that Capitalism was what the people with all our money, drunk or sober, sane or insane, decided to do today. So I straightened that out, and explained that the opinion was my grandfather's, not my own.

"I heard your speech was worse than Mr. Slazinger's," she said.

"I certainly hope not," I said. "I was trying to show how outdated my grandfather's opinions were. I wanted people to laugh. They did."

"I heard you said Jesus Christ was un-American," she said, her tape recorder running all the time.

So I unscrambled that one for her. The original had been another of Grandfather's sayings. He repeated Karl Marx's prescription for an ideal society, "From each according to his abilities, to each according to his needs." And then he asked me, meaning it to be a wry joke, "What could be more un-American, Gene, than sounding like the Sermon on the Mount?"

"What about putting all the Jews in a concentration camp in Idaho?" said Kimberley.

"What about what-what-what?" I asked in bewilderment. At last, at last, and too late, too late, I understood that this stupid girl was as dangerous as a cobra. It would be catastrophic if she spread the word that I was an anti-Semite, especially with so many Jews, having interbred with Gentiles, now sending their children to Tarkington.

"In all my life, I never said anything like that," I promised.

"Maybe it wasn't Idaho," she said.

"Wyoming?" I said.

"OK, Wyoming," she said. "Lock 'em all up, right?"

"I only said 'Wyoming' because I was married in Wyoming," I said. "I've never been to Idaho or even thought about Idaho. I'm just trying to figure out what you've got so all mixed up and upside down. It doesn't sound even a little bit like me."

"Jews," she said.

"That was my grandfather again," I said.

"He hated Jews, right?" she said.

"No, no, no," I said. "He admired a lot of them."

"But he still wanted to put them in concentration camps," she said. "Right?"

The origin of this most poisonous misunderstanding was in my account in Chapel of riding around with Grandfather in his car one Sunday morning in Midland City, Ohio, when I was a little boy. He, not I, was mocking all organized religions.

When we passed a Catholic church, I recalled, he said, "You think your dad's a good chemist? They're turning soda crackers into meat in there. Can your dad do that?"

When we passed a Pentecostal church, he said, "The mental giants in there believe that every word is true in a book put together by a bunch of preachers 300 years after the birth of Christ. I hope you won't be that dumb about words set in type when you grow up."

I would later hear, incidentally, that the woman my father got involved with when I was in high school, when he jumped out a window with his pants down and got bitten by a dog and tangled in a clothesline and so on, was a member of that Pentecostal church.

What he said about Jews that morning was actually another kidding of Christianity. He had to explain to me, as I would have to explain to Kimberley, that the Bible consisted of 2 separate works, the New Testament and the Old Testament. Religious Jews gave credence only to what was supposedly their own history, the Old Testament, whereas Christians took both works seriously.

"I pity the Jews," said Grandfather, "trying to get through life with only half a Bible."

And then he added, "That's like trying to get from here to San Francisco with a road map that stops at Dubuque, Iowa."

I was angry now. "Kimberley," I asked, "did you by any chance tell the Board of Trustees that I said these things? Is that what they want to see me about?"

"Maybe," she said. She was acting cute. I thought this was a dumb answer. It was in fact accurate. The Trustees had a lot more they wanted to discuss than misrepresentations of my Chapel lecture.

I found her both repulsive and pitiful. She thought she was such a heroine and I was such a viper! Now that I had caught on to what she had been up to, she was thrilled to show me that she was proud and unafraid. Little did she know that I had once thrown a man almost as big as she out of a helicopter. What was to prevent me from throwing her out a tower window? The thought of doing that to her crossed my mind. I was so insulted! That would teach her not to insult me!

The man I threw out of the helicopter had spit in my face and bitten my hand. I had taught him not to insult me.

She was pitiful because she was a dimwit from a brilliant family and believed that she at last had done something brilliant, too, in getting the goods on a person whose ideas were criminal. I didn't know yet that her Rhodes Scholar father, a Phi Beta Kappa from Princeton, had put her up to this. I thought she had noted her father's conviction, often expressed in his columns and on his TV show, and no doubt at home, that a few teachers who secretly hated their country were making young people lose faith in its future and leadership.

I thought that, just on her own, she had resolved to find such a villain and get him fired, proving that she wasn't so dumb, after all, and that she was really Daddy's little girl.

Wrong.

"Kimberley," I said, as an alternative to throwing her out the window, "this is ridiculous."

Wrong.

"All right," I said, "we're going to settle this in a hurry."

Wrong.

I would stride into the Trustees' meeting, I thought, shoulders squared, and radiant with righteous indignation, the most popular teacher on campus, and the only faculty member who had medals from the Vietnam War. When it comes right down to it, that is why they fired me, although I don't believe they themselves realized that that was why they fired me: I had ugly, personal knowledge of the disgrace that was the Vietnam War.

None of the Trustees had been in that war, and neither

had Kimberley's father, and not one of them had allowed a son or a daughter to be sent over there. Across the lake in the prison, of course, and down in the town, there were plenty of somebody's sons who had been sent over there.

12

I met just 2 people when I crossed the Quadrangle to Samoza Hall. One was Professor Marilyn Shaw, head of the Department of Life Sciences. She was the only other faculty member who had served in Vietnam. She had been a nurse. The other was Norman Everett, an old campus gardener like my grandfather. He had a son who had been paralyzed from the waist down by a mine in Vietnam and was a permanent resident in a Veterans Administration hospital over in Schenectady.

The seniors and their families and the rest of the faculty were having lunch in the Pavilion. Everybody got a lobster which had been boiled alive.

I never considered making a pass at Marilyn, although she was reasonably attractive and unattached. I don't know why that is. There may have been some sort of incest taboo operating, as though we were brother and sister, since we had both been in Vietnam.

She is dead now, buried next to the stable, in the shadow of Musket Mountain when the Sun goes down. She was evidently hit by a stray bullet. Who in his right mind would have taken dead aim at her?

Remembering her now, I wonder if I wasn't in love with

her, even though we avoided talking to each other as much as possible.

Maybe I should put her on a very short list indeed: all the women I loved. That would be Marilyn, I think, and Margaret during the first 4 years or so of our marriage, before I came home with the clap. I was also very fond of Harriet Gummer, the war correspondent for *The Des Moines Register,* who, it turns out, bore me a son after our love affair in Manila. I think I felt what could be called love for Zuzu Johnson, whose husband was crucified. And I had a deep, thoroughly reciprocated, multidimensioned friendship with Muriel Peck, who was a bartender at the Black Cat Café the day I was fired, who later became a member of the English Department.

End of list.

Muriel, too, is buried next to the stable, in the shadow of Musket Mountain when the Sun goes down.

Harriet Gummer is also dead, but out in Iowa.

Hey, girls, wait for me, wait for me.

I don't expect to break a world's record with the number of women I made love to, whether I loved them or not. As far as I am concerned, the record set by Georges Simenon, the French mystery writer, can stand for all time. According to his obituary in *The New York Times,* he copulated with 3 different women a day for years and years.

Marilyn Shaw and I hadn't known each other in Vietnam, but we had a friend in common there, Sam Wakefield. Afterward, he had hired both of us for Tarkington, and then committed suicide for reasons unclear even to himself, judging from the plagiarized note he left on his bedside table.

He and his wife, who would become Tarkington's Dean of Women, were sleeping in separate rooms by then.

Sam Wakefield, in my opinion, saved Marilyn's and my lives before he gave up on his own. If he hadn't hired both of us for Tarkington, where we both became very good teachers of the learning-disabled, I don't know what would have become of either of us. When we passed yet again like ships in the night on the Quadrangle, with me on my way to get fired, I was, incredibly, a tenured Full Professor of Physics and she was a tenured Full Professor of Life Sciences!

When I was still a teacher here, I asked GRIOT™, the most popular computer game at the Pahlavi Pavilion, what might have become of me after the war instead of what really happened. The way you play GRIOT™, of course, is to tell the computer the age and race and degree of education and present situation and drug use, if any, and so on of a person. The person doesn't have to be real. The computer doesn't ask if the person is real or not. It doesn't care about anything. It especially doesn't care about hurting people's feelings. You load it up with details about a life, real or imagined, and then it spits out a story about what was likely to happen to him or her. This story is based on what has happened to real persons with the same general specifications.

GRIOT™ won't work without certain pieces of information. If you leave out race, for instance, it flashes the words "ethnic origin" on its screen, and stops cold. If it doesn't know that, it can't go on. The same with education.

I didn't tell GRIOT™ that I had landed a job I loved here. I told it only about my life up to the end of the Vietnam War. It knew all about the Vietnam War and the sorts of veterans it had produced. It made me a burned-out case, on the basis of my length of service over there, I think. It had me becoming a wife-beater and an alcoholic, and winding up all alone on Skid Row.

If I had access to GRIOT™ now, I might ask it what might have happened to Marilyn Shaw if Sam Wakefield hadn't rescued her. But the escaped convicts smashed up the one in the Pavilion soon after I showed them how to work it.

They hated it, and I didn't blame them. I was immediately sorry that I had let them know of its existence. One by one they punched in their race and age and what their parents did, if they knew, and how long they'd gone to school and what drugs they'd taken and so on, and GRIOT™ sent them straight to jail to serve long sentences.

I have no idea how much GRIOT™ back then may have known about Vietnam nurses. The manufacturers claimed then as now that no program in stores was more than 3 months old, and so every program was right up-to-date about what had really happened to this or that sort of person at the time you bought it. The programmers, supposedly, were constantly updating GRIOT™ with the news of the day about plumbers, about podiatrists, about Vietnam boat people and Mexican wetbacks, about drug smugglers, about paraplegics, about everyone you could think of within the continental limits of the United States and Canada.

There is some question now, I've heard, about whether GRIOT™ is as deep and up-to-date as it used to be, since Parker Brothers, the company that makes it, has been taken over by Koreans. The new owners are moving the whole operation to Indonesia, where labor costs next to nothing. They say they will keep up with American news by satellite. One wonders.

I don't need any help from GRIOT™ to know that Marilyn Shaw had a much rougher war than I did. All the soldiers she had to deal with were wounded, and all of them expected of her what was more often than not impossible: that she make them whole again.

I know that she was married, and that her husband back home divorced her and married somebody else while she was still over there, and that she didn't care. She and Sam Wakefield may have been lovers over there. I never asked.

That seems likely. After the war he went looking for her and found her taking a course in Computer Science at New York University. She didn't want to be a nurse anymore. He told her that maybe she should try being a teacher instead. She asked him if there was a chapter of Alcoholics Anonymous in Scipio, and he said there was.

After he shot himself, Marilyn, Professor Shaw, fell off the wagon for about a week. She disappeared, and I was given the job of finding her. I discovered her downtown, drunk and asleep on a pool table in the back room of the Black Cat Café. She was drooling on the felt. One hand was on the cue ball, as though she meant to throw it at something when she regained consciousness.

As far as I know, she never took another drink.

GRIOT™, in the old days anyway, before the Koreans promised to make Parker Brothers lean and mean in Indonesia, didn't come up with the same biography every time you gave it a certain set of facts. Like life itself, it offered a variety of possibilities, spitting out endings according to what the odds for winning or losing or whatever were known to be.

After GRIOT™ put me on Skid Row 15 years ago, I had it try again. I did a little better, but not as well as I was doing here. It had me stay in the Army and become an instructor at West Point, but unhappy and bored. I lost my wife again, and still drank too much, and had a succession of woman friends who soon got sick of me and my depressions. And I died of cirrhosis of the liver a second time.

GRIOT™ didn't have many alternatives to jail for the escaped convicts, though. If it came up with a parole, it soon put the ex-con back in a cage again.

The same thing happened if GRIOT™ was told that the jailbird was Hispanic. It was somewhat more optimistic about Whites, if they could read and write, and had never been in a mental hospital or been given a Dishonorable Discharge from the Armed Forces. Otherwise, they might as well be Black or Hispanic.

The wild cards among jailbirds, as far as GRIOT™ was concerned, were Orientals and American Indians.

When the Supreme Court handed down its decision that prisoners should be segregated according to race, many jurisdictions did not have enough Oriental or American Indian criminals to make separate institutions for them economically feasible. Hawaii, for example, had only 2 American Indian prisoners, and Wyoming, my wife's home state, had only 1 Oriental.

Under such circumstances, said the Court, Indians and/or Orientals should be made honorary Whites, and treated accordingly.

This state has plenty of both, however, particularly after Indians began to make tax-free fortunes smuggling drugs over unmapped trails across the border from Canada. So the Indians had a prison all their own at what their ancestors used to call "Thunder Beaver," what we call "Niagara Falls." The Orientals have their own prison at Deer Park, Long Island, conveniently located only 50 kilometers from their heroin-processing plants in New York City's Chinatown.

When you dare to think about how huge the illegal drug business is in this country, you have to suspect that practically everybody has a steady buzz on, just as I did during my last 2 years in high school, and just as General Grant did during the Civil War, and just as Winston Churchill did during World War II.

So Marilyn Shaw and I passed yet again like ships in the night on the Quadrangle. It would be our last encounter there. Without either of us knowing that it would be the last time, she said something that in retrospect is quite moving to me. What she said was derived from our exploratory conversation at the cocktail party that had welcomed us to the faculty so long ago.

I had told her about how I met Sam Wakefield at the Cleveland Science Fair, and what the first words were that he ever spoke to me. Now, as I hastened to my doom, she played back those words to me: "What's the hurry, Son?"

13

THE Chairman of the Board of Trustees that fired me 10 years ago was Robert W. Moellenkamp of West Palm Beach, himself a graduate of Tarkington and the father of 2 Tarkingtonians, 1 of whom had been my student. As it happened, he was on the verge of losing his fortune, which was nothing but paper, in Microsecond Arbitrage, Incorporated. That swindle claimed to be snapping up bargains in food and shelter and clothing and fuel and medicine and raw materials and machinery and so on before people who really needed them could learn of their existence. And then the company's computers, supposedly, would get the people who really needed whatever it was to bid against each other, running profits right through the roof. It was able to do this with its clients' money, supposedly, because its computers were linked by satellites to marketplaces in every corner of the world.

The computers, it would turn out, weren't connected to anything but each other and their credulous clients like Tarkington's Board Chairman. He was high as a kite on printouts describing brilliant trades he had made in places like Tierra del Fuego and Uganda and God knows where else, when he agreed with the Panjandrum of American Conservatism, Jason Wilder, that it was time to fire me.

Microsecond Arbitrage was his angel dust, his LSD, his heroin, his jug of Thunderbird wine, his cocaine.

I myself have been addicted to older women and housekeeping, which my court-appointed lawyer tells me might be germs we could make grow into a credible plea of insanity. The most amazing thing to him was that I had never masturbated.

"Why not?" he said.

"My mother's father made me promise never to do it, because it would make me lazy and crazy," I said.

"And you believed him?" he said. He is only 23 years old, fresh out of Syracuse.

And I said, "Counselor, in these fast-moving times, with progress gone hog-wild, grandfathers are bound to be wrong about everything."

Robert W. Moellenkamp hadn't heard yet that he and his wife and kids were as broke as any convict in Athena. So when I came into the Board Room back in 1991, he addressed me in the statesmanlike tones of a prudent conservator of a noble legacy. He nodded in the direction of Jason Wilder, who was then simply a Tarkington parent, not a member of the Board. Wilder sat at the opposite end of the great oval table with a manila folder, a tape recorder and cassettes, and a Polaroid photograph deployed before him.

I knew who he was, of course, and something of how his mind worked, having read his newspaper column and watched his television show from time to time. But we had not met before. The Board members on either side of him had crowded into one another in order to give him plenty of room for some kind of performance.

He was the only celebrity there. He was probably the only true celebrity ever to set foot in that Board Room.

There was 1 other non-Trustee present. That was the

College President, Henry "Tex" Johnson, whose wife Zuzu, as I've already said, I used to make love to when he was away from home any length of time. Zuzu and I had broken up for good about a month before, but we were still on speaking terms.

"Please take a seat, Gene," said Moellenkamp. "Mr. Wilder, who I guess you know is Kimberley's father, has a rather disturbing story he wants to tell to you."

"I see," I said, a good soldier doing as he was told. I wanted to keep my job. This was my home. When the time came, I wanted to retire here and then be buried here. That was before it was clear that glaciers were headed south again, and that anybody buried here, including the gang by the stable, along with Musket Mountain itself, would eventually wind up in Pennsylvania or West Virginia. Or Maryland.

Where else could I become a Full Professor or a college teacher of any rank, with nothing but a Bachelor of Science Degree from West Point? I couldn't even teach high school or grade school, since I had never taken any of the required courses in education. At my age, which was then 51, who would hire me for anything, and especially with a demented wife and mother-in-law in tow.

I said to the Trustees and Jason Wilder, "I believe I know most of what the story is, ladies and gentlemen. I've just been with Kimberley, and she gave me a pretty good rehearsal for what I'd better say here.

"When listening to her charges against me, I can only hope you did not lose sight of what you yourselves have learned about me during my 15 years of faithful service to Tarkington. This Board itself, surely, can provide all the character witnesses I could ever need. If not, bring in parents and students. Choose them at random. You know and I know that they will all speak well of me."

I nodded respectfully in Jason Wilder's direction. "I am

glad to meet you in person, sir. I read your columns and watch your TV show regularly. I find what you have to say invariably thought-provoking, and so do my wife and her mother, both of them invalids." I wanted to get that in about my 2 sick dependents, in case Wilder and a couple of new Trustees hadn't heard about them.

Actually, I was laying it on pretty thick. Although Margaret and her mother read to each other a lot, taking turns, and usually by flashlight in a tent they'd made inside the house out of bedspreads and chairs or whatever, they never read a newspaper. They didn't like television, either, except for *Sesame Street,* which was supposedly for children. The only time they saw Jason Wilder on the little screen as far as I can remember, my mother-in-law started dancing to him as though he were modern music.

When one of his guests on the show said something, she froze. Only when Wilder spoke did she start to dance again.

I certainly wasn't going to tell him that.

"I want to say first," said Wilder, "that I am in nothing less than awe, Professor Hartke, of your magnificent record in the Vietnam War. If the American people had not lost their courage and ceased to support you, we would be living in a very different and much better world, and especially in Asia. I know, too, of your kindness and understanding toward your wife and her mother, to which I am glad to apply the same encomium your behavior earned in Vietnam, 'beyond the call of duty.' So I am sorry to have to warn you that the story I am about to tell you may not be nearly as simple or easy to refute as my daughter may have led you to expect."

"Whatever it is, sir," I said, "let's hear it. Shoot."

So he did. He said that several of his friends had attended Tarkington or sent their children here, so that he was favorably impressed with the institution's successes with the learning-disabled long before he entrusted his own daughter to us. An usher and a bridesmaid at his wedding, he said, had earned Associate in the Arts and Sciences Degrees in Scipio. The usher had gone on to be Ambassador to Iceland. The bridesmaid was on the Board of Directors of the Chicago Symphony Orchestra.

He felt that Tarkington's highly unconventional techniques would be useful if applied to the country's notoriously beleaguered inner-city schools, and he planned to say so after he had learned more about them. The ratio of teachers to students at Tarkington, incidentally, was then 1 to 6. In inner-city schools, that ratio was then 1 to 65.

There was a big campaign back then, I remember, to get the Japanese to buy up inner-city public schools the way they were buying up prisons and hospitals. But they were too smart. They wouldn't touch schools for unwelcome children of unwelcome parents with a 10-foot pole.

He said he hoped to write a book about Tarkington called "Little Miracle on Lake Mohiga" or "Teaching the Unteachable." So he wired his daughter for sound and told her to follow the best teachers in order to record what they said and how they said it. "I wanted to learn what it was that made them good, Professor Hartke, without their knowing they were being studied," he said. "I wanted them to go on being whatever they were, warts and all, without any self-consciousness."

This was the first I heard of the tapes. That chilling news explained Kimberley's lurking, lurking, lurking all the time. Wilder spared me the suspense, at least, of wondering what all of Kimberley's apparatus might have overheard. He punched the playback button on the recorder before him, and I heard myself telling Paul Slazinger, privately, I'd thought, that the two principal currencies of the planet were the Yen and fellatio. This was so early in the academic year that classes hadn't begun yet! This was during Freshman Orientation Week, and I had just told the incoming Class of 1994 that merchants and tradespeople in the town below preferred to be paid in Japanese Yen rather than dollars, so that the freshmen might want their parents to give them their allowances in Yen.

I had told them, too, that they were never to go into the Black Cat Café, which the townspeople considered their private club. It was one place they could go and not be reminded of how dependent they were on the rich kids on the hill, but I didn't say that. Neither did I say that free-lance prostitutes were sometimes found there, and in the past had been the cause of outbreaks of venereal disease on campus.

I had kept it simple for the freshmen: "Tarkingtonians are more than welcome anywhere in town but the Black Cat Café."

If Kimberley recorded that good advice, her father did not play it back for me. He didn't even play back what Slazinger had said to me, and it was during a coffee break, that stimulated me to name the planet's two most acceptable currencies. He was the agent provocateur.

What he said, as I recall, was, "They want to get paid in Yen?" He was as new to Scipio as any freshman, and we had just met. I hadn't read any of his books, and so far as I knew, neither had anybody else on the faculty. He was a last-minute choice for Writer in Residence, and had come to orientation because he was lonesome and had nothing else to do. He wasn't supposed to be there, and he was so old, so old! He had been sitting among all those teenagers as though he were just another rich kid who had bottomed out on his Scholastic Aptitude Test, and he was old enough to be their grandfather!

He had fought in World War II! That's how old he was.

So I said to him, "They'll take dollars if they have to, but you'd better have a wheelbarrow."

And he wanted to know if the merchants and tradespeople would also accept fellatio. He used a vernacular word for fellatio in the plural.

But the tape began right after that, with my saying, as though out of the blue, and as a joke, of course, only it didn't sound like a joke during the playback, that, in effect, the whole World was for sale to anyone who had Yen or was willing to perform fellatio.

14

So that was twice within an hour that I was accused of cynicism that was Paul Slazinger's, not mine. And he was in Key West, well out of reach of punishment, having been unemployment-proofed for 5 years with a Genius Grant from the MacArthur Foundation. In saying what I had about Yen and fellatio, I was being sociable with a stranger. I was echoing him to make him feel at home in new surroundings.

As far as that goes, Professor Damon Stern, head of the History Department and my closest male friend here, spoke as badly of his own country as Slazinger and I did, and right into the faces of students in the classroom day after day. I used to sit in on his course and laugh and clap. The truth can be very funny in an awful way, especially as it relates to greed and hypocrisy. Kimberley must have made recordings of his words, too, and played them back for her father. Why wasn't Damon fired right along with me?

My guess is that he was a comedian, and I was not. He wanted students to leave his presence feeling good, not bad, so the atrocities and stupidities he described were in the distant past. There was nothing a student could do about them but laugh, laugh, laugh.

Whereas Slazinger and I talked about the last half of the

20th Century, in which we had both been seriously wounded physically and psychologically, which was nothing anybody but a sociopath could laugh about.

I, too, might have been acceptable as a comedian if all Kimberley had taped was what I said about Yen and fellatio. That was good, topical Mohiga Valley humor, what with the Japanese taking over the prison across the lake and arousing curiosity among the natives about the relative values of different national currencies. The Japanese were willing to pay their local bills in either dollars or Yen. These bills were for small-ticket items, hardware or toiletries or whatever, which the prison needed in a hurry, usually ordered by telephone. Big-ticket items in quantity came from Japanese-owned suppliers in Rochester or beyond.

So Japanese currency had started to circulate in Scipio. The prison administrators and guards were rarely seen in town, however. They lived in barracks to the east of the prison, and lived lives as invisible to this side of the lake as those of the prisoners.

To the limited extent that anybody on this side of the lake thought about the prison at all until the mass escape, people were generally glad to have the Japanese in charge. The new proprietor had cut waste and corruption to almost nothing. What they charged the State for punishing its prisoners was only 75 percent of what the State used to pay itself for identical services.

The local paper, *The Valley Sentinel,* sent a reporter over there to see what the Japanese were doing differently. They were still using the steel boxes on the back of trucks and showing old TV shows, including news, in no particular order and around the clock. The biggest change was that Athena was drug-free for the first time in its history, and rich prisoners weren't able to buy privileges. The guards weren't easily fooled or corrupted, either, since they understood so little English, and wanted nothing more than to finish up their 6 months overseas and go home again.

A normal tour of duty in Vietnam was twice that long and 1,000 times more dangerous. Who could blame the educated classes with political connections for staying home?

One new wrinkle by the Japanese the reporter didn't mention was that the guards wore surgical masks and rubber gloves when they were on duty, even up in the towers and atop the walls. That wasn't to keep them from spreading infections, of course. It was to ensure that they didn't take any of their loathsome charges' loathsome diseases back home with them.

When I went to work over there, I refused to wear gloves and a mask. Who could teach anybody anything while wearing such a costume?

So now I have tuberculosis.

Cough, cough, cough.

Before I could protest to the Trustees that I certainly wouldn't have said what I'd said about Yen and fellatio if I'd thought there was the slightest chance that a student could hear me, the background noises on the tape changed. I realized that I was about to hear something I had said in a different location. There was the pop-pop-pop of Ping-Pong balls, and a card player asked, "Who dealt this mess?" Somebody else asked somebody else to bring her a hot fudge sundae without nuts on top. She was on a diet, she said. There were rumblings like distant artillery, which were really the sound of bowling balls in the basement of the Pahlavi Pavilion.

Oh Lordy, was I ever drunk that night at the Pavilion. I

was out of control. And it was a disgrace that I should have appeared before students in such a condition. I will regret it to my dying day. Cough.

It was on a cold night near the end of November of 1990, 6 months before the Trustees fired me. I know it wasn't December, because Slazinger was still on campus, talking openly of suicide. He hadn't yet received his Genius Grant.

When I came home from work that afternoon, to tidy up the house and make supper, I found an awful mess. Margaret and Mildred, both hags by then, had torn bedsheets into strips. I had laundered the sheets that morning, and was going to put them on our beds that night. What did they care?

They had constructed what they said was a spider web. At least it wasn't a hydrogen bomb.

White cotton strips spliced end to end crisscrossed every which way in the front hall and living room. The newel post of the stairway was connected to the inside doorknob of the front door, and the doorknob was connected to the living room chandelier, and so on ad infinitum.

The day hadn't begun auspiciously anyway. I had found all 4 tires of my Mercedes flat. A bunch of high school kids from down below, high on alcohol or who knows what, had come up during the night like Vietcong and gone what they called "coring" again. They not only had let the air out of the tires of every expensive car they could find in the open on campus, Porsches and Jaguars and Saabs and BMWs and so on, but had taken out the valve cores. At home, I had heard, they had jars full of valve cores or necklaces of valve cores to prove how often they had gone coring. And they got my Mercedes. They got my Mercedes every time.

So when I found myself tangled in Margaret and Mildred's spider web, my nervous system came close to the breaking

118

point. I was the one who was going to have to clean up this mess. I was the one who was going to have to remake the beds with other sheets, and then buy more sheets the next day. I have always liked housework, or at least not minded it as much as most people seem to. But this was housework beyond the pale!

I had left the house so neat in the morning! And Margaret and Mildred weren't getting any fun out of watching my reactions when I was tangled up in their spider web. They were hiding someplace where they couldn't see or hear me. They expected me to play hide-and-seek, with me as "it."

Something in me snapped. I wasn't going to play hide-and-seek this time. I wasn't going to take down the spider web. I wasn't going to prepare supper. Let them come creeping out of their hiding places in an hour or whatever. Let them wonder, as I had when I walked into the spider web, what on Earth had happened to their previously dependable, forgiving Universe?

Out into the cold night I went, with no destination in mind save for good old oblivion. I found myself in front of the house of my best friend, Damon Stern, the entertaining professor of History. When he was a boy in Wisconsin, he had learned how to ride a unicycle. He had taught his wife and kids how to ride one, too.

The lights were on, but nobody was home. The family's 4 unicycles were in the front hall and the car was gone. They never got cored. They were smart. They drove one of the last Volkswagen Bugs still running.

I knew where they kept the liquor. I poured myself a couple of stiff shots of bourbon, in lieu of their absent body warmth. I don't think I had had a drink for a month before that.

I got this hot rush in my belly. Out into the night I went again. I was automatically looking for an older woman who would make everything all right by becoming the beast with two backs with me.

A coed would not do, not that a coed would have had anything to do with somebody as old and relatively poor as me. I couldn't even have promised her a better grade than she deserved. There were no grades at Tarkington.

But I wouldn't have wanted a coed in any case. The only sort of woman who excites me is an older one in uncomfortable circumstances, full of doubts not only about herself but about the value of life itself. Although I never met her personally, the late Marilyn Monroe comes to mind, maybe 3 years before she committed suicide.

Cough, cough, cough.

If there is a Divine Providence, there is also a wicked one, provided you agree that making love to off-balance women you aren't married to is wickedness. My own feeling is that if adultery is wickedness then so is food. Both make me feel so much better afterward.

Just as a hungry person knows that somewhere not far away somebody is preparing good things to eat, I knew that night that not far away was an older woman in despair. There had to be!

Zuzu Johnson was out of the question. Her husband was home, and she was hosting a dinner party for a couple of grateful parents who were giving the college a language laboratory. When it was finished, students would be able to sit in soundproof booths and listen to recordings of any one of more than 100 languages and dialects made by native speakers.

The lights were on in the sculpture studio of Norman Rockwell Hall, the art building, the only structure on campus named after a historical figure rather than the donating family. It was another gift from the Moellenkamps, who may have felt that too much was named after them already.

There was a whirring and rumbling coming from inside the sculpture studio. Somebody was playing with the crane in there, making it run back and forth on its tracks overhead. Whoever it was had to be playing, since nobody ever made a piece of sculpture so big that it could be moved only by the mighty crane.

After the prison break, there was some talk on the part of the convicts of hanging somebody from it, and running him back and forth while he strangled. They had no particular candidate in mind. But then the Niagara Power and Light Company, which was owned by the Unification Church Korean Evangelical Association, shut off all our electricity.

Outside Rockwell Hall that night, I might have been back on a patrol in Vietnam. That is how keen my senses were. That was how quick my mind was to create a whole picture from the slightest clues.

I knew that the sculpture studio was locked up tight after 6:30 P.M., since I had tried the door many times, thinking that I might sometime bring a lover there. I had considered getting a key somehow at the start of the semester and learned from Building and Grounds that only they and that year's Artist in Residence, the sculptress Pamela Ford Hall, were allowed to have keys. This was because of vandalism by either students or Townies in the studio the year before.

They knocked off the noses and fingers of replicas of Greek statues, and defecated in a bucket of wet clay. That sort of thing.

So that had to be Pamela Ford Hall in there making the crane go back and forth. And the crane's restless travels had to represent unhappiness, not any masterpiece she was creating. What use did she have for a crane, or even a wheelbarrow, since she worked exclusively in nearly weightless polyurethane. And she was a recent divorcée without children. And, because she knew my reputation, I'm sure, she had been avoiding me.

I climbed up on the studio's loading dock. I thumped my fist on its enormous sliding door. The door was motor driven. She had only to press a button to let me in.

The crane stopped going back and forth. There was a hopeful sign!

She asked through the door what I wanted.

"I wanted to make sure you were OK in there," I said.

"Who are you to care whether I'm OK or not in here?" she said.

"Gene Hartke," I said.

She opened the door just a crack and stared out at me, but didn't say anything. Then she opened the door wider, and I could see she was holding an uncorked bottle of what would turn out to be blackberry brandy.

"Hello, Soldier," she said.

"Hi," I said very carefully.

And then she said, "What took you so long?"

15

PAMELA sure got me drunk that night, and we made love. And then I spilled my guts about the Vietnam War in front of a bunch of students at the Pahlavi Pavilion. And Kimberley Wilder recorded me.

I had never tasted blackberry brandy before. I never want to taste it again. It did bad things to me. It made me a crybaby about the war. That is something I swore I would never be.

If I could order any drink I wanted now, it would be a Sweet Rob Roy on the Rocks, a Manhattan made with Scotch. That was another drink a woman introduced me to, and it made me laugh instead of cry, and fall in love with the woman who said to try one.

That was in Manila, after the excrement hit the air-conditioning in Saigon. She was Harriet Gummer, the war correspondent from Iowa. She had a son by me without telling me.

His name? Rob Roy.

After we made love, Pamela asked me the same question Harriet had asked me in Manila 15 years earlier. It was something they both had to know. They both asked me if I had killed anybody in the war.

I said to Pamela what I had said to Harriet: "If I were a fighter plane instead of a human being, there would be little pictures of people painted all over me."

I should have gone straight home after saying that. But I went over to the Pavilion instead. I needed a bigger audience for that great line of mine.

So I barged into a group of students sitting in front of the great fireplace in the main lounge. After the prison break, that fireplace would be used for cooking horse meat and dogs. I got between the students and the fire, so there was no way they could ignore me, and I said to them, "If I were a fighter plane instead of a human being, there would be little pictures of people painted all over me."

I went on from there.

I was so full of self-pity! That was what I found unbearable when Jason Wilder played back my words to me. I was so drunk that I acted like a victim!

The scenes of unspeakable cruelty and stupidity and waste I described that night were no more horrible than ultrarealistic shows about Vietnam, which had become staples of TV entertainment. When I told the students about the severed human head I saw nestled in the guts of a water buffalo, to them, I'm sure, the head might as well have been made of wax, and the guts those of some big animal which may or may not have belonged to a real water buffalo.

What difference could it make whether the head was or was not wax, or whether the guts were or were not those of a water buffalo?

No difference.

124

"Professor Hartke," Jason Wilder said to me gently, reasonably, when the tape had reached its end, "why on Earth would you want to tell such tales to young people who need to love their country?"

I wanted to keep my job so much, and the house which came with it, that my reply was asinine. "I was telling them history," I said, "and I had had a little too much to drink. I don't usually drink that much."

"I'm sure," he said. "I am told that you are a man with many problems, but that alcohol has not appeared among them with any consistency. So let us say that your performance in the Pavilion was a well-intended history lesson of which you accidentally lost control."

"That's what it was, sir," I said.

His balletic hands flitted in time to the logic of his thoughts before he spoke again. He was a fellow pianist. And then he said, "First of all, you were not hired to teach History. Second of all, the students who come to Tarkington need no further instructions in how it feels to be defeated. They would not be here if they themselves had not failed and failed. The Miracle on Lake Mohiga for more than a century now, as I see it, has been to make children who have failed and failed start thinking of victory, stop thinking about the hopelessness of it all."

"There was just that one time," I said, "and I'm sorry."

Cough. One cough.

Wilder said he didn't consider a teacher who was negative about everything a teacher. "I would call a person like that an 'unteacher.' He's somebody who takes things out of young people's heads instead of putting more things in."

"I don't know as I'm negative about everything," I said.

"What's the first thing students see when they walk into the library?" he said.

"Books?" I said.

"All those perpetual-motion machines," he said. "I saw that display, and I read the sign on the wall above it. I had no idea then that you were responsible for the sign."

He was talking about the sign that said "THE COMPLICATED FUTILITY OF IGNORANCE."

"All I knew was that I didn't want my daughter or anybody's child to see a message that negative every time she comes into the library," he said. "And then I found out it was you who was responsible for it."

"What's so negative about it?" I said.

"What could be a more negative word than 'futility'?" he said.

" 'Ignorance,' " I said.

"There you are," he said. I had somehow won his argument for him.

"I don't understand," I said.

"Precisely," he said. "You obviously do not understand how easily discouraged the typical Tarkington student is, how sensitive to suggestions that he or she should quit trying to be smart. That's what the word 'futile' means: 'Quit, quit, quit.' "

"And what does 'ignorance' mean?" I said.

"If you put it up on the wall and give it the prominence you have," he said, "it's a nasty echo of what so many Tarkingtonians were hearing before they got here: 'You're dumb, you're dumb, you're dumb.' And of course they aren't dumb."

"I never said they were," I protested.

"You reinforce their low self-esteem without realizing what you are doing," he said. "You also upset them with humor appropriate to a barracks, but certainly not to an institution of higher learning."

"You mean about Yen and fellatio?" I said. "I would never have said it if I'd thought a student could hear me."

"I am talking about the entrance hall of the library again," he said.

"I can't think of what else is in there that might have offended you," I said.

"It wasn't I who was offended," he said. "It was my daughter."

"I give up," I said. I wasn't being impudent. I was abject.

"On the same day Kimberley heard you talk about Yen and fellatio, before classes had even begun," he said, "a senior led her and the other freshmen to the library and solemnly told them that the bell clappers on the wall were petrified penises. That was surely barracks humor the senior had picked up from you."

For once I didn't have to defend myself. Several of the Trustees assured Wilder that telling freshmen that the clappers were penises was a tradition that antedated my arrival on campus by at least 20 years.

But that was the only time they defended me, although 1 of them had been my student, Madelaine Astor, née Peabody, and 5 of them were parents of those I had taught. Madelaine dictated a letter to me afterward, explaining that Jason Wilder had promised to denounce the college in his column and on his TV show if the Trustees did not fire me.

So they dared not come to my assistance.

She said, too, that since she, like Wilder, was a Roman Catholic, she was shocked to hear me say on tape that Hitler was a Roman Catholic, and that the Nazis painted crosses on their tanks and airplanes because they considered themselves a Christian army. Wilder had played that tape right after I had been cleared of all responsibility for freshmen's being told that the clappers were penises.

Once again I was in deep trouble for merely repeating what somebody else had said. It wasn't something my grandfather had said this time, or somebody else who couldn't be hurt by the Trustees, like Paul Slazinger. It was something my best friend Damon Stern had said in a History class only a couple of months before.

If Jason Wilder thought I was an unteacher, he should have heard Damon Stern! Then again, Stern never told the awful truth about supposedly noble human actions in recent times. Everything he debunked had to have transpired before 1950, say.

So I happened to sit in on a class where he talked about Hitler's being a devout Roman Catholic. He said something I hadn't realized before, something I have since discovered most Christians don't want to hear: that the Nazi swastika was intended to be a version of a Christian cross, a cross made out of axes. Stern said that Christians had gone to a lot of trouble denying that the swastika was just another cross, saying it was a primitive symbol from the primordial ooze of the pagan past.

And the Nazis' most valuable military decoration was the Iron Cross.

And the Nazis painted regular crosses on all their tanks and airplanes.

I came out of that class looking sort of dazed, I guess. Who should I run into but Kimberley Wilder?

"What did he say today?" she said.

"Hitler was a Christian," I said. "The swastika was a Christian cross."

She got it on tape.

I didn't rat on Damon Stern to the Trustees. Tarkington wasn't West Point, where it was an honor to squeal.

Madelaine agreed with Wilder, too, she said in her letter, that I should not have told my Physics students that the Russians, not the Americans, were the first to make a hydrogen bomb that was portable enough to be used as a weapon.

"Even if it's true," she wrote, "which I don't believe, you had no business telling them that."

She said, moreover, that perpetual motion was possible, if only scientists would work harder on it.

She had certainly backslid intellectually since passing her orals for her Associate in the Arts and Sciences Degree.

I used to tell classes that anybody who believed in the possibility of perpetual motion should be boiled alive like a lobster.

I was also a stickler about the Metric System. I was famous for turning my back on students who mentioned feet or pounds or miles to me.

They hated that.

I didn't dare teach like that in the prison across the lake, of course.

Then again, most of the convicts had been in the drug business, and were either Third World people or dealt with Third World people. So the Metric System was old stuff to them.

Rather than rat on Damon Stern about the Nazis' being Christians, I told the Trustees that I had heard it on National Public Radio. I said I was very sorry about having passed it on to a student. "I feel like biting off my tongue," I said.

"What does Hitler have to do with either Physics or Music Appreciation?" said Wilder.

I might have replied that Hitler probably didn't know any more about physics than the Board of Trustees, but that he loved music. Every time a concert hall was bombed, I heard somewhere, he had it rebuilt immediately as a matter of top priority. I think I may actually have learned that from National Public Radio.

I said instead, "If I'd known I upset Kimberley as much as

you say I did, I would certainly have apologized. I had no idea, sir. She gave no sign."

What made me weak was the realization that I had been mistaken to think that I was with family there in the Board Room, that all Tarkingtonians and their parents and guardians had come to regard me as an uncle. My goodness—the family secrets I had learned over the years and kept to myself! My lips were sealed. What a faithful old retainer I was! But that was all I was to the Trustees, and probably to the students, too.

I wasn't an uncle. I was a member of the Servant Class. They were letting me go.

Soldiers are discharged. People in the workplace are fired. Servants are let go.

"Am I being fired?" I asked the Chairman of the Board incredulously.

"I'm sorry, Gene," he said, "but we're going to have to let you go."

The President of the college, Tex Johnson, sitting two chairs away from me, hadn't let out a peep. He looked sick. I surmised mistakenly that he had been scolded for having let me stay on the faculty long enough to get tenure. He was sick about something more personal, which still had a lot to do with Professor Eugene Debs Hartke.

He had been brought in as President from Rollins College down in Winter Park, Florida, where he had been Provost, after Sam Wakefield did the big trick of suicide. Henry "Tex" Johnson held a Bachelor's Degree in Business Administration from Texas Tech in Lubbock, and claimed to be a descendant of a man who had died in the Alamo. Damon Stern, who was always turning up little-known facts of history, told me, incidentally, that the Battle of the Alamo was about slavery. The brave men who died there wanted to secede from Mexico because it was against the law to own slaves in Mexico. They were fighting for the right to own slaves.

Since Tex's wife and I had been lovers, I knew that his ancestors weren't Texans, but Lithuanians. His father, whose name certainly wasn't Johnson, was a Lithuanian second mate on a Russian freighter who jumped ship when it put in for emergency repairs at Corpus Christi. Zuzu told me that Tex's father was not only an illegal immigrant but the nephew of the former Communist boss of Lithuania.

So much for the Alamo.

I turned to him at the Board meeting, and I said, "Tex—for pity sakes, say something! You know darn good and well I'm the best teacher you've got! I don't say that. The students do! Is the whole faculty going to be brought before this Board, or am I the only one? Tex?"

He stared straight ahead. He seemed to have turned to cement. "Tex?" Some leadership!

I put the same question to the Chairman, who had been pauperized by Microsecond Arbitrage but didn't know it yet. "Bob—" I began.

He winced.

I began again, having gotten the message in spades that I was a servant and not a relative: "Mr. Moellenkamp, sir—" I said, "you know darn well, and so does everybody else here, that you can follow the most patriotic, deeply religious American who ever lived with a tape recorder for a year, and then prove that he's a worse traitor than Benedict Arnold, and a worshipper of the Devil. Who doesn't say things in a moment of passion or absentmindedness that he doesn't wish he could take back? So I ask again, am I the only one this was done to, and if so, why?"

He froze.

"Madelaine?" I said to Madelaine Astor, who would later write me such a dumb letter.

She said she did not like it that I had told students that a new Ice Age was on its way, even if I had read it in *The New York Times.* That was another thing I'd said that Wilder had on tape. At least it had something to do with science, and at least it wasn't something I had picked up from Slazinger or Grandfather Wills or Damon Stern. At least it was the real me.

"The students here have enough to worry about," she said. "I know I did."

She went on to say that there had always been people who had tried to become famous by saying that the World was going to end, but the World hadn't ended.

There were nods of agreement all around the table. I don't think there was a soul there who knew anything about science.

"When I was here you were predicting the end of the World," she said, "only it was atomic waste and acid rain that were going to kill us. But here we are. I feel fine. Doesn't everybody else feel fine? So pooh."

She shrugged. "About the rest of it," she said, "I'm sorry I heard about it. It made me sick. If we have to go over it again, I think I'll just leave the room."

Heavens to Betsy! What could she have meant by "the rest of it"? What could it be that they had gone over once, and were going to have to go over again with me there? Hadn't I already heard the worst?

No.

16

"THE rest of it" was in a manila folder in front of Jason Wilder. So there is Manila playing a big part in my life again. No Sweet Rob Roys on the Rocks this time.

In the folder was a report by a private detective hired by Wilder to investigate my sex life. It covered only the second semester, and so missed the episode in the sculpture studio. The gumshoe recorded 3 of 7 subsequent trysts with the Artist in Residence, 2 with a woman from a jewelry company taking orders for class rings, and maybe 30 with Zuzu Johnson, the wife of the President. He didn't miss a thing Zuzu and I did during the second semester. There was only 1 misunderstood incident: when I went up into the loft of the stable, where the Lutz Carillon had been stored before there was a tower and where Tex Johnson was crucified 2 years ago. I went up with the aunt of a student. She was an architect who wanted to see the pegged post-and-beam joinery up there. The operative assumed we made love up there. We hadn't.

We made love much later that afternoon, in a toolshed by the stable, in the shadow of Musket Mountain when the Sun goes down.

I wasn't to see the contents of Wilder's folder for another 10 minutes or so. Wilder and a couple of others wanted to go on discussing what really bothered them about me, which was what I had been doing, supposedly, to the students' minds. My sexual promiscuity among older women wasn't of much interest to them, the College President excepted, save as a handy something for which I could be fired without raising the gummy question of whether or not my rights under the First Amendment of the Constitution had been violated.

Adultery was the bullet they would put in my brain, so to speak, after I had been turned to Swiss cheese by the firing squad.

To Tex Johnson, the closet Lithuanian, the contents of the folder were more than a gadget for diddling me out of tenure. They were a worse humiliation for Tex than they were for me.

At least they said that my love affair with his wife was over.

He stood up. He asked to be excused. He said that he would just as soon not be present when the Trustees went over for the second time what Madelaine had called "the rest of it."

He was excused, and was apparently about to leave without saying anything. But then, with one hand on the doorknob, he uttered two words chokingly, which were the title of a novel by Gustave Flaubert. It was about a wife who was bored with her husband, who had an exceedingly silly love affair and then committed suicide.

"*Madame Bovary,*" he said. And then he was gone.

He was a cuckold in the present, and crucifixion awaited him in the future. I wonder if his father would have jumped ship in Corpus Christi if he had known what an unhappy end his only son would come to under American Free Enterprise.

I had read *Madame Bovary* at West Point. All cadets in my day had to read it, so that we could demonstrate to cultivated people that we, too, were cultivated, should we ever face that challenge. Jack Patton and I read it at the same time for the same class. I asked him afterward what he thought of it. Predictably, he said he had to laugh like hell.

He said the same thing about *Othello* and *Hamlet* and *Romeo and Juliet.*

I confess that to this day I have come to no firm conclusions about how smart or dumb Jack Patton really was. This leaves me in doubt about the meaning of a birthday present he sent me in Vietnam shortly before the sniper killed him with a beautiful shot in Hué, pronounced "whay." It was a gift-wrapped copy of a stroke magazine called *Black Garterbelt.* But did he send it to me for its pictures of women naked except for black garterbelts, or for a remarkable science fiction story in there, "The Protocols of the Elders of Tralfamadore"?

But more about that later.

I have no idea how many of the Trustees had read *Madame Bovary.* Two of them would have had to have it read aloud to them. So I was not alone in wondering why Tex Johnson would have said, his hand on the doorknob, *"Madame Bovary."*

If I had been Tex, I think I might have gotten off the campus as fast as possible, and maybe drowned my sorrows among the nonacademics at the Black Cat Café. That was where I was going to wind up that afternoon. It would have been funny in retrospect if we had wound up as a couple of sloshed buddies at the Black Cat Café.

Imagine my saying to him or his saying to me, both of us drunk as skunks, "I love you, you old son of a gun. Do you know that?"

One Trustee had it in for me on personal grounds. That was Sydney Stone, who was said to have amassed a fortune of more than $1,000,000,000 in 10 short years, mainly in commissions for arranging sales of American properties to foreigners. His masterpiece, maybe, was the transfer of ownership of my father's former employer, E. I. Du Pont de Nemours & Company, to I. G. Farben in Germany.

"There is much I could probably forgive, if somebody put a gun to my head, Professor Hartke," he said, "but not what you did to my son." He himself was no Tarkingtonian. He was a graduate of the Harvard Business School and the London School of Economics.

"Fred?" I said.

"In case you haven't noticed," he said, "I have only 1 son in Tarkington. I have only 1 son anywhere." Presumably this 1 son, without having to lift a finger, would himself 1 day have $1,000,000,000.

"What did I do to Fred?" I said.

"You know what you did to Fred," he said.

What I had done to Fred was catch him stealing a Tarkington beer mug from the college bookstore. What Fred Stone did was beyond mere stealing. He took the beer mug off the shelf, drank make-believe toasts to me and the cashier, who were the only other people there, and then walked out.

I had just come from a faculty meeting where the campus theft problem had been discussed for the umpteenth time. The manager of the bookstore told us that only one comparable institution had a higher percentage of its merchandise stolen than his, which was the Harvard Coop in Cambridge.

So I followed Fred Stone out to the Quadrangle. He was headed for his Kawasaki motorcycle in the student parking lot. I came up behind him and said quietly, with all possible politeness, "I think you should put that beer mug back where you got it, Fred. Either that or pay for it."

"Oh, yeah?" he said. "Is that what you think?" Then he smashed the mug to smithereens on the rim of the Vonnegut Memorial Fountain. "If that's what you think," he said, "then you're the one who should put it back."

I reported the incident to Tex Johnson, who told me to forget it.

But I was mad. So I wrote a letter about it to the boy's father, but never got an answer until the Board meeting.

"I can never forgive you for accusing my son of theft," the father said. He quoted Shakespeare on behalf of Fred. I was supposed to imagine Fred's saying it to me.

" 'Who steals my purse steals trash; 'tis something, nothing,' " he said. " ' 'Twas mine, 'tis his, and has been slave to thousands,' " he went on, " 'but he that filches from me my good name robs me of that which not enriches him and makes me poor indeed.' "

"If I was wrong, sir, I apologize," I said.

"Too late," he said.

17

THERE was 1 Trustee I was sure was my friend. He would have found what I said on tape funny and interesting. But he wasn't there. His name was Ed Bergeron, and we had had a lot of good talks about the deterioration of the environment and the abuses of trust in the stock market and the banking industry and so on. He could top me for pessimism any day.

His wealth was as old as the Moellenkamps', and was based on ancestral oil fields and coal mines and railroads which he had sold to foreigners in order to devote himself full-time to nature study and conservation. He was President of the Wildlife Rescue Federation, and his photographs of wildlife on the Galápagos Islands had been published in *National Geographic.* The magazine gave him the cover, too, which showed a marine iguana digesting seaweed in the sunshine, right next to a skinny penguin who was no doubt having thoughts about entirely different issues of the day, whatever was going on that day.

Not only was Ed Bergeron my doomsday pal. He was also a veteran of several debates about environmentalism with Jason Wilder on Wilder's TV show. I haven't found a tape of any of those ding-dong head-to-heads in this library, but there used to be 1 at the prison. It would bob up about every

6 months on the TV sets there, which were running all the time.

In it, I remember, Wilder said that the trouble with conservationists was that they never considered the costs in terms of jobs and living standards of eliminating fossil fuels or doing something with garbage other than dumping it in the ocean, and so on.

Ed Bergeron said to him, "Good! Then I can write the epitaph for this once salubrious blue-green orb." He meant the planet.

Wilder gave him his supercilious, vulpine, patronizing, silky debater's grin. "A majority of the scientific community," he said, "would say, if I'm not mistaken, that an epitaph would be premature by several thousand years." That debate took place maybe 6 years before I was fired, which would be back in 1985, and I don't know what scientific community he was talking about. Every kind of scientist, all the way down to chiropractors and podiatrists, was saying we were killing the planet fast.

"You want to hear the epitaph?" said Ed Bergeron.

"If we must," said Wilder, and the grin went on and on. "I have to tell you, though, that you are not the first person to say the game was all over for the human race. I'm sure that even in Egypt before the first pyramid was constructed, there were men who attracted a following by saying, 'It's all over now.' "

"What is different about now as compared with Egypt before the first pyramid was built—" Ed began.

"And before the Chinese invented printing, and before Columbus discovered America," Jason Wilder interjected.

"Exactly," said Bergeron.

"The difference is that we have the misfortune of knowing what's really going on," said Bergeron, "which is no fun at all. And this has given rise to a whole new class of preening, narcissistic quacks like yourself who say in the service of rich and shameless polluters that the state of the atmosphere and the water and the topsoil on which all life depends is as debatable as how many angels can dance on the fuzz of a tennis ball."

He was angry.

When this old tape was played at Athena before the great escape, it kindled considerable interest. I watched it and listened with several students of mine. Afterward one of them said to me, "Who right, Professor—beard or mustache?" Wilder had a mustache. Bergeron had a beard.

"Beard," I said.

That may have been almost the last word I said to a convict before the prison break, before my mother-in-law decided that it was at last time to talk about her big pickerel.

Bergeron's epitaph for the planet, I remember, which he said should be carved in big letters in a wall of the Grand Canyon for the flying-saucer people to find, was this:

WE COULD HAVE SAVED IT,
BUT WE WERE TOO DOGGONE CHEAP.

Only he didn't say "doggone."

But I would never see or hear from Ed Bergeron again. He resigned from the Board soon after I was fired, and so would miss being taken hostage by the convicts. It would have been interesting to hear what he had to say to and about that particular kind of captor. One thing he used to say to me, and to a class of mine he spoke to one time, was that man was the weather now. Man was the tornadoes, man was the hailstones, man was the floods. So he might have said that Scipio was Pompeii, and the escapees were a lava flow.

He didn't resign from the Board on account of my firing. He had at least two personal tragedies, one right on top of the other. A company he inherited made all sorts of products out of asbestos, whose dust proved to be as carcinogenic as any substance yet identified, with the exception of epoxy cement and some of the radioactive stuff accidentally turned loose in the air and aquifers around nuclear weapons factories and power plants. He felt terrible about this, he told me, although he had never laid eyes on any of the factories that made the stuff. He sold them for practically nothing, since the company in Singapore that bought them got all the lawsuits along with the machinery and buildings, and an inventory of finished materials which was huge and unsalable in this country. The people in Singapore did what Ed couldn't bring himself to do, which was to sell all those floor tiles and roofing and so on to emerging nations in Africa.

And then his son Bruce, Tarkington Class of '85, who was a homosexual, joined the Ice Capades as a chorus boy. That was all right with Ed, who understood that some people were born homosexual and that was that. And Bruce was so happy with the ice show. He was not only a good skater but maybe the best male or female dancer at Tarkington. Bruce used to come over to the house and dance with my mother-in-law sometimes, just for the sake of dancing. He said she was the best dance partner he had ever had, and she returned the compliment.

I didn't tell her when, 4 years after he graduated, he was found strangled with his own belt, and with something like 100 stab wounds, in a motel outside of Dubuque. So there was Dubuque again.

18

S HAKESPEARE.

I think William Shakespeare was the wisest human being I ever heard of. To be perfectly frank, though, that's not saying much. We are impossibly conceited animals, and actually dumb as heck. Ask any teacher. You don't even have to ask a teacher. Ask anybody. Dogs and cats are smarter than we are.

If I say that the Trustees of Tarkington College were dummies, and that the people who got us involved in the Vietnam War were dummies, I hope it is understood that I consider myself the biggest dummy of all. Look at where I am now, and how hard I worked to get here and nowhere else. Bingo!

And if I feel that my father was a horse's fundament and my mother was a horse's fundament, what can I be but another horse's fundament? Ask my kids, both legitimate and illegitimate. They know.

I didn't have a Chinaman's chance with the Trustees, if I may be forgiven a racist cliché—not with the sex stuff Wilder had concealed in the folder. When I defended myself against him, I had no idea how well armed he was—a basic situation in the funniest slapstick comedies.

I argued that it was a teacher's duty to speak frankly to students of college age about all sorts of concerns of humankind, not just the subject of a course as stated in the catalogue. "That's how we gain their trust, and encourage them to speak up as well," I said, "and realize that all subjects do not reside in neat little compartments, but are continuous and inseparable from the one big subject we have been put on Earth to study, which is life itself."

I said that the doubts I might have raised in the students' minds about the virtues of the Free Enterprise System, when telling them what my grandfather believed, could in the long run only strengthen their enthusiasm for that system. It made them think up reasons of their own for why Free Enterprise was the only system worth considering. "People are never stronger," I said, "than when they have thought up their own arguments for believing what they believe. They stand on their own 2 feet that way."

"Did you or did you not say that the United States was a crock of doo-doo?" said Wilder.

I had to think a minute. This wasn't something Kimberley had gotten on tape. "What I may have said," I replied, "is that all nations bigger than Denmark are crocks of doo-doo, but that was a joke, of course."

I now stand behind that statement 100 percent. All nations bigger than Denmark are crocks of doo-doo.

Jason Wilder had heard enough. He asked the Trustees to pass the folder from hand to hand down the table to me. He said, "Before you see what's inside, you should know that this Board promised me that its contents would never be mentioned outside this room. It will remain in your sole possession, provided that you submit your resignation immediately."

"My goodness—" I said, "what could be in here? And what made Tex Johnson run out of the room the way he did?"

"The bottom-most document," said Wilder, "was painful for him to read."

"What can it be?" I said. I honestly couldn't imagine how I might have caused Tex pain. When I made love to his wife, I only wanted to make the 2 of us happier. I didn't think of her as somebody's wife. When I make love to a woman, the farthest thing from my mind is whom she may be married to. I can't speak for Zuzu, but I myself had no wish to cause Tex even a little pain. When Zuzu spoke contemptuously of him, I had to remember who he was, and then I stuck up for him.

My first impression of the bottom-most document in the folder is that it was a timetable of some sort, maybe for the bus from Scipio to Rochester, a not very subtle hint that I should get out of town as soon as possible. But then I realized that what was doing all the arriving and departing was me, and that the depot, so to speak, was the home of the College President.

The accuracy of the times and dates was attested to by Terrence W. Steel, Jr., whom I had known simply as Terry. I hadn't known his full name, and believed him to be what he was said to be, a new gardener working for Buildings and Grounds. He was in fact the private detective Wilder hired to get the goods on me. What little he had told me about himself may have been invented by GRIOT™, or much of it could have been true. Who knows? Who cares?

He told me, I remember, that his wife had discovered she was a lesbian, and fell in love with a female junior high school dietitian. Then both women disappeared along with his 3 kids. GRIOT™ could have cooked that up.

The timetable about me and Zuzu was signed by the detective and notarized. I knew the Notary. Everybody did. He was Lyle Hooper, the Fire Chief and owner of the Black

144

Cat Café. He, too, would be killed soon after the prison break. That document with his seal was all I needed to see in order to understand that my tenure was down the toilet.

Wilder said that the rest of the papers in the folder were affidavits gathered by his detective. They attested to my having been a shameless adulterer from the moment I and my family hit Scipio. "I expect you to agree with me," he said, "that your behavior in this valley would fall dead center into even the narrowest definition of moral turpitude."

I put the folder flat on the table to indicate that I had no need to look inside. My gesture was like folding a poker hand. In so doing, I would lay it on top of the school's annual Treasurer's Report, one copy of which had been put at every seat before the meeting. I would inadvertently take the report with me when I left, learning later from it something I hadn't known before. The college had sold all its property in the town below, including the ruins of the brewery and the wagon factory and the carpet mills and the land under the Black Cat Café, to the same Japanese corporation which owned the prison.

And then the Treasurer had put the proceeds of the sale, less real estate commissions and lawyers' fees, into preferred stock in Microsecond Arbitrage.

"This is not a happy moment in my life," said Wilder.

"Nor mine," I said.

"Unfortunately for all of us," he said, "the moving finger writes; and, having writ, moves on."

"You said a mouthful," I said.

Now the Chairman of the Board, Robert Moellenkamp, spoke up. He was illiterate, but legendary among Tarkingtonians, and no doubt back home, too, for his phenomenal memory. Like the father of the founder of the college, his ancestor, he could learn by heart anything that was read out loud to him 3 times or so. I knew several convicts at Athena, also illiterate, who could do that, too.

He wanted to quote Shakespeare now. "I want it on the record," he said, "that this has been an extremely painful episode for me as well." And then he delivered this speech from Shakespeare's *Romeo and Juliet,* in which the dying Mercutio, Romeo's gallant and witty best friend, describes the wound he received in a duel:

"No, 'tis not so deep as a well, nor so wide as a church door; but 'tis enough, 'twill serve: ask for me tomorrow, and you shall find me a grave man. I am peppered, I warrant, for this world. A plague on both your houses!"

The two houses, of course, were the Montagues and the Capulets, the feuding families of Romeo and Juliet, whose nitwit hatred would indirectly cause Mercutio's departure for Paradise.

I have lifted this speech from Bartlett's *Familiar Quotations.* If more people would acknowledge that they got their pearls of wisdom from that book instead of the original, it might clear the air.

If there really had been a Mercutio, and if there really were a Paradise, Mercutio might be hanging out with teenage Vietnam draftee casualties now, talking about what it felt like to die for other people's vanity and foolishness.

19

WHEN I heard a few months later, after I had gone to work at Athena, that Robert Moellenkamp had been wiped out and then some by Microsecond Arbitrage, and had had to sell his boats and his horses and his El Greco and all that, I assumed he quit the Board. Tarkington's Trustees were expected to give a lot of money to the college every year. Otherwise why would Lowell Chung's mother, who had to have everything that was said at meetings translated into Chinese, have been tolerated as a member of the Board?

Actually, I don't think Mrs. Chung would have become a member if another Trustee, a Caucasian Tarkington classmate of Moellenkamp's, John W. Fedders, Jr., hadn't grown up in Hong Kong, and so could serve as her interpreter. His father was an importer of ivory and rhinoceros horns, which many Orientals believed to be aphrodisiacs. He also traded, it was suspected, in industrial quantities of opium. Fedders was perhaps the most conceited man I ever saw out of uniform. He thought his fluency in Chinese made him as brilliant as a nuclear physicist, as though 1,000,000,000 other people, including, no doubt, 1,000,000 morons, couldn't speak Chinese.

When I met with the Trustees 2 years ago, and they had

become hostages in the stable, I was surprised to see Moellenkamp. He had been allowed to stay on the Board, even though he didn't have a nickel. Mrs. Chung had dropped out by then. Fedders was there. Wilder, as I've said, had since become a Trustee. There were some other new Trustees I didn't know.

All the Trustees survived the ordeal of captivity, with nothing to eat but horse meat roasted over burning furniture in the huge fireplace in the Pavilion, although Fedders would be the worse for an untreated heart attack. While he was going through the worst of it, he spoke Chinese.

I wouldn't be under indictment now if I hadn't paid a compassionate visit to the hostages. They wouldn't have known that I was within 1,000 kilometers of Scipio. But when I appeared to them, seemingly free to come and go as I pleased, and treated with deference by the Black man who was actually guarding me, they jumped to the conclusion that I was the mastermind behind the great escape.

It was a racist conclusion, based on the belief that Black people couldn't mastermind anything. I will say so in court.

In Vietnam, though, I really was the mastermind. Yes, and that still bothers me. During my last year there, when my ammunition was language instead of bullets, I invented justifications for all the killing and dying we were doing which impressed even me! I was a genius of lethal hocus pocus!

You want to know how I used to begin my speeches to fresh troops who hadn't yet been fed into the meat grinder? I squared my shoulders and threw out my chest so they could see all my ribbons, and I roared through a bullhorn, "Men, I want you to listen, and to listen good!"

And they did, they did.

148

I have been wondering lately how many human beings I actually killed with conventional weaponry. I don't believe it was my conscience which suggested that I do this. It was the list of women I was making, trying to remember all the names and faces and places and dates, which led to the logical question: "Why not list all you've killed?"

So I think I will. It can't be a list of names, since I never knew the name of anybody I killed. It has to be a list of dates and places. If my list of women isn't to include high school or prostitutes, then my list of those whose lives I took shouldn't include possibles and probables, or those killed by artillery or air strikes called in by me, and surely not all those, many of them Americans, who died as an indirect result of all my hocus pocus, all my blah blah blah.

I have long had a sort of ballpark figure in my head. I am quite sure that I killed more people than did my brother-in-law. I hadn't been working as a teacher at Athena very long before it occurred to me that I had almost certainly killed more people than had the mass murderer Alton Darwin or anybody else serving time in there. That didn't trouble me, and still doesn't. I just think it is interesting.

It is like an old movie. Does that mean that something is wrong with me?

My lawyer, a mere stripling, has paid me a call. Since I have no money, the Federal Government is paying him to protect me from injustice. Moreover, I cannot be tortured or otherwise compelled to testify against myself. What a Utopia!

Among my fellow prisoners here, and the 1,000s upon 1,000s of those across the lake, you better believe there's a lot of jubilation about the Bill of Rights.

I told my lawyer about the two lists I am making. How can he help me if I don't tell him everything.

"Why are you making them?" he said.

"To speed things up on Judgment Day," I said.

"I thought you were an Atheist," he said. He was hoping the Prosecuting Attorney wouldn't get wind of that.

"You never know," I said.

"I'm Jewish," he said.

"I know that, and I pity you," I said.

"Why do you pity me?" he said.

I said, "You're trying to get through life with only half a Bible. That's like trying to get from here to San Francisco with a road map that stops at Dubuque, Iowa."

I told him I wanted to be buried with my 2 lists, so that, if there really was going to be a Judgment Day, I could say to the Judge, "Judge, I have found a way to save you some precious time in Eternity. You don't have to look me up in the Book in Which All Things Are Recorded. Here's a list of my worst sins. Send me straight to Hell, and no argument."

He asked to see the 2 lists, so I showed him what I had written down so far. He was delighted, and especially by their messiness. There were all sorts of marginal notes about this or that woman or this or that corpse.

"The messier the better," he said.

"How so?" I said.

And he said, "Any fair-minded jury looking at them will have to believe that you are in a deeply disturbed mental state, and probably have been for quite some time. They will already believe that all you Vietnam veterans are crazy, because that's their reputation."

"But the lists aren't based on hallucinations," I protested. "I'm not getting them from a radio set the CIA or the flying-saucer people put in my skull while I was sleeping. It all really happened."

"All the same," he said serenely. "All the same, all the same."

150

20

AFTER Robert Moellenkamp, broke-and-didn't-know-it, said so grandly, "A plague on both your houses!" Jason Wilder commented that he did not feel, in the case under discussion, my case, that 2 houses were involved.

"I don't believe there is 2 of anything involved," he said. "I venture to say that even Mr. Hartke now agrees that this Board cannot conceive of any alternative to accepting his resignation. Am I right, Mr. Hartke?"

I got to my feet. "This is the second worst day of my life," I said. "The first was the day we got kicked out of Vietnam. Shakespeare has been quoted twice so far. It so happens that I can quote him, too. I have always been bad at memorizing, but I had an English teacher in high school who insisted that everyone in her class know his most famous lines by heart. I never expected to speak them as being meaningful to me in real life, but now's the time. Here goes:

" 'To be, or not to be: that is the question: Whether 'tis nobler in the mind to suffer the slings and arrows of outrageous fortune, or to take arms against a sea of troubles, and by opposing end them?

" 'To die: to sleep; no more; and by a sleep to say we end the heart-ache and the thousand natural shocks that flesh is heir to, 'tis a consummation devoutly to be wished.

" 'To die, to sleep; to sleep: perchance to dream: ay, there's the rub; for in that sleep of death what dreams may come when we have shuffled off this mortal coil, must give us pause.' "

There was more to that speech, of course, but that was all the teacher, whose name was Mary Pratt, required us to memorize. Why overdo? It was certainly enough for the occasion, raising as it did the specter of having yet another Vietnam veteran on the faculty killing himself on school property.

I fished the key to the bell tower from my pocket and threw it into the middle of the circular table. The table was so big that somebody was going to have to climb up on it to retrieve the key, or maybe find a long stick somewhere.

"Good luck with the bells," I said. I was out of there.

I departed Samoza Hall by the same route Tex Johnson had taken. I sat down on a bench at the edge of the Quadrangle, across from the library, next to the Senior Walk. It was nice to be outside.

Damon Stern, my best friend on the faculty, happened by and asked me what I was doing there.

I said I was sunning myself. I wouldn't tell anybody I had been fired until I found myself sitting at the bar of the Black Cat Café. So Professor Stern felt free to talk cheerful nonsense. He owned a unicycle, and he could ride it, and he said he was considering riding it in the academic procession to the graduation ceremonies, which were then only about an hour in the future.

"I'm sure there are strong arguments on both sides," I said.

He had grown up in Shelby, Wisconsin, where practically everybody, including grandmothers, could ride a unicycle. The thing was, a circus had gone broke while playing Shelby

60 years earlier and had abandoned a lot of its equipment, including several unicycles. So more and more people there learned how to ride them, and ordered more unicycles for themselves and their families. So Shelby became and remains today, so far as I know, the Unicycling Capital of the World.

"Do it!" I said.

"You've convinced me," he said. He was happy. He was gone, and my thoughts rode the breeze and the sunbeams back to when I was still in uniform, but home from the war, and was offered a job at Tarkington. That happened in a Chinese restaurant on Harvard Square in Cambridge, Massachusetts, where I was dining with my mother-in-law and my wife, both of them still sane, and my two legitimate children, Melanie, 11, and Eugene, Jr., 8. My illegitimate son, Rob Roy, conceived in Manila only 2 weeks before, must have been the size of a BB shot.

I had been ordered to Cambridge in order to take an examination for admission as a graduate student to the Physics Department of the Massachusetts Institute of Technology. I was to earn a Master's Degree, and then return to West Point as a teacher, but still a soldier, a soldier to the end.

My family, except for the BB, was awaiting me at the Chinese restaurant while I walked there in full uniform, ribbons and all. My hair was cut short on top and shaved down to the skin on the sides and back. People looked at me as though I were a freak. I might as well have been wearing nothing but a black garterbelt.

That was how ridiculous men in uniform had become in academic communities, even though a major part of Harvard's and MIT's income came from research and development having to do with new weaponry. I would have been dead if it weren't for that great gift to civilization from the

Chemistry Department of Harvard, which was napalm, or sticky jellied gasoline.

It was near the end of the humiliating walk that somebody said to somebody else behind me, "My goodness! Is it Halloween?"

I did not respond to that insult, did not give some draft-dodging student burst eardrums and a collapsed windpipe to think about. I kept on going because my mind was swamped with much deeper reasons for unhappiness. My wife had moved herself and the kids from Fort Bragg to Baltimore, where she was going to study Physical Therapy at Johns Hopkins University. Her recently widowed mother had moved in with them. Margaret and Mildred had bought a house in Baltimore with money left to them by my father-in-law. It was their house, not mine. I didn't know anybody in Baltimore.

What the heck was I supposed to do in Baltimore? It was exactly as though I had been killed in Vietnam, and now Margaret had to make a new life for herself. And I was a freak to my own children. They, too, looked at me as though I were wearing nothing but a black garterbelt.

And wouldn't my wife and kids be proud of me when I told them that I hadn't been able to answer more than a quarter of the questions on the examination for admission to graduate studies in Physics at MIT?

Welcome home!

As I was about to go into the Chinese restaurant, two pretty girls came out. They, too, showed contempt for me and my haircut and my uniform. So I said to them, "What's the matter? Haven't you ever before seen a man wearing nothing but a black garterbelt?"

Black garterbelts were on my mind, I suppose, because I missed Jack Patton so much. I had survived the war, but he hadn't, and the present he sent me only a few days before he was shot dead, as I said before, was a skin magazine called *Black Garterbelt.*

So there we were in that restaurant, with me on my third Sweet Rob Roy. Margaret and her mother, again acting as though I were 6 feet under in Arlington National Cemetery, did all the ordering. They had it served family style. Nobody asked me how I had done on the exam. Nobody asked me what it was like to be home from the war.

The others gabbled on to each other about all the tourist sights they had seen that day. They hadn't come along to keep me company and give me moral support. They were there to see "Old Ironsides" and the belfry where Paul Revere had waved the lantern, signaling that the British were coming by land, and so on.

Yes, and, speaking of belfries, it was on this same enchanted evening that I was told that my wife, the mother of my children, had a remarkable number of ancestors and collateral relatives with bats in their belfries on her mother's side. This was news to me, and to Margaret, too. We knew that Mildred had grown up in Peru, Indiana. But all she had ever said about Peru was that Cole Porter had been born there, too, and that she had been very glad to get out of there.

Mildred had let us know that her childhood had been unhappy, but that was a long way from saying that she, which meant my wife and kids, too, was from a notorious family of loonies there.

It turned out that my mother-in-law had run into an old friend from her hometown, Peru, Indiana, during the tour of "Old Ironsides." Now the old friend and his wife were at the table next to ours. When I went to urinate, the old friend came with me, and told me what a hard life Mildred had had in high school, with both her mother and her mother's mother in the State Hospital for the Insane down in Indianapolis.

"Her mother's brother, who she loved so much," he went on, shaking the last droplets from the end of his weenie, "also went nuts in her senior year, and set fires all over town. If I was her, I would have taken off like a scalded cat for Wyoming, too."

As I say, this was news to me.

"Funny thing—" he went on, "it never seemed to hit any of them until they were middle-aged."

"If I'm not laughing," I said, "that's because I got out on the wrong side of the bed today."

No sooner had I returned to our table than a young man passing behind me could not resist the impulse to touch my bristly haircut. I went absolutely ape-poop! He was slight, and had long hair, and wore a peace symbol around his neck. He looked like the singer Bob Dylan. For all I know or care, he may actually have been Bob Dylan. Whoever he was, I knocked him into a waiter carrying a heavily loaded tray.

Chinese food flew everywhere!

Pandemonium!

I ran outside. Everybody and everything was my enemy. I was back in Vietnam!

But a Christ-like figure loomed before me. He was wearing a suit and tie, but he had a long beard, and his eyes were full of love and pity. He seemed to know all about me, and he really did. He was Sam Wakefield, who had resigned his commission as a General, and gone over to the Peace Movement, and become President of Tarkington College.

He said to me what he had said to me so long ago in Cleveland, at the Science Fair: "What's the hurry, Son?"

21

REMEMBERING my homecoming from Vietnam always puts me in mind of Bruce Bergeron, a student of mine at Tarkington. I have already mentioned Bruce. He joined the Ice Capades as a chorus boy after winning his Associate in the Arts and Sciences Degree, and was murdered in Dubuque. His father was President of the Wildlife Rescue Federation.

When I had Bruce in Music Appreciation I played a recording of Tchaikovsky's *1812 Overture.* I explained to the class that the composition was about an actual event in history, the defeat of Napoleon in Russia. I asked the students to think of some major event in their own lives, and to imagine what kind of music might best describe it. They were to think about it for a week before telling anybody about the event or the music. I wanted their brains to cook and cook with music, with the lid on tight.

The event Bruce Bergeron set to music in his head was getting stuck between floors in an elevator when he was maybe 6 years old, on the way with a Haitian nanny to a post-Christmas white sale at Bloomingdale's department store in New York City. They were supposed to be going to the American Museum of Natural History, but the nanny, without permission from her employers, wanted to send some bargain bedding to relatives in Haiti first.

The elevator got stuck right below the floor where the white sale was going on. It was an automatic elevator. There was no operator. It was jammed. When it became obvious that the elevator was going to stay there, somebody pushed the alarm button, which the passengers could hear clanging far below. According to Bruce, this was the first time in his life that he had ever been in some kind of trouble that grownups couldn't take care of at once.

There was a 2-way speaker in the elevator, and a woman's voice came on, telling the people to stay calm. Bruce remembered that she made this particular point: Nobody was to try to climb out through the trapdoor in the ceiling. If anybody did that, Bloomingdale's could not be responsible for whatever might happen to him or her afterward.

Time went by. More time went by. To little Bruce it seemed that they had been trapped there for a century. It was probably more like 20 minutes.

Little Bruce believed himself to be at the center of a major event in American history. He imagined that not only his parents but the President of the United States must be hearing about it on television. When they were rescued, he thought, bands and cheering crowds would greet him.

Little Bruce expected a banquet and a medal for not panicking, and for not saying he had to go to the bathroom.

The elevator suddenly jolted upward a few centimeters, stopped. It jolted upward a meter, an aftershock. The doors slithered open, revealing the white sale in progress behind ordinary customers, who were simply waiting for the next elevator, without any idea that there had been something wrong with that one.

They wanted the people in there to get out so that they could get in.

There wasn't even somebody from the management of

the store to offer an anxious apology, to make certain that everybody was all right. All the actions relative to freeing the captives had taken place far away—wherever the machinery was, wherever the alarm gong was, wherever the woman was who had told them not to panic or climb out the trapdoor.

That was that.

The nanny bought some bedding, and then she and little Bruce went on to the American Museum of Natural History. The nanny made him promise not to tell his parents that they had been to Bloomingdale's, too—and he never did.

He still hadn't told them when he spilled the beans in Music Appreciation.

"You know what you have described to perfection?" I asked him.

"No," he said.

I said, "What it was like to come home from the Vietnam War."

22

I read about World War II. Civilians and soldiers alike, and even little children, were proud to have played a part in it. It was impossible, seemingly, for any sort of person not to feel a part of that war, if he or she was alive while it was going on. Yes, and the suffering or death of soldiers and sailors and Marines was felt at least a little bit by everyone.

But the Vietnam War belongs exclusively to those of us who fought in it. Nobody else had anything to do with it, supposedly. Everybody else is as pure as the driven snow. We alone are stupid and dirty, having fought such a war. When we lost, it served us right for ever having started it. The night I went temporarily insane in a Chinese restaurant on Harvard Square, everybody was a big success but me.

Before I blew up, Mildred's old friend from Peru, Indiana, spoke as though we were in separate businesses, as though I were a podiatrist, maybe, or a sheet-metal contractor, instead of somebody who had risked his life and sacrificed common sense and decency on his behalf.

As it happened, he himself was in the medical-waste disposal game in Indianapolis. That's a nice business to learn about in a Chinese restaurant, with everybody dangling who knows what from chopsticks.

He said that his workaday problems had as much to do with aesthetics as with toxicity. Those were both his words, "aesthetics" and "toxicity."

He said, "Nobody likes to find a foot or a finger or whatever in a garbage can or a dump, even though it is no more dangerous to public health than the remains of a rib roast."

He asked me if I saw anything on his and his wife's table that I would like to sample, that they had ordered too much.

"No, thank you, sir," I said.

"But telling you that," he said, "is coals to Newcastle."

"How so?" I said. I was trying not to listen to him, and was looking in exactly the wrong place for distraction, which was the face of my mother-in-law. Apparently this potential lunatic with no place else to go had become a permanent part of our household. It was a fait accompli.

"Well—you've been in war," he said. The way he said it, it was clear that he considered the war to have been my war alone. "I mean you people must have had to do a certain amount of cleaning up."

That was when the kid patted my bristles. My brains blew up like a canteen of nitroglycerin.

My lawyer, much encouraged by the 2 lists I am making, and by the fact that I have never masturbated and like to clean house, asked me yesterday why it was that I never swore. He found me washing windows in this library, although nobody had ordered me to do that.

So I told him my maternal grandfather's idea that obscenity and blasphemy gave most people permission not to listen respectfully to whatever was being said.

I repeated an old story Grandfather Wills had taught me, which was about a town where a cannon was fired at noon every day. One day the cannoneer was sick at the last minute and was too incapacitated to fire the cannon.

So at high noon there was silence.

All the people in the town jumped out of their skins when the sun reached its zenith. They asked each other in astonishment, "Good gravy! What was that?"

My lawyer wanted to know what that had to do with my not swearing.

I replied that in an era as foulmouthed as this one, "Good gravy" had the same power to startle as a cannon shot.

There on Harvard Square, back in 1975, Sam Wakefield again made himself the helmsman of my destiny. He told me to stay out on the sidewalk, where I felt safe. I was shaking like a leaf. I wanted to bark like a dog.

He went into the restaurant, and somehow calmed everybody down, and offered to pay for all damages from his own pocket right then and there. He had a very rich wife, Andrea, who would become Tarkington's Dean of Women after he committed suicide. Andrea died 2 years before the prison break, and so is not buried with so many others next to the stable, in the shadow of Musket Mountain when the Sun goes down.

She is buried next to her husband in Bryn Mawr, Pennsylvania. The glacier could still shove the 2 of them into West Virginia or Maryland. Bon Voyage!

Andrea Wakefield was the 2nd person I spoke to after Tarkington fired me. Damon Stern was the first. I am talking about 1991 again. Practically everybody else was eating lobsters. Andrea came up to me after meeting Stern farther down on the Senior Walk.

"I thought you would be in the Pavilion eating lobster," she said.

"Not hungry," I said.

"I can't stand it that they're boiled alive," she said. "You know what Damon Stern just told me?"

"I'm sure it was interesting," I said.

"During the reign of Henry the 8th of England," she said, "counterfeiters were boiled alive."

"Show biz," I said. "Were they boiled alive in public?"

"He didn't say," she said. "And what are you doing here?"

"Enjoying the sunshine," I said.

She believed me. She sat down next to me. She was already wearing her academic gown for the faculty parade to graduation. Her cowl identified her as a graduate of the Sorbonne in Paris, France. In addition to her duties as Dean, dealing with unwanted pregnancies and drug addiction and the like, she also taught French and Italian and oil painting. She was from a genuinely distinguished old Philadelphia family, which had given civilization a remarkable number of educators and lawyers and physicians and artists. She actually may have been what Jason Wilder and several of Tarkington's Trustees believed themselves to be, obviously the most highly evolved creatures on the planet.

She was a lot smarter than her husband.

I always meant to ask her how a Quaker came to marry a professional soldier, but I never did.

Too late now.

Even at her age then, which was about 60, 10 years older than me, Andrea was the best figure skater on the faculty. I think figure skating, if Andrea Wakefield could find the right partner, was eroticism enough for her. General Wakefield couldn't skate for sour apples. The best partner she had on ice at Tarkington, probably, was Bruce Bergeron—the boy who was trapped in an elevator at Bloomingdale's, who became the youth who couldn't get into any college but Tarkington, who became the man who joined the chorus of an ice show and then was murdered by somebody who presumably hated homosexuals, or loved one too much.

Andrea and I had never been lovers. She was too contented and old for me.

163

"I want you to know I think you're a Saint," said Andrea.

"How so?" I said.

"You're so nice to your wife and mother-in-law."

"It's easier than what I did for Presidents and Generals and Henry Kissinger," I said.

"But this is voluntary," she said.

"So was that," I said. "I was real gung-ho."

"When you realize how many men nowadays dissolve their marriages when they become the least little bit inconvenient or uncomfortable," she said, "all I can think is that you're a Saint."

"They didn't want to come up here, you know," I said. "They were very happy in Baltimore, and Margaret would have become a physical therapist."

"It isn't this valley that made them sick, is it?" she said. "It isn't this valley that made my husband sick."

"It's a clock that made them sick," I said. "It would have struck midnight for both of them, no matter where they were."

"That's how I feel about Sam," she said. "I can't feel guilty."

"Shouldn't," I said.

"When he resigned from the Army and went over to the peace movement," she said, "I think he was trying to stop the clock. Didn't work."

"I miss him," I said.

"Don't let the war kill you, too," she said.

"Don't worry," I said.

"You still haven't found the money?" she said.

She was talking about the money Mildred had gotten for the house in Baltimore. While Mildred was still fairly sane, she deposited it in the Scipio branch of the First National

Bank of Rochester. But then she withdrew it in cash when the bank was bought by the Sultan of Brunei, without telling me or Margaret that she had done so. Then she hid it somewhere, but she couldn't remember where.

"I don't even think about it anymore," I said. "The most likely thing is that somebody else found it. It could have been a bunch of kids. It could have been somebody working on the house. Whoever it was sure isn't going to say so."

We were talking about $45,000 and change.

"I know I should give a darn, but somehow I can't give a darn," I said.

"The war did that to you," she said.

"Who knows?" I said.

As we chatted in the sunshine, a powerful motorcycle came to life with a roar in the valley, in the region of the Black Cat Café. Then another one spoke, and yet another.

"Hell's Angels?" she said. "You mean it's really going to happen?"

The joke was that Tex Johnson, the College President, having seen one too many motorcycle movies, believed that the campus might actually be assaulted by Hell's Angels someday. This fantasy was so real to him that he had bought an Israeli sniper's rifle, complete with a telescopic sight, and ammunition for it from a drugstore in Portland, Oregon. He and Zuzu were visiting Zuzu's half sister. That was the same weapon which would eventually get him crucified.

But now Tex's anticipation of an assault by Hell's Angels didn't seem so comical after all. A mighty doomsday chorus of basso profundo 2-wheelers was growing louder and louder and coming closer and closer. There could be no doubt about it! Whoever it was, whatever it was, its destination could only be Tarkington!

23

I<small>T</small> wasn't Hell's Angels.

It wasn't lower-class people of any kind.

It was a motorcade of highly successful Americans, most on motorcycles, but some in limousines, led by Arthur Clarke, the fun-loving billionaire. He himself was on a motorcycle, and on the saddle behind him, holding on for dear life, her skirt hiked up to her crotch, was Gloria White, the 60-year-old lifelong movie star!

Bringing up the rear were a sound truck and a flatbed carrying a deflated hot-air balloon. When the balloon was inflated at the center of the Quadrangle it would turn out to be shaped like a castle Clarke owned in Ireland!

Cough, cough. Silence. Two more: Cough, cough. There, I'm OK now. Cough. That's it. I really am OK now. Peace.

This wasn't Arthur C. Clarke, the science fiction writer who wrote all the books about humanity's destiny in other parts of the Universe. This was Arthur K. Clarke, the billionaire speculator and publisher of magazines and books about high finance.

Cough. I beg your pardon. A little blood this time. In the immortal words of the Bard of Avon:

"Out, damned spot! out, I say! One; two: why, then, 'tis time to do't. Hell is murky! Fie, my lord, fie! a soldier, and afeard? What need we fear who knows it, when none can call our power to account? Who would have thought the old man to have had so much blood in him?"

Amen. And especial thanks to Bartlett's *Familiar Quotations.*

I read a lot of science fiction when I was in the Army, including Arthur C. Clarke's *Childhood's End,* which I thought was a masterpiece. He was best known for the movie *2001,* the very year in which I am writing and coughing now.

I saw *2001* twice in Vietnam. I remember 2 wounded soldiers in wheelchairs in the front row at 1 of those showings. The whole front row was wheelchairs. The 2 soldiers had had their feet wrecked some way, but seemed to be OK from the knees on up, and they weren't in any pain. They were awaiting transportation back to the States, I guess, where they could be fitted with prostheses. I don't think either of them was older than 18. One was black and 1 was white.

After the lights went up, I heard the black one say to the white one, "You tell *me:* What was that all about?"

The white one said, "I dunno, I dunno. I'll be happy if I can just get back to Cairo, Illinois."

He didn't pronounce it *"ky-*roe." He pronounced it *"kay-*roe."

My mother-in-law from Peru, Indiana, pronounces the name of her hometown *"pee-*roo," not *"puh-roo."*

Old Mildred pronounces the name of another Indiana town, Brazil, as "brazzle."

Arthur K. Clarke was coming to Tarkington to get an honorary Grand Contributor to the Arts and Sciences Degree.

The College was prevented by law from awarding any sort of degree which sounded as though the recipient had done serious work to get it. Paul Slazinger, the former Writer in Residence, I remember, objected to real institutions of higher learning giving honorary degrees with the word "Doctor" in them anywhere. He wanted them to use "Panjandrum" instead.

When the Vietnam War was going on, though, a kid could stay out of it by enrolling at Tarkington. As far as Draft Boards were concerned, Tarkington was as real a college as MIT. This could have been politics.

It must have been politics.

Everybody knew Arthur Clarke was going to get a meaningless certificate. But only Tex Johnson and the campus cops and the Provost had advance warning of the spectacular entrance he planned to make. It was a regular military operation. The motorcycles, and there were about 30 of them, and the balloon had been trucked into the parking lot behind the Black Cat Café at dawn.

And then Clarke and Gloria White and the rest of them, including Henry Kissinger, had been brought down from the Rochester airport in limousines, followed by the sound truck. Kissinger wouldn't ride a motorcycle. Neither would some others, who came all the way to the Quadrangle by limousine.

Just like the people on the motorcycles, though, the people in the limousines wore gold crash helmets decorated with dollar signs.

It's a good thing Tex Johnson knew Clarke was coming by motorcycle, or Tex just might have shot him with the Israeli rifle he had bought in Oregon.

Clarke's big arrival wasn't a half-bad dress rehearsal for Judgment Day. St. John the Divine in the Bible could only imagine such an absolutely knockout show with noise and smoke and gold and lions and eagles and thrones and celebrities and marvels up in the sky and so on. But Arthur K. Clarke had created a real one with modern technology and tons of cash!

The gold-helmeted motorcyclists formed a hollow square on the Quadrangle, facing outward, making their mighty steeds roar and roar.

Workmen in white coveralls began to inflate the balloon.

The sound truck ripped the air to shreds with the recorded racket of a bagpipe band.

Arthur Clarke, astride his bike, was looking in my direction. That was because great pals of his on the Board of Trustees were waving to him from the building right behind me. I found myself deeply offended by his proof that big money could buy big happiness.

I yawned elaborately. I turned my back on him and his show. I walked away as though I had much better things to do than gape at an imbecile.

Thus did I miss seeing the balloon snap its cable and, as unattached as myself, sail over the prison across the lake.

All the prisoners over there could see of the outside world was sky. Some of them in the exercise yard saw a castle up there for just a moment. What on Earth could the explanation be?

"There are more things in heaven and earth, Horatio, than are dreamt of in your philosophy."—Bartlett's *Familiar Quotations*

That empty castle with its mooring snapped, a plaything of the wind, was a lot like me. We were so much alike, in fact, that I myself would pay a surprise visit to the prison before the Sun went down.

If the balloon had been as close to the ground as I was, it

would have been blown this way and that at first, before it gained sufficient altitude for the prevailing wind to take it across the lake. What caused me to change course, however, wasn't random gusts but the possibility of running into this person or that one who had the power to make me even more uncomfortable. I particularly did not want to run into Zuzu Johnson or the departing Artist in Residence, Pamela Ford Hall.

But life being what it was, I would of course run into both of them.

I would rather have faced Zuzu than Pamela, since Pamela had gone all to pieces and Zuzu hadn't. But as I say, I would have to face them both.

I wasn't what had shoved Pamela over the edge. It was her 1-woman show in Buffalo a couple of months earlier. What went wrong with it seemed funny to everybody but her, and it was in the papers and on TV. For a couple of days she was the light side of the news, comic relief from reports of the rapid growth of glaciers at the poles and the desert where the Amazon rain forest used to be. And I am sure there was another oil spill. There was always another oil spill.

If Denver and Santa Fe and Le Havre, France, hadn't been evacuated yet because of atomic wastes in their water supplies, they soon would be.

What happened to Pamela's 1-woman show also gave a lot of people an opportunity to jeer at modern art, which only rich people claimed to like.

As I've said, Pamela worked in polyurethane, which is easy to carve and weighs almost nothing, and smells like urine when it's hot. Her figures, moreover, were small, women in full skirts, sitting and hunched over so you couldn't see their faces. A shoebox could have contained any 1 of them.

So they were displayed on pedestals in Buffalo, but they weren't glued down. Wind was not considered a problem, since there were 3 sets of doors between her stuff and the main entrance to the museum, which faced Lake Erie.

The museum, the Hanson Centre for the Arts, was brand-new, a gift to the city from a Rockefeller heir living in Buffalo who had come into a great deal of money from the sale of Rockefeller Center in Manhattan to the Japanese. This was an old lady in a wheelchair. She hadn't stepped on a mine in Vietnam. I think it was just old age that knocked the pins out from under her, and all the waiting for Rockefeller properties to be sold off so she could have some dough for a change.

The press was there because this was the Centre's grand opening. Pamela Ford Hall's first 1-woman show, which she called "Bagladies," was incidental, except that it was mounted in the gallery, where a string quartet was playing and champagne and canapés were being served. This was black-tie.

The donor, Miss Hanson, was the last to arrive. She and her wheelchair were set down on the top step outside. Then all 3 sets of doors between Pam's bagladies and the North Pole were thrown open wide. So all the bagladies were blown off their pedestals. They wound up on the floor, piled up against the hollow baseboards which concealed hot heating pipes.

TV cameras caught everything but the smell of hot polyurethane. What a relief from mundane worries! Who says the news has to be nothing but grim day after day?

24

P

AMELA was sulking next to the stable. The stable wasn't in the shadow of Musket Mountain yet. It would be another 7 hours before the Sun went down.

This was years before the prison break, but there were already 2 bodies and 1 human head buried out that way. Everybody knew about the 2 bodies, which had been interred with honors and topped with a tombstone. The head would come as a complete surprise when more graves were dug with a backhoe at the end of the prison break.

Whose head was it?

The 2 bodies everybody knew about belonged to Tarkington's first teacher of Botany and German and the flute, the brewmaster Hermann Shultz and his wife Sophia. They died within 1 day of each other during a diphtheria epidemic in 1893. They were in fairly fresh graves the day I was fired, although their joint grave marker was 98 years old. Their bodies and tombstone were moved there to make room for the Pahlavi Pavilion.

The mortician from down in town who took charge of moving the bodies back in 1987 reported that they were remarkably well preserved. He invited me to look, but I told him I was willing to take his word for it.

Can you imagine that? After all the corpses I saw in Vietnam, and in many cases created, I was squeamish about looking at 2 more which had absolutely nothing to do with me. I am at a loss for an explanation. Maybe I was thinking like an innocent little boy again.

I have leafed through the Atheist's Bible, Bartlett's *Familiar Quotations,* for some sort of comment on unexpected squeamishness. The best I can do is something Lady Macbeth said to her henpecked husband:

"Fie! a soldier, and afeared?"

Speaking of Atheism, I remember one time when Jack Patton and I went to a sermon in Vietnam delivered by the highest-ranking Chaplain in the Army. He was a General.

The sermon was based on what he claimed was a well-known fact, that there were no Atheists in foxholes.

I asked Jack what he thought of the sermon afterward, and he said, "There's a Chaplain who never visited the front."

The mortician, who is himself now in a covered trench by the stable, was Norman Updike, a descendant of the valley's early Dutch settlers. He went on to tell me with bow-wow cheerfulness back in 1987 that people were generally mistaken about how quickly things rot, turn into good old dirt or fertilizer or dust or whatever. He said scientists had discovered well-preserved meat and vegetables deep in city dumps, thrown away presumably years and years ago. Like Hermann and Sophia Shultz, these theoretically biodegradable works of Nature had failed to rot for want of moisture, which was life itself to worms and fungi and bacteria.

"Even without modern embalming techniques," he said,

173

"ashes to ashes and dust takes much, much longer than most people realize."

"I'm encouraged," I said.

I did not see Pamela Ford Hall by the stable until it was too late for me to head off in the opposite direction. I was distracted from watching out for her and Zuzu by a parent who had fled the bagpipe music on the Quadrangle. He commented that I seemed very depressed about something.

I still hadn't told anybody I had been fired, and I certainly didn't want to share the news with a stranger. So I said I couldn't help being unhappy about the ice caps and the deserts and the busted economy and the race riots and so on.

He told me to cheer up, that 1,000,000,000 Chinese were about to throw off the yoke of Communism. After they did that, he said, they would all want automobiles and tires and gasoline and so forth.

I pointed out that virtually all American industries having to do with automobiles either were owned or had been run out of business by the Japanese.

"And what is to prevent you from doing what I've done?" he said. "It's a free country." He said that his entire portfolio consisted of stocks in Japanese corporations.

Can you imagine what 1,000,000,000 Chinese in automobiles would do to each other and what's left of the atmosphere?

I was so intent on getting away from that typical Ruling Class chowderhead that I did not see Pamela until I was right next to her. She was sitting on the ground drinking blackberry brandy, with her back to the Shultzes' tombstone. She was gazing up at Musket Mountain. She had a serious alcohol problem. I didn't blame myself for that. The worst problem in the life of any alcoholic is alcohol.

The inscription on the grave marker was facing me.

HERMANN SHULTZ
1830–1893
SOPHIA HIMMLER SHULTZ
1841–1893
FREETHINKERS

The diphtheria epidemic that killed so many people in this valley took place when almost all of Tarkington's students were away on vacation.

That was certainly lucky for the students. If school had been in session during the epidemic, many, many of them might have wound up with the Shultzes, first where the Pavilion now stands, and then next to the stable, in the shadow of Musket Mountain when the Sun goes down.

And then the student body got lucky again 2 years ago. They were all away on a recess between semesters when habitual criminals overran this insignificant little country town.

Miracles.

I have looked up who the Freethinkers were. They were members of a short-lived sect, mostly of German descent, who believed, as did my Grandfather Wills, that nothing but sleep awaited good and evil persons alike in the Afterlife, that science had proved all organized religions to be baloney, that God was unknowable, and that the greatest use a person could make of his or her lifetime was to improve the quality of life for all in his or her community.

Hermann and Sophia Shultz weren't the only victims of the diphtheria epidemic. Far from it! But they were the only ones who asked to be buried on the campus, which they said on their deathbeds was holy ground to them.

Pamela wasn't surprised to see me. She was insulated against surprises by alcohol. The first thing she said to me was, "No." I hadn't said anything yet. She thought I had come to make love to her. I could understand why she might think that.

I myself had started thinking that.

And then she said, "This has certainly been the best year of my life, and I want to thank you for being such a big part of it." This was irony. She was being corrosively insincere.

"When are you leaving?" I said.

"Never," she said. "My transmission is shot." She was talking about her 12-year-old Buick 4-door sedan, which she had gotten as part of her divorce settlement from her ex-husband. He used to mock her efforts to become a serious artist, even slapping or kicking her from time to time. So he must have laughed even harder than everybody else when her 1-woman show was blown off its pedestals in Buffalo.

She said a new transmission was going to cost $850 down in town, and that the mechanic wanted to be paid in Yen, and that he hinted that the repairs would cost a lot less if she would go to bed with him. "I don't suppose you ever found out where your mother-in-law hid the money," she said.

"No," I said.

"Maybe I should go looking for it," she said.

"I'm sure somebody else found it, and just isn't saying anything," I said.

"I never asked you to pay for anything before," she said.
"How about you buy me a new transmission? Then, when
anybody asks me, 'Where did you get that beautiful transmission?' I can answer, 'An old lover gave that to me. He is
a very famous war hero, but I am not free to reveal his
name.' "

"Who is the mechanic?" I asked.

"The Prince of Wales," she said. "If I go to bed with him,
he will not only fix my transmission, he will make me the
Queen of England. You never made me Queen of England."

"Was it Whitey VanArsdale?" I said. This was a mechanic
down in town who used to tell everybody that he or she had
a broken transmission. He did it to me with the car I had
before the Mercedes, which was a 1979 Chevy station
wagon. I got a second opinion, from a student, actually. The
transmission was fine. All I'd wanted in the first place was a
grease job. Whitey VanArsdale, too, is now buried next to
the stable. He ambushed some convicts and got ambushed
right back. His victory lasted 10 minutes, if that. It was,
"Bang," and then, a few minutes later, "Bang, bang," right
back.

Pamela, sitting on the ground with her back to the tombstone, didn't do to me what Zuzu Johnson would soon do to
me, which was to identify me as a major cause of her unhappiness. The closest Pam came to doing that, I guess, was
when she said I had never made her the Queen of England.
Zuzu's complaint would be that I had never seriously intended to make her my wife, despite all our talk in bed about
our running off to Venice, which neither one of us had ever
seen. She would open a flower shop there, I promised her,
since she was so good at gardening. I would teach English
as a second language or help local glassblowers get their
wares into American department stores, and so on.

Zuzu was also a pretty good photographer, so I said she
would soon be hanging around where the gondolas took on

passengers, and selling tourists Polaroid pictures of themselves in gondolas right then and there.

When it came to dreaming up a future for ourselves, we left GRIOT™ in the dust.

I considered those dreams of Venice part of lovemaking, my erotic analogue to Zuzu's perfume. But Zuzu took them seriously. She was all set to go. And I couldn't go because of my family responsibilities.

Pamela knew about my love affair with Zuzu, and all the hocus pocus about Venice. Zuzu told her.

"You know what you ought to say to any woman dumb enough to fall in love with you?" she asked me. Her gaze was on Musket Mountain, not on me.

"No," I said.

And she said, " 'Welcome to Vietnam.' "

She was sitting over the Shultzes in their caskets. I was standing over a severed head which would be dug up by a backhoe in 8 years. The head had been in the ground so long that it was just a skull.

A specialist in Forensic Medicine from the State Police happened to be down here when the skull showed up in the backhoe's scoop, so he had a look at it, told us what he thought. He didn't think it was an Indian, which was my first guess. He said it had belonged to a white woman maybe 20 years old. She hadn't been bludgeoned or shot in the head, so he would have to see the rest of the skeleton before theorizing about what might have killed her.

But the backhoe never brought up another bone.

Decapitation, alone, of course, could have done the job.

He wasn't much interested. He judged from the patina on the skull that its owner had died long before we were born. He was here to examine the bodies of people who had been killed after the prison break, and to make educated guesses about how they had died, by gunshot or whatever.

He was especially fascinated by Tex Johnson's body. He had seen almost everything in his line of work, he told me, but never a man who had been crucified, with spikes through the palms and feet and all.

I wanted him to talk more about the skull, but he changed the subject right back to crucifixion. He sure knew a lot about it.

He told me one thing I'd never realized: that the Jews, not just the Romans, also crucified their idea of criminals from time to time. Live and learn!

How come I'd never heard that?

Darius, King of Persia, he told me, crucified 3,000 people he thought were enemies in Babylon. After the Romans put down the slave revolt led by Spartacus, he said, they crucified 6,000 of the rebels on either side of the Appian Way!

He said that the crucifixion of Tex Johnson was unconventional in several ways besides Tex's being dead or nearly dead when they spiked him to timbers in the stable loft. He hadn't been whipped. There hadn't been a cross-beam for him to carry to his place of execution. There was no sign over his head saying what his crime was. And there was no spike in the upright, whose head would abrade his crotch and hindquarters as he turned this way and that in efforts to become more comfortable.

As I said at the beginning of this book, if I had been a professional soldier back then, I probably would have crucified people without thinking much about it, if ordered to do so.

Or I would have ordered underlings to do it, and told them how to do it, if I had been a high-ranking officer.

I might have taught recruits who had never had anything to do with crucifixions, who maybe had never even seen one before, a new word from the vocabulary of military science of that time. The word was *crurifragium.* I myself learned it from the Medical Examiner, and I found it so interesting that I went and got a pencil and wrote it down.

It is a Latin word for "breaking the legs of a crucified person with an iron rod in order to shorten his time of suffering." But that still didn't make crucifixion a country club.

What kind of an animal would do such a thing? The old me, I think.

The late unicyclist Professor Damon Stern asked me one time if I thought there would be a market for religious figures of Christ riding a unicycle instead of spiked to a cross. It was just a joke. He didn't want an answer, and I didn't give him one. Some other subject must have come up right away.

But I would tell him now, if he hadn't been killed while trying to save the horses, that the most important message of a crucifix, to me anyway, was how unspeakably cruel supposedly sane human beings can be when under orders from a superior authority.

But listen to this: While idly winnowing through old local newspapers here, I think I have discovered whom that probably Caucasian, surely young and female skull belonged to. I want to rush out into the prison yard, formerly the Quadrangle, shouting "Eureka! Eureka!"

My educated guess is that the skull belonged to Letitia Smiley, a reputedly beautiful, dyslexic Tarkington senior who disappeared from the campus in 1922, after winning the traditional Women's Barefoot Race from the bell tower to the President's House and back again. Letitia Smiley was crowned Lilac Queen as her prize, and she burst into tears for reasons nobody could understand. Something obviously was bothering her. People were agreed, I learn from a newspaper of the time, that Letitia Smiley's tears were not happy tears.

One suspicion had to be, although nobody said so for publication, that Miss Smiley was pregnant—possibly by a member of the student body or faculty. I am playing detective now, with nothing but a skull and old newspapers to go on. But at least I have what the police were unable to find back then: what might be proof positive in the hands of a forensic cranial expert that Letitia Smiley was no longer among the living. The morning after she was crowned Lilac Queen, her bed was found to contain a dummy made of rolled-up bath towels. A souvenir football given to her by an admirer at Union College in Schenectady was the dummy's head. On it was painted: "Union 31, Hobart 3."

After that: thin air.

A dentist would be no help in identifying the skull, since whoever owned it never had so much as a single cavity to be filled. Whoever it was had perfect teeth. Who is alive today who could tell us whether or not Letitia Smiley, who herself would be 100 years old now, in the year 2001, had perfect teeth?

That was how a lot of the more mutilated bodies of soldiers in Vietnam were positively identified, by their imperfect teeth.

There is no statute of limitations on murder, the most terrible crime of all, they say. But how old would her killer be by now? If he was who I think he was, he would be 135. I think he was none other than Kensington Barber, the Provost of Tarkington College at the time. He would spend his last days in the State Hospital for the Insane up in Batavia.

I think it was he, empowered to make bed checks in both the women's and the men's dormitories, who made the dummy whose head was a football.

I think Letitia Smiley was dead by then.

And it was a matter of public record that it was the Provost who found the dummy.

The medical examiner from the State Police said it was odd that there was no hair still stuck to the skull. He thought it might have been scalped or boiled before it was buried, to make it that much harder to identify. And what have I discovered? That Letitia was famous in her short life for her long golden hair. The newspaper description of the race she won goes on and on about her golden hair.

Yes, and the same story gives Kensington Barber as the sole source of the assertion that Letitia had been deeply troubled by a stormy romance with a much older man down in Scipio. The Provost wished that he or somebody knew the name of the man, so that the police could question him.

In another story, Barber told a reporter that he had planned to take his family to Europe that summer but would stay in Scipio instead, in order to do all he could to clear up the mystery of what had become of Letitia Smiley. Such dedication to duty!

He had a wife and 2 kids, and he sent them to Europe without him. Since the campus was virtually deserted in the summertime, except for the maintenance staff, which took orders from him, he could easily have ensured his own privacy by sending the workmen to another part of the campus while he buried small parts of Letitia, possibly using a posthole digger.

I have to wonder, too, in light of my own experiences in public-relations hocus pocus and the recent history of my Government, if there weren't a lot of people back in 1922 who could put 2 and 2 together as easily as I have now. For the sake of the reputation of what had become Scipio's principal business, the college, there could have been a massive cover-up.

Kensington Barber would have a nervous breakdown at the end of the summer, and be committed, as I've said, to Batavia. The President of Tarkington at that time, who was Herbert Van Arsdale, no relation to Whitey VanArsdale, the dishonest mechanic, ascribed the Provost's crackup to exhaustion brought on by his tireless efforts to solve the mystery of the disappearance of the golden-haired Lilac Queen.

25

My lawyer found only one thing really interesting in my theory about the Lilac Queen, and that was about the broad purple hair ribbons worn by all the girls in that footrace, right up to the last race before the prison break. The escaped convicts discovered spools and spools of that ribbon in a closet in the office of the Dean of Women. Alton Darwin had them cut it up into armbands as a sort of uniform, a quick way to tell friend from foe. Of course, skin color already did a pretty good job of that.

The significance of the purple armbands, my lawyer says, is that I never put one on. This would help to prove that I was truly neutral.

The convicts didn't create a new flag. They flew the Stars and Stripes from the bell tower. Alton Darwin said they weren't against America. He said, "We *are* America."

So I took my leave of Pamela Ford Hall on the afternoon Tarkington fired me. I would never see her again. The only real favor I ever did for her, I suppose, was to tell her to get a second opinion before letting Whitey VanArsdale sell her a new transmission. She did that, I heard, and it turned out that her old transmission was perfectly OK.

It and the rest of the car took her all the way down to Key West, where the former Writer in Residence Paul Slazinger had settled in, living well on his Genius Grant from the MacArthur Foundation. I hadn't realized that he and she had been an item when they were both at Tarkington, but I guess they were. She certainly never told me about it. At any rate, when I was working over at Athena, I got an announcement of their impending wedding down there, forwarded from Scipio.

But evidently that fell through. I imagine her drinking and her insistence on pursuing an art career, even though she wasn't talented, frightened the old novelist.

Slazinger was no prize himself, of course.

After the prison break, I told the GRIOT™ here all I knew about Pamela, and asked it to guess what might become of her after her breakup with Paul Slazinger. GRIOT™ had her die of cirrhosis of the liver. I gave the machine the same set of facts a second time, and it had her freezing to death in a doorway in Chicago.

The prognosis was not good.

After leaving Pamela, whose basic problem wasn't me but alcohol, I started to climb Musket Mountain, intending to think things out under the water tower. But I was met by Zuzu Jackson, who was coming down. She said she had been under the water tower for hours, trying to think up dreams to replace those we had had of running off to Venice.

She said that maybe she would run off to Venice alone, and take Polaroid pictures of tourists getting in and out of gondolas.

The prognosis for her was a lot better than for Pamela, short-term anyway. At least she wasn't an addict, and at least she wasn't all alone in the world, even if all she had was Tex.

185

And at least she hadn't been held up as an object of public ridicule from coast to coast.

And she could see the humorous side of things. She said, I remember, that the loss of the Venice dream had left her a walking corpse, but that a zombie was an ideal mate for a College President.

She went on like that for a little while, but she didn't cry, and she ran out of steam pretty quick. The last thing she said was that she didn't blame me. "I take full responsibility," she said, speaking over her shoulder as she walked away, "for falling in love with such an obvious jerk."

Fair enough!

I decided not to climb Musket Mountain after all. I went home instead. It would be wiser to think things out in my garage, where other loose cannons from my past were unlikely to interrupt me. But when I got there I found a man from United Parcel Service ringing the bell. I didn't know him. He was new to town, or he wouldn't have asked why all the blinds were drawn. Anybody who had been in Scipio any length of time knew why the blinds were drawn.

Crazy people lived in there.

I told him somebody was sick in there, and asked what I could do for him.

He said he had this big box for me from St. Louis, Missouri.

I said I didn't know anybody in St. Louis, Missouri, and wasn't expecting a big box from anywhere. But he proved to me that it was addressed to me all right, so I said, "OK, let's see it." It turned out to be my old footlocker from Vietnam, which I had left behind when the excrement hit the air-conditioning, when I was ordered to take charge of the evacuation from the roof of the embassy.

Its arrival was not a complete surprise. Several months earlier I had received a notice of its existence in a huge

Army warehouse that was indeed on the edge of St. Louis, where all sorts of unclaimed personal property of soldiers was stored, stuff ditched on battlefields or whatever. Some idiot must have put my footlocker on one of the last American planes to flee Vietnam, thus depriving the enemy of my razor, my toothbrush, my socks and underwear, and, as it happened, the late Jack Patton's final birthday present to me, a copy of *Black Garterbelt*. A mere 14 years later, the Army said they had it, and asked me if I wanted it. I said, "Yes." A mere 2 years more went by, and then, suddenly, here it was at my doorstep. Some glaciers move faster than that.

So I had the UPS man help me lug it into the garage. It wasn't very heavy. It was just unwieldy.

The Mercedes was parked out front. I hadn't noticed yet that kids from the town had cored it again. All 4 tires were flat again.

Cough, cough.

The UPS man was really only a boy still. He was so child-like and new to his job that he had to ask me what was inside the box.

"If the Vietnam War was still going on," I said, "it might have been you in there." I meant he might have wound up in a casket.

"I don't get it," he said.

"Never mind," I said. I knocked off the lock and hasp with a hammer. I lifted the lid of what was indeed a sort of casket to me. It contained the remains of the soldier I used to be. On top of everything else, lying flat and face up, was that copy of *Black Garterbelt*.

"Wow," said the kid. He was awed by the woman on the magazine cover. He might have been an Astronaut on his first trip in space.

"Have you ever considered being a soldier?" I asked him. "I think you'd make a good one."

I never saw him again. He could have been fired soon after that, and gone looking for work elsewhere. He certainly wasn't going to last long as a UPS man if he was going to hang around like a kid on Christmas morning until he found out what was inside all the different packages.

I stayed in the garage. I didn't want to go into the house. I didn't want to go outdoors again, either. So I sat down on my footlocker and read "The Protocols of the Elders of Tralfamadore" in *Black Garterbelt*. It was about intelligent threads of energy trillions of light-years long. They wanted mortal, self-reproducing life forms to spread out through the Universe. So several of them, the Elders in the title, held a meeting by intersecting near a planet called Tralfamadore. The author never said why the Elders thought the spread of life was such a hot idea. I don't blame him. I can't think of any strong arguments in favor of it. To me, wanting every habitable planet to be inhabited is like wanting everybody to have athlete's foot.

The Elders agreed at the meeting that the only practical way for life to travel great distances through space was in the form of extremely small and durable plants and animals hitching rides on meteors that ricocheted off their planets.

But no germs tough enough to survive a trip like that had yet evolved anywhere. Life was too easy for them. They were a bunch of creampuffs. Any creature they infected, chemically speaking, was as challenging as so much chicken soup.

There were people on Earth at the time of the meeting, but they were just more hot slop for the germs to swim in. But they had extra-large brains, and some of them could talk. A few could even read and write! So the Elders focused in on them, and wondered if people's brains might not invent survival tests for germs which were truly horrible.

They saw in us a potential for chemical evils on a cosmic scale. Nor did we disappoint them.

What a story!

It so happened, according to this story, that the legend of Adam and Eve was being written down for the first time. A woman was doing it. Until then, that charming bunkum had been passed from generation to generation by word of mouth.

The Elders let her write down most of the origin myth just the way she had heard it, the way everybody told it, until she got very close to the end. Then they took control of her brain and had her write down something which had never been part of the myth before.

It was a speech by God to Adam and Eve, supposedly. This was it, and life would become pure hell for microorganisms soon afterward: "Fill the Earth and subdue it; and have dominion over the fish of the sea and over the birds of the air and over every living thing that moves on the Earth."

Cough.

26

So the people on Earth thought they had instructions from the Creator of the Universe Himself to wreck the joint. But they were going at it too slowly to satisfy the Elders, so the Elders put it into the people's heads that they themselves were the life forms that were supposed to spread out through the Universe. This was a preposterous idea, of course. In the words of the nameless author: "How could all that meat, needing so much food and water and oxygen, and with bowel movements so enormous, expect to survive a trip of any distance whatsoever through the limitless void of outer space? It was a miracle that such ravenous and cumbersome giants could make a roundtrip for a 6-pack to the nearest grocery store."

The Elders, incidentally, had given up on influencing the humanoids of Tralfamadore, who were right below where they were meeting. The Tralfamadorians had senses of humor and so knew themselves for the severely limited lunkers, not to say crazy lunkers, they really were. They were immune to the kilovolts of pride the Elders jazzed their brains with. They laughed right away when the idea popped up in their heads that they were the glory of the Universe, and that they were supposed to colonize other planets with their incomparable magnificence. They knew exactly how clumsy and dumb they were, even though they could talk and some of them could read and write and do math. One author wrote a series of side-splitting satires about Tralfamadorians arriving on other planets with the intention of spreading enlightenment.

But the people here on Earth, being humorless, found the same idea quite acceptable.

It appeared to the Elders that the people here would believe anything about themselves, no matter how preposterous, as long as it was flattering. To make sure of this, they performed an experiment. They put the idea into Earthlings' heads that the whole Universe had been created by one big male animal who looked just like them. He sat on a throne with a lot of less fancy thrones all around him. When people died they got to sit on those other thrones forever because they were such close relatives of the Creator.

The people down here just ate that up!

Another thing the Elders liked about Earthlings was that they feared and hated other Earthlings who did not look and talk exactly as they did. They made life a hell for each other as well as for what they called "lower animals." They actually thought of strangers as lower animals. So all the Elders had to do to ensure that germs were going to experience really hard times was to tell us how to make more effective weapons by studying Physics and Chemistry. The Elders lost no time in doing this.

They caused an apple to fall on the head of Isaac Newton.

They made young James Watt prick up his ears when his mother's teakettle sang.

The Elders made us think that the Creator on the big throne hated strangers as much as we did, and that we would be doing Him a big favor if we tried to exterminate them by any and all means possible.

That went over big down here.

So it wasn't long before we had made the deadliest poisons in the Universe, and were stinking up the air and water and topsoil. In the words of the author, and I wish I knew his name, "Germs died by the trillions or failed to reproduce because they could no longer cut the mustard."

But a few survived and even flourished, even though almost all other life forms on Earth perished. And when all other life forms vanished, and this planet became as sterile as the Moon, they hibernated as virtually indestructible spores, capable of waiting as long as necessary for the next lucky hit by a meteor. Thus, at last, did space travel become truly feasible.

If you stop to think about it, what the Elders did was based on a sort of trickle-down theory. Usually when people talk about the trickle-down theory, it has to do with economics. The richer people at the top of a society become, supposedly, the more wealth there is to trickle down to the people below. It never really works out that way, of course, because if there are 2 things people at the top can't stand, they have to be leakage and overflow.

But the Elders' scheme of having the misery of higher animals trickle down to microorganisms worked like a dream.

There was a lot more to the story than that. The author taught me a new term, which was "Finale Rack." This was apparently from the vocabulary of pyrotechnicians, specialists in loud and bright but otherwise harmless nighttime explosions for climaxes of patriotic holidays. A Finale Rack was a piece of milled lumber maybe 3 meters long and 20 centimeters wide and 5 centimeters thick, with all sorts of mortars and rocket launchers nailed to it, linked in series by a single fuse.

When it seemed that a fireworks show was over, that was when the Master Pyrotechnician lit the fuse of the Finale Rack.

That is how the author characterized World War II and the few years that followed it. He called it "the Finale Rack of so-called Human Progress."

If the author was right that the whole point of life on Earth was to make germs shape up so that they would be ready to ship out when the time came, then even the greatest human being in history, Shakespeare or Mozart or Lincoln or Voltaire or whoever, was nothing more than a Petri dish in the truly Grand Scheme of Things.

In the story, the Elders of Tralfamadore were indifferent, to say the least, to all the suffering going on. When 6,000 rebellious slaves were crucified on either side of the Appian Way back in good old 71 B.C., the elders would have been delighted if a crucified person had spit into the face of a Centurion, giving him pneumonia or TB.

If I had to guess when "The Protocols of the Elders of Tralfamadore" was written, I would have to say, "A long, long time ago, after World War II but before the Korean War, which broke out in 1950, when I was 10." There was no mention of Korea as part of the Finale Rack. There was a lot of talk about making the planet a paradise by killing all the bugs and germs, and generating electricity with atomic energy so cheaply that it wouldn't even be metered, and making it possible for everybody to have an automobile that would make him or her mightier than 200 horses and 3 times faster than a cheetah, and incinerating the other half of the planet in case the people there got the idea that it was their sort of intelligence that was supposed to be exported to the rest of the Universe.

The story was very likely pirated from some other publication, so the omission of the author's name may have been intentional. What sort of writer, after all, would submit a work of fiction for possible publication in *Black Garterbelt*?

I did not realize at the time how much that story affected me. Reading it was simply a way of putting off for just a little while my looking for another job and another place to live at the age of 51, with 2 lunatics in tow. But down deep the story was beginning to work like a buffered analgesic. What a relief it was, somehow, to have somebody else confirm what I had come to suspect toward the end of the Vietnam War, and particularly after I saw the head of a human being pillowed in the spilled guts of a water buffalo on the edge of a Cambodian village, that Humanity is going somewhere really nice was a myth for children under 6 years old, like the Tooth Fairy and the Easter Bunny and Santa Claus.

Cough.

I'll tell you one germ that's ready to take off for the belt of Orion or the handle on the Big Dipper or whatever right now, somewhere on Earth, and that's the gonorrhea I brought home from Tegucigalpa, Honduras, back in 1967. For a while there, it looked like I was going to have it for the rest of my life. By now it probably can eat broken glass and razor blades.

The TB germs which make me cough so much now, though, are pussycats. There are several drugs on the market which they have never learned to handle. The most potent of these was ordered for me weeks ago, and should be arriving from Rochester at any time. If any of my germs are thinking of themselves as space cadets, they can forget it. They aren't going anywhere but down the toilet.

Bon voyage!

But listen to this: You know the 2 lists I've been working on, 1 of the women I've made love to, and 1 of the men, women, and children I've killed? It is becoming ever clearer that the lengths of the lists will be virtually identical! What a coincidence! When I started out with my list of lovers, I thought that however many of them there were might serve as my epitaph, a number and nothing more. But by golly if that same number couldn't stand for the people I've killed!

There's another miracle on the order of Tarkington's students being on vacation during the diphtheria epidemic, and then again during the prison break. How much longer can I go on being an Atheist?

"There are more things in heaven and earth . . ."

27

HERE is how I got a job at the prison across the lake on the same day Tarkington College fired me:

I came out of the garage, having read that germs, not people, were the darlings of the Universe. I got into my Mercedes, intending to go down to the Black Cat Café to pick up gossip, if I could, about anybody who was hiring anybody to do practically any kind of work anywhere in this valley. But all 4 tires went *bloomp, bloomp, bloomp.*

All 4 tires had been cored by Townies the night before. I got out of the Mercedes and realized that I had to urinate. But I didn't want to do it in my own house. I didn't want to talk to the crazy people in there. How is that for excitement? What germ ever lived a life so rich in challenges and opportunities?

At least nobody was shooting at me, and I wasn't wanted by the police.

So I went into the tall weeds of a vacant lot across the street from and below my house, which was built on a slope. I whipped out my ding-dong and found it was aimed down at a beautiful white Italian racing bicycle lying on its side. The bicycle was so full of magic and innocence, hiding there. It might have been a unicorn.

After urinating elsewhere, I set that perfect artificial animal upright. It was brand-new. It had a seat like a banana. Why had somebody thrown it away? To this day I do not know. Despite our enormous brains and jam-packed libraries, we germ hotels cannot expect to understand absolutely everything. My guess is that some kid from a poor family in the town below came across it while skulking around the campus. He assumed, as would I, that it belonged to some Tarkington student who was superrich, who probably had an expensive car and more beautiful clothes than he could ever wear. So he took it, as would I when my turn came. But he lost his nerve, as I would not, and hid it in the weeds rather than face arrest for grand larceny.

As I would soon find out the hard way, the bike actually belonged to a poor person, a teenage boy who worked in the stable after school, who had scrimped and saved until he could afford to buy as splendid a bicycle as had ever been seen on the campus of Tarkington.

To play with my mistaken scenario of the bike's belonging to a rich kid: It seemed possible to me that some rich kid had so many expensive playthings that he couldn't be bothered with taking care of this one. Maybe it wouldn't fit into the trunk of his Ferrari Gran Turismo. You wouldn't believe all the treasures, diamond earrings, Rolex watches, and on and on, that wound up unclaimed in the college's Lost and Found.

Do I resent rich people? No. The best or worst I can do is notice them. I agree with the great Socialist writer George Orwell, who felt that rich people were poor people with money. I would discover this to be the majority opinion in the prison across the lake as well, although nobody over there had ever heard of George Orwell. Many of the inmates themselves had been poor people with money before they were caught, with the most costly cars and jewelry and watches and clothes. Many, as teenage drug dealers, had no doubt owned bicycles as desirable as the one I found in the weeds in the highlands of Scipio.

When convicts found out that my car was nothing but a 4-door, 6-cylinder Mercedes, they often scorned or pitied me. It was the same with many of the students at Tarkington. I might as well have owned a battered pickup truck.

So I walked that bicycle out of the weeds and onto the steep slope of Clinton Street. I wouldn't have to pedal or turn a corner in order to deliver myself to the front door of the Black Cat Café. I would have to use the brakes, however, and I tested those. If the brakes didn't work, I would go off the end of the dock of the old barge terminal and, alley-oop, straight into Lake Mohiga.

I straddled the banana-shaped saddle, which turned out to be surprisingly considerate of my sensitive crotch and hindquarters. Sailing down a hill on that bicycle in the sunshine wasn't anything like being crucified.

I parked the bike in plain view in front of the Black Cat Café, noting several champagne corks on the sidewalk and in the gutter. In Vietnam they would have been cartridge cases. This was where Arthur K. Clarke had formed up his motorcycle gang for its unopposed assault on Tarkington. The troops and their ladies had first drunk champagne. There were also remains of sandwiches, and I stepped on one, which I think was either cucumber or watercress. I scraped it off on the curbing, left it there for germs. I'll tell you this, though: No germ is going to leave the Solar System eating sissy stuff like that.

Plutonium! Now there's the stuff to put hair on a microbe's chest.

I entered the Black Cat Café for the first time in my life. This was my club now, since I had been busted down to

Townie. Maybe, after a few drinks, I'd go back up the hill and let air out of the tires of some of Clarke's motorcycles and limousines.

I bellied up to the bar and said, "Give me a wop." That was what I had heard people down in the town called Budweiser beer, ever since Italians had bought Anheuser-Busch, the company that made Budweiser. The Italians got the St. Louis Cardinals, too, as part of the deal.

"Wop coming up," said the barmaid. She was just the kind of woman I would go for right now, if I didn't have TB. She was in her late 30s, and had had a lot of bad luck recently, and didn't know where to turn next. I knew her story. So did everybody else in town. She and her husband restored an old-time ice cream parlor 2 doors up Clinton Street from the Black Cat Café. But then her husband died because he had inhaled so much paint remover. The germs inside him couldn't have felt too great, either.

Who knows, though? The Elders of Tralfamadore may have had her husband restore the ice cream parlor just so we could have a new strain of germs capable of surviving a passage through a cloud of paint remover in outer space.

Her name was Muriel Peck, and her husband Jerry Peck was a direct descendant of the first President of Tarkington College. His father grew up in this valley, but Jerry was raised in San Diego, California, and then he went to work for an ice cream company out there. The ice cream company was bought by President Mobutu of Zaire, and Jerry was let go. So he came here with Muriel and their 2 kids to discover his roots.

Since he already knew ice cream, it made perfect sense for him to buy the old ice cream parlor. It would have been better for all concerned if he had known a little less about ice cream and a little more about paint remover.

Muriel and I would eventually become lovers, but not until I had been working at Athena Prison for 2 weeks. I finally got nerve enough to ask her, since she and Jerry had both majored in Literature at Swarthmore College, if either of them had ever taken the time to read a label on a can of paint remover.

"Not until it was much too late," she said.

Over at the prison I would encounter a surprising number of convicts who had been damaged not by paint remover but by paint. When they were little they had eaten chips or breathed dust from old lead-based paint. Lead poisoning had made them very stupid. They were all in prison for the dumbest crimes imaginable, and I was never able to teach any of them to read and write.

Thanks to them, do we now have germs which eat lead?

I know we have germs which eat petroleum. What their story is, I do not know. Maybe they're that Honduran gonorrhea.

28

JERRY Peck was in a wheelchair with a tank of oxygen in his lap at the grand opening of the Mohiga Ice Cream Emporium. But he and Muriel had a nice little hit on their hands. Tarkingtonians and Townies alike were pleased by the decor and the luscious ice cream.

After the place had been open for only 6 months, though, a man came in and photographed everything. Then he pulled out a tape and made measurements which he wrote down in a book. The Pecks were flattered, and asked him if he was from an architectural magazine or what. He said that he worked for the architect who was designing the new student recreation center up on the hill, the Pahlavi Pavilion. The Pahlavis wanted it to have an ice cream parlor identical to theirs, right down to the last detail.

So maybe it wasn't paint remover that killed Jerry Peck after all.

The Pavilion also put the valley's only bowling alley out of business. It couldn't survive on the business of Townies alone. So anybody in this area who wanted to bowl and wasn't connected to Tarkington had to go 30 kilometers to the north, to the alleys next to the Meadowdale Cinema

Complex, across the highway from the National Guard Armory.

It was a slow time of day at the Black Cat Café. There may have been a few prostitutes in vans in the parking lot out back but none inside.

The owner, Lyle Hooper, who was also Chief of the Volunteer Fire Department and a Notary, was at the other end of the bar, doing some kind of bookkeeping. Until the very end of his life, he would never admit that the availability of prostitutes in his parking lot accounted in large measure for the business he did in liquor and snacks, and for the condom machine in the men's room.

To the Elders of Tralfamadore, of course, that condom machine would represent a threat to their space program.

Lyle Hooper surely knew about my sexual exploits, since he had notarized the affidavits in my portfolio. But he never mentioned them to me, or so far as I know to anyone. He was the soul of discretion.

Lyle was probably the best-liked man in this valley. Townies were so fond of him, men and women alike, that I never heard one call the Black Cat Café a whorehouse. Up on the hill, of course, it was called almost nothing else.

The Townies protected the image he had of himself, in spite of State Police raids and visits from the County Health Department, as a family man who ran a place of refreshment whose success depended entirely on the quality of the drinks and snacks he served. This kindly conspiracy protected Lyle's son Charlton, as well. Charlton grew to be 2 meters tall, and was a New York State High School All-Star basketball center in his senior year at Scipio High School, and all he ever had to say about his father was that he ran a restaurant.

Charlton was such a phenomenal basketball player that he

was invited to try out for the New York Knickerbockers, which were still owned by Americans back then. He accepted a full scholarship to MIT instead, and became a top scientist running the huge subatomic particle accelerator called "the Supercollider" outside Waxahachie, Texas.

As I understand it, the scientists down there forced invisible particles to reveal their secrets by making them go *splat* on photographic plates. That isn't all that different from the way we treated suspected enemy agents in Vietnam sometimes.

Have I already said that I threw one out of a helicopter?

The Townies didn't have to protect the sensibilities of Lyle's wife by never saying why the Black Cat Café was so prosperous. She had left him. She discovered in midlife that she was a lesbian, and ran off with the high school's girls' gym teacher to Bermuda, where they gave and probably still give sailing lessons.

I made a pass at her one time at an Annual Town-and-Gown Mixer up on the hill. I knew she was a lesbian before *she* did.

At the very end of his life 2 years ago, though, when Lyle Hooper was a prisoner of the escaped convicts up in the bell tower, he was addressed by his captors as "Pimp." It was, "Hey, Pimp, how you like the view?" and "What you think we ought to do with you, Pimp?" and so on. It was cold and wet up there. Snow or rain blown into the belfry fell down through a myriad of bullet holes in the ceiling. Those had been made from below by escaped convicts when they realized that a sniper was up there among the bells.

There was no electricity. All electric and telephone service had been shut off. When I visited Lyle up there, he knew the story of those holes, knew the sniper had been crucified in the stable loft. He knew that the escaped convicts hadn't decided yet what to do with him. He knew that he had committed what was in their eyes murder pure and simple. He and Whitey VanArsdale had ambushed and killed 3 escaped convicts who were on their way up the old towpath to the head of the lake, to negotiate with the police and politicians and soldiers at the roadblock there. The would-be negotiators were carrying flags of truce, white pillowcases on broomsticks, when Lyle Hooper and Whitey VanArsdale shot them dead.

And then Whitey was himself shot dead almost immediately, but Lyle was taken prisoner.

But what bothered Hooper most when I talked to him up in the bell tower was that his captors called him nothing but "Pimp."

At this point in my story, and in order to simplify the telling, and not to make any political point, let me from now on call the escaped convicts in Scipio what they called themselves, which was "Freedom Fighters."

So Lyle Hooper was without question responsible for the death of 3 Freedom Fighters carrying flags of truce. The Freedom Fighter who was guarding him in the tower when I came to see him, moreover, was the half brother and former partner in the crack business, along with their grandmother, of 1 of the Freedom Fighters he or Whitey had killed.

But all Lyle could talk about was the pain of being called a pimp. To many if not most of the Freedom Fighters, of course, it was no particular insult to call someone a pimp.

Lyle told me that he had been raised by his paternal grandmother, who made him promise to leave the world a better place than when he found it. He said, "Have I done that, Gene?"

I said he had. Since he was facing execution, I certainly wasn't going to tell him that, in my experience anyway, ambushes made the world seem an even worse place than it was before.

"I ran a nice, clean place, raised a wonderful son," he said. "Put out a lot of fires."

It was the Trustees who told the Freedom Fighters that Lyle ran a whorehouse. Otherwise they would have thought he was just a restaurateur and Fire Chief.

Lyle Hooper's mood up there in the bell tower reminded me of my father's mood after he was let go by Barrytron, and he went on a cruise down the Inland Waterway on the East Coast, from City Island in New York City to Palm Beach, Florida. This was on a motor yacht owned by his old college roommate, a man named Fred Handy. Handy had also studied chemical engineering, but then had gone into junk bonds instead. He heard that Father was deeply depressed. He thought the cruise might cheer Dad up.

But all the way to Palm Beach, where Handy had a waterfront estate, down the East River, down Barnegat Bay, up Delaware Bay and down Chesapeake Bay, down the Dismal Swamp Canal, and on and on, the yacht had to nuzzle its way through a shore-to-shore, horizon-to-horizon carpet of bobbing plastic bottles. They had contained brake fluid and laundry bleach and so on.

Father had had a lot to do with the development of those bottles. He knew, too, that they could go on bobbing for 1,000 years. They were nothing to be proud of.

In a way, those bottles called him what the Freedom Fighters called Lyle Hooper.

Lyle's despairing last words as he was led out of the bell

tower to be executed in front of Samoza Hall might be an apt epitaph for my father:

OK, I ADMIT IT.
IT REALLY WAS A
WHOREHOUSE.

29

LYLE Hooper's last words, I think we can say with the benefit of hindsight in the year 2001, might serve as an apt epitaph for a plurality of working adults in industrialized nations during the 20th Century. How could they help themselves, when so many of the jobs they or their mates could get had to do with large-scale deceptions, legal thefts from public treasuries, or the wrecking of the food chain, the topsoil, the water, or the atmosphere?

After Lyle Hooper was executed, with a bullet behind the ear, I visited the Trustees in the stable. Tex Johnson was still spiked to the cross-timbers in the loft overhead, and they knew it.

But before I tell about that, I had better finish my story of how I got a job at Athena.

So there I was back in 1991, nursing a Budweiser, or "wop," at the bar of the Black Cat Café. Muriel Peck was telling me how exciting it had been to see all the motorcycles and limousines and celebrities out front. She couldn't believe that she had been that close to Gloria White and Henry Kissinger.

Several of the merry roisterers had come inside to use the

toilet or get a drink of water. Arthur K. Clarke had provided everything but water and toilets. So Muriel had dared to ask some of them who they were and what they did.

Three of the people were Black. One Black was an old woman who had just won $57,000,000 in the New York State Lottery, and the other 2 were baseball players who made $3,000,000 a year.

A white man, who kept apart from the rest, and, according to Muriel, didn't seem to know what to make of himself, was a daily book reviewer for *The New York Times.* He had given a rave review to Clarke's autobiography, *Don't Be Ashamed of Money.*

One man who came in to use the toilet, she said, was a famous author of horror stories that had been made into some of the most popular movies of all time. I had in fact read a couple of them in Vietnam, about innocent people getting murdered by walking corpses with axes and knives and so on.

I passed 1 of them on to Jack Patton, I remember, and asked him later what he thought of it. And then I stopped him from answering, saying, "You don't have to tell me, Jack. I already know. It made you want to laugh like hell."

"Not only that, Major Hartke," he replied. "I thought of what his next book should be about."

"What's that?" I asked.

"A B-52," he said. "Gore and guts everywhere."

One user of the toilet, who confessed to Muriel that he had diarrhea, and asked if she had anything behind the bar to stop it, was a retired Astronaut whom she recognized but couldn't name. She had seen him again and again in commercials for a sinus-headache remedy and a retirement community in Cocoa Beach, Florida, near Cape Kennedy.

So Arthur K. Clarke, along with all his other activities, was a whimsical people-collector. He invited people he didn't really know, but who had caught his eye for 1 reason or another, to his parties, and they came, they came. Another one, Muriel told me, was a man who had inherited from his father a painting by Mark Rothko that had just been sold to the Getty Museum in Malibu, California, for $37,000,000, a new record for a painting by an American.

Rothko himself had long since committed suicide.

He had had enough.

He was out of here.

"She's so short," Muriel said to me. "I was so surprised how short she was."

"Who's so short?" I said.

"Gloria White," she said.

I asked her what she thought of Henry Kissinger. She said she loved his voice.

I had seen him up on the Quadrangle. Although I had been an instrument of his geopolitics, I felt no connection between him and me. His face was certainly familiar. He might have been, like Gloria White, somebody who had been in a lot of movies I had seen.

I dreamed about him once here in prison, though. He was a woman. He was a Gypsy fortune-teller who looked into her crystal ball but wouldn't say anything.

I said to Muriel, "You worry me."

"I what?" she said.

"You look tired," I said. "Do you get enough sleep?"

"Yes, thank you," she said.

"Forgive me," I said. "None of my business. It's just that you were so full of life while you were talking about the motorcycle people. When you stopped, it was as though you took off a mask, and you seemed as though you were suddenly all wrung out."

Muriel knew vaguely who I was. She had seen me with Margaret and Mildred in tow at least twice a week during the short time the ice cream parlor was in business. So I did not have to tell her that I, too, practically speaking, was without a mate. And she had seen with her own eyes how kind and patient I was with my worse than useless relatives.

So she was already favorably disposed to me. She trusted me, and responded with undisguised gratitude to my expressions of concern for her happiness.

"If you want to know the truth," she said, "I hardly sleep at all, I worry so much about the children." She had 2 of them. "The way things are going," she said, "I don't see how I can afford to send even 1 of them to college. I'm from a family where everybody went to college and never thought a thing about it. But that's all over now. Neither 1 is an athlete."

We might have become lovers that night, I think, instead of 2 weeks from then, if an ugly mountain of a man hadn't entered raging, demanding to know, "All right, where is he? Where's that kid?"

He was asking about the kid who worked at Tarkington's stable after school, whose bicycle I had stolen. I had left the kid's bike in plain view out front. Every other place of business on Clinton Street was boarded up, from the barge terminal to halfway up the hill. So the only place the boy could be, he thought, was inside the Black Cat Café or, worse, inside one of the vans out back in the parking lot.

I played dumb.

We went outside with him to find out what bicycle he could possibly be talking about. I offered him the theory that the boy was a good boy, and nowhere near the Black Cat Café, and that some bad person had borrowed the bike and left it there. So he put the bike on the back of his beat-up pickup truck, and said he was late for an appointment for a job interview at the prison across the lake.

"What kind of a job?" I asked.

And he said, "They're hiring teachers over there."

I asked if I could come with him.

He said, "Not if you're going to teach what I want to teach. What do you want to teach?"

"Anything you don't want to teach," I said.

"I want to teach shop," he said. "You want to teach shop?"

"No," I said.

"Word of honor?" he said.

"Word of honor," I said.

"OK," he said, "get in, get in."

30

To understand how the lower ranks of guards at Athena in those days felt about White people, and never mind Black people, you have to realize that most of them were recruited from Japan's northernmost island, Hokkaido. On Hokkaido the primitive natives, the Ainus, thought to be very ugly because they were so pallid and hairy, were White people. Genetically speaking, they are just as white as Nancy Reagan. Their ancestors long ago had made the error, when humiliated by superior Asiatic civilizations, of shambling north instead of west to Europe, and eventually, of course, to the Western Hemisphere.

Those White people on Hokkaido had sure missed a lot. They were way behind practically everybody. And when the man who wanted to teach shop and I presented ourselves at the gate to the road that led through the National Forest to the prison, the 2 guards on duty there were fresh from Hokkaido. For all the respect our being Whites inspired in them, we might as well have been a couple of drunk and disorderly Arapahos.

The man who wanted to teach shop said his name was John Donner. On the way over he asked me if I had seen him on the Phil Donahue show on TV. That was a 1-hour show every weekday afternoon, which featured a small group of real people, not actors, who had had the same sort of bad thing happen to them, and had triumphed over it or were barely coping or whatever. There were 2 very similar programs in competition with *Donahue*, and the old novelist Paul Slazinger used to watch all 3 simultaneously, switching back and forth.

I asked him why he did that. He said he didn't want to miss the moment when, suddenly, there was absolutely nothing left to talk about.

I told John Donner that, unfortunately, I couldn't watch any of those shows, since I taught Music Appreciation in the afternoon, and then Martial Arts after that. I asked him what his particular *Donahue* show had been about.

"People who were raised in foster homes and got beat up all the time," he said.

I would see plenty of *Donahue* reruns at the prison, but not Donner's. That show would have been coals to Newcastle at Athena, where practically everybody had been beaten regularly and severely when he was a little kid.

I didn't see Donner on TV over there, but I did see myself a couple of times, or somebody who looked a whole lot like me in the distance, on old footage of the Vietnam War.

I even yelled 1 time at the prison, "There I am! There I am!"

Convicts gathered behind me, looking at the TV and saying, "Where? Where? Where?"

But they were too late. I was gone again.

Where did I go?

Here I am.

31

J OHN Donner could have been a pathological liar. He could have made that up about being on *Donahue*. There was something very fishy about him. Then again, he could have been living under the Federal Witness Protection Program, with a new name and a fake biography GRIOT™ had written out for him. Statistically speaking, GRIOT™ would have to put it into a biography every so often, I suppose, that the fictitious subject was on *Donahue*.

He claimed that the boy he lived with was his son. But he could have kidnapped that kid whose bike I stole. They had come to town only about 18 months before, and kept to themselves.

I am sure his last name wasn't Donner. I have known several Donners. One was a year behind me at the Academy. Two were unrelated Tarkingtonians. One was a First Sergeant in Vietnam who had his arm blown off by a little boy with a homemade handgrenade. Every one of those Donners knew the story of the infamous Donner Party, which got caught in a blizzard back in 1846 while trying to cross the Sierra Nevada Mountains in wagons to get to California. Their wagons were very likely made right here in Scipio.

I have just looked up the details in the *Encyclopaedia Britannica,* published in Chicago and owned by a mysterious Egyptian arms dealer living in Switzerland. Rule Britannia!

Those who survived the blizzard did so by becoming cannibals. The final tally, and several women and children were eaten, was 47 survivors out of 87 people who had begun the trip.

Now there's a subject for *Donahue:* people who have eaten people.

People who can eat people are the luckiest people in the world.

But when I asked the man who claimed his last name was Donner if he was any relation to the man who led the Donner Party, he didn't know what I was talking about.

Whoever he really was, he and I wound up side by side on a hard bench in the waiting room outside the office of Athena's Warden, Hiroshi Matsumoto.

While we sat there, incidentally, some supplier to the prison was stealing the bicycle from the back of Donner's pickup truck.

A mere detail!

Donner told the truth about 1 thing at least. The Warden was ready to interview applicants for a teaching job. But we were the only 2 applicants. Donner said he heard about the job opening on the National Public Radio station in Rochester. That isn't the sort of station people looking for work are likely to listen to. It is much too sophisticated.

That was the only area station I know of, incidentally, which said it was tragic, not funny, what happened to Pamela Ford Hall's 1-woman show in Buffalo.

There was a Japanese TV set in front of us. There were Japanese TV sets all over the prison. They were like portholes on an ocean liner. The passengers were in a state of suspended animation until the big ship got where it was going. But anytime they wanted, the passengers could look through a porthole and see the real world out there.

Life was like an ocean liner to a lot of people who weren't in prison, too, of course. And their TV sets were portholes through which they could look while doing nothing, to see all the World was doing with no help from them.

Look at it go!

At Athena, though, the TVs showed nothing but very old shows from a large library of tapes 2 doors down from the office of Warden Matsumoto's office.

The tapes weren't played in any particular order. A guard who might not even understand English kept the central VCR stoked with whatever came to hand, just as though the cassettes were charcoal briquettes and the VCR was a hibachi back on Hokkaido.

But this whole scheme was an American invention taken over by the Japanese, like the VCR and the TV sets. Back when races were mixed in prisons, the adopted son of a member of the Board of Directors of the Museum of Broadcasting was sent to Athena for having strangled a girlfriend behind the Metropolitan Museum of Art. So the father had hundreds of tapes of TV shows in the library of the Museum of Broadcasting duplicated and presented to the prison. His dream, apparently, was that the tapes would provide the basis for a course at Athena in Broadcasting, which industry some of the inmates might consider entering after they got out, if they ever got out.

But the course in Broadcasting never materialized. So the tapes were run over and over again as something better than nothing for the convicts to look at while they were serving time.

The adopted son of the donor of the tapes came back into the news briefly at the time the prison populations were being segregated according to race. There was talk of paroling him and a lot of others rather than transferring them to other prisons.

But the parents of the girl he had murdered behind the museum, who were well connected socially, demanded that he serve his full sentence, which, as I recall it, was 99 years. He was adopted, as I say. It came out that his biological father had also been a murderer.

So he now may be on one of the aircraft carriers or missile cruisers in New York Harbor that have been converted into prison ships.

While Donner and I waited to see the Warden, we watched the assassination of President John F. Kennedy. Bingo! The back of his head flew off. His wife, wearing a pillbox hat, crawled out over the trunk of the convertible limousine.

And then the show cut to the police station in Dallas as Lee Harvey Oswald, the ex-Marine who supposedly shot the President with a mail-order Italian rifle, was shot in the guts by the owner of a local strip joint. Oswald said, "Ow." There, yet again, was that "Ow" heard round the world.

Who says history has to be boring?

Meanwhile, out in the prison parking lot, somebody who had delivered food or whatever to the prison was taking the bicycle out of Donner's truck and putting it in his own, and taking off. It was like the murder of the Lilac Queen back in 1922, a perfect crime.

Cough.

There is even talk now of turning our nuclear submarines into jails for persons who, like myself, are awaiting trial.

They wouldn't submerge, of course, and the rocket and tor-
pedo tubes and all the electronic equipment would be sold
for junk, leaving more space for cells.

If the entire submarine fleet were converted into jails, I've
heard, the cells would be filled up at once. When this place
stopped being a college and became a prison, it was filled to
the brim before you could say "Jack Robinson."

I was called into the Warden's Office first. When I came
back out, with not only a job but a place to live, the TV set
was displaying a program I had watched when I was a boy,
Howdy Doody. Buffalo Bob, the host, was about to be
sprayed with seltzer water by Clarabell the Clown.

They were in black and white. That's how old that show
was.

I told Donner the Warden wanted to see him, but he
didn't seem to know who I was. I felt as though I were trying
to wake up a mean drunk. I used to have to do that a lot in
Vietnam. A couple of times the mean drunks were Generals.
The worst was a visiting Congressman.

I thought I might have to fight Donner before he realized
that *Howdy Doody* wasn't the main thing going on.

Warden Hiroshi Matsumoto was a survivor of the atom-
bombing of Hiroshima, when I was 5 and he was 8. When
the bomb was dropped, he was playing soccer during school
recess. He chased a ball into a ditch at one end of the playing
field. He bent over to pick up the ball. There was a flash and
wind. When he straightened up, his city was gone. He was
alone on a desert, with little spirals of dust dancing here and
there. But I would have to know him for more than 2 years
before he told me that.

His teachers and schoolmates were executed without trial
for the crime of Emperor Worship.

Like St. Joan of Arc, they were burned alive.

Crucifixion as a mode of execution for the very worst criminals was outlawed by the first Christian Roman Emperor, who was Constantine the Great.

Burning and boiling were still OK.

If I had had more time to think about it, I might not have applied for a job at Athena, realizing that I would have had to admit that I had served in Vietnam, killing or trying to kill nothing but Orientals. And my interviewer would surely be Oriental.

Yes, and no sooner did Warden Matsumoto hear that I was a West Pointer than he said with terrible heaviness, "Then of course you spent time in Vietnam."

I thought to myself, "Oh oh. There goes the ball game."

I misread him completely, not knowing then that the Japanese considered themselves to be as genetically discrete from other Orientals as from me or Donner or Nancy Reagan or the pallid, hairy Ainus, say.

"A soldier does what he is ordered to do," I said. "I never felt good about what I had to do." This wasn't entirely true. I had gotten high as a kite on the fighting now and then. I actually killed a man with my bare hands 1 time. He had tried to kill me. I barked like a dog and laughed afterward, and then threw up.

My confession that I had served in Vietnam, to my amazement, made Warden Matsumoto feel that we were almost brothers! He came out from behind his desk to take me by the hand and stare into my eyes. It was an odd experience for me, simply from the physical standpoint, since he was wearing a surgical mask and rubber gloves.

"So we both know what it is," he said, "to be shipped to an alien land on a dangerous mission of vainglorious lunacy!"

32

WHAT an afternoon!

Only 3 hours before, I had been so at peace in my bell tower. Now I was inside a maximum-security prison, with a masked and gloved Japanese national who insisted that the United States was his Vietnam!

What is more, he had been in the middle of student antiwar protests over here when the Vietnam War was going on. His corporation had sent him to the Harvard Business School to study the minds of the movers and shakers who were screwing up our economy for their own immediate benefit, taking money earmarked for research and development and new machinery and so on, and putting it into monumental retirement plans and year-end bonuses for themselves.

During our interview, he used all the antiwar rhetoric he had heard at Harvard in the '60s to denounce his own country's overseas disaster. We were a quagmire. There was no light at the end of the tunnel over here, and on and on.

Until that moment, I had not given a thought to the mental state of members of the ever-growing army of Japanese nationals in this country, who had to make a financial go of all the properties their corporations had bought out from under us. And it really must have felt to most of them like a war overseas about Heaven knows what, and especially since, as was my case in Vietnam, they were color-coded in contrast with the majority of the native population.

On the subject of color-coding: You might have expected that a lot of black people would be shot after the prison break, even though they weren't escaped convicts. The state of mind of Whites in this valley, certainly, was that any Black male had to be an escapee.

Shoot first, and ask questions afterward. I sure used to do that.

But the only person who wasn't an escapee who got shot just for being black was a nephew of the Mayor of Troy. And he was only winged. He lost the use of his right hand, but that has since been repaired by the miracle of microsurgery.

He was left-handed anyway.

He was winged when he was where he wasn't supposed to be, where nobody of any race was supposed to be. He was camping in the National Forest, which is against the law. He didn't even know there had been a prison break.

And then: *Bang!*

And here I am capitalizing "Black" and "White" sometimes, and then not capitalizing them, and not feeling right about how the words look either way. That could be because sometimes race seems to matter a tremendous lot, and other times race seems to matter a little less than that. And I keep wanting to say "so-called Black" or "so-called black." My guess is that well over half the inmates at Athena, and now in this prison here, had white or White ancestors. Many appear to be mostly white, but they get no credit for that.

Imagine what that must feel like.

I myself have claimed a black ancestor, since this is a prison for Blacks only, and I don't want to be transferred out of here. I need this library. You can imagine what sorts of

221

libraries they must have on the aircraft carriers and missile cruisers which have been converted into prison ships.

This is home.

My lawyer says I am smart not to want to be transferred, but for other reasons. A transfer might put me back in the news again, and raise a popular clamor for my punishment.

As matters stand now, I am forgotten by the general public, and so, for that matter, is the prison break. The break was big news on TV for only about 10 days.

And then it was displaced as a headliner by a lone White girl. She was the daughter of a gun nut in rural northern California. She wiped out the Prom Committee of her high school with a Chinese handgrenade from World War II.

Her father had one of the World's most complete collections of handgrenades.

Now his collection isn't as complete as it used to be, unless, of course, he had more than 1 Chinese handgrenade from the Finale Rack.

Warden Matsumoto became chattier and chattier during my job interview. Before he was sent to Athena, he said, he ran a hospital-for-profit his corporation had bought in Louisville. He loved the Kentucky Derby. But he hated his job.

I told him I used to go to the horse races in Saigon every chance I got.

He said, "I only wish our Chairman of the Board back in Tokyo could have spent just one hour with me in our emergency room, turning away dying people because they could not afford our services."

"You had a body count in Vietnam, I believe?" he said.

It was true. We were ordered to count how many people we killed so that higher headquarters, all the way back to

Washington, D.C., could estimate how much closer, even if it was only a teeny-weeny bit closer, all our efforts were bringing us to victory. There wasn't any other way to keep score.

"So now we count dollars the way you used to count bodies," he said. "What does that bring us closer to? What does it mean? We should do with those dollars what you did with the bodies. Bury and forget them! You were luckier with your bodies than we are with all our dollars."

"How so?" I said.

"All anybody can do with bodies is burn them or bury them," he said. "There isn't any nightmare afterwards, when you have to invest them and make them grow."

"What a clever trap your Ruling Class set for us," he went on. "First the atomic bomb. Now this."

"Trap?" I echoed wonderingly.

"They looted your public and corporate treasuries, and turned your industries over to nincompoops," he said. "Then they had your Government borrow so heavily from us that we had no choice but to send over an Army of Occupation in business suits. Never before has the Ruling Class of a country found a way to stick other countries with all the responsibilities their wealth might imply, and still remain rich beyond the dreams of avarice! No wonder they thought the comatose Ronald Reagan was a great President!"

His point was well taken, it seems to me.

When Jason Wilder and all the rest of the Trustees were hostages in the stable, and I paid them a call, I got the distinct impression that they regarded Americans as foreigners. What nationality that made them is hard to say.

They were all White, and they were all Male, since Lowell Chung's mother had died of tetanus. She died before the doctors could understand what was killing her. None of them had ever seen a case of tetanus before, because practically everybody in this country in the old days had been immunized.

Now that public health programs have pretty much fallen apart, and no foreigners are interested in running them, which is certainly understandable, quite a number of cases of tetanus, and especially among children, are turning up again.

So most doctors know what it looks like now. Mrs. Chung had the misfortune to be a pioneer.

The hostages told me about that. One of the first things I said to them was, "Where is Madam Chung?"

I thought I should reassure the Trustees after the execution of Lyle Hooper. His corpse had been shown to them as a warning, I suppose, against their making any plans for derring-do. That body was surely icing on the cake of terror, so to speak. The College President, after all, was dangling from spikes in the loft above.

One of the hostages said in a TV interview after he was liberated that he would never forget the sound of Tex Johnson's head bouncing on the steps as Tex was dragged up to the loft feet first. He tried to imitate the sound. He said, *"Bloomp, bloomp, bloomp,"* the same sound a flat tire makes.

What a planet!

The hostages expressed pity for Tex, but none for Lyle Hooper, and none for all the other faculty members and Townies who were also dead. The locals were too insignificant for persons on their social level to think about. I don't fault them for this. I think they were being human.

The Vietnam War couldn't have gone on as long as it did, certainly, if it hadn't been human nature to regard persons

1 didn't know and didn't care to know, even if they were in agony, as insignificant. A few human beings have struggled against this most natural of tendencies, and have expressed pity for unhappy strangers. But, as History shows, as History yells: "They have never been numerous!"

Another flaw in the human character is that everybody wants to build and nobody wants to do maintenance.

And the worst flaw is that we're just plain dumb. Admit it!

You think Auschwitz was intelligent?

When I tried to tell the hostages a little about their captors, about their childhoods and mental illnesses, and their not caring if they lived or died, and what prison was like, and so on, Jason Wilder actually closed his eyes and covered his ears. He was being theatrical rather than practical. He didn't cover his ears so well that he couldn't hear me.

Others shook their heads and indicated in other ways that such information was not only tiresome but offensive. It was as though we were in a thunderstorm, and I had begun lecturing on the circulation of electrical charges in clouds, and the formation of raindrops, and the paths chosen by lightning strokes, and what thunder was, and on and on. All they wanted to know was when the storm would stop, so they could go on about their business.

What Warden Matsumoto had said about people like them was accurate. They had managed to convert their wealth, which had originally been in the form of factories or stores or other demanding enterprises, into a form so liquid and abstract, negotiable representations of money on paper, that there were few reminders coming from anywhere that they might be responsible for anyone outside their own circle of friends and relatives.

They didn't rage against the convicts. They were mad at the Government for not making sure that escapes from prison were impossible. The more they ran on like that, the clearer it became that it was their Government, not mine or the convicts' or the Townies'. Its first duty, moreover, was to protect them from the lower classes, not only in this country but everywhere.

Were people on Easy Street ever any different?

Think again about the crucifixions of Jesus and the 2 thieves, and the 6,000 slaves who followed the gladiator Spartacus.

Cough.

My body, as I understand it, is attempting to contain the TB germs inside me in little shells it builds around them. The shells are calcium, the most common element in the walls of many prisons, including Athena. This place is ringed by barbed wire. So was Auschwitz.

If I die of TB, it will be because my body could not build prisons fast enough and strong enough.

Is there a lesson there? Not a cheerful one.

If the Trustees were bad, the convicts were worse. I would be the last person to say otherwise. They were devastators of their own communities with gunfights and robberies and rapes, and the merchandising of brain-busting chemicals and on and on.

But at least they saw what they were doing, whereas people like the Trustees had a lot in common with B-52 bombardiers way up in the stratosphere. They seldom saw the devastation they caused as they moved the huge portion of this country's wealth they controlled from here to there.

226

Unlike my Socialist grandfather Ben Wills, who was a no-body, I have no reforms to propose. I think any form of government, not just Capitalism, is whatever the people who have all our money, drunk or sober, sane or insane, decide to do today.

Warden Matsumoto was an odd duck. Many of his quirks were no doubt a consequence of his having had an atomic bomb dropped on him in childhood. The buildings and trees and bridges and so on which had seemed so substantial van-ished like fantasies.

As I've said, Hiroshima was suddenly a blank tableland with little dust devils spinning here and there.

After the flash, little Hiroshi Matsumoto was the only real thing on the table. He began a long, long walk in search of anything else that was also real. When he reached the edge of the city, he found himself among structures and creatures both real and fantastic, living people with their skins hang-ing on their exposed muscles and bones like draperies, and so on.

These images about the bombing are all his, by the way. But I wouldn't hear them from him until I had been teach-ing at the prison and living next door to him by the lake for 2 long years.

Whatever else being atom-bombed had done to him, it had not destroyed his conscience. He had hated turning away poor people from the emergency room at the hospital-for-profit he ran in Louisville. After he took over the prison-for-profit at Athena, he thought there ought to be some sort of educational program there, even though his corporation's contract with New York State required him to keep the prisoners from escaping and nothing more.

He worked for Sony. He never worked for anybody but Sony.

"New York State," he said, "does not believe that education can rehabilitate the sort of criminal who ends up at Athena or Attica or Sing Sing." Attica and Sing Sing were for Hispanics and Whites respectively, who, like the inmates at Athena, had been convicted of at least 1 murder and 2 other violent crimes. The other 2 were likely to be murders, too.

"I don't believe it, either," he said. "I do know this, though: 10 percent of the people inside these walls still have minds, but there is nothing for those minds to play with. So this place is twice as painful for them as it is for the rest. A good teacher just might be able to give their minds new toys, Math or Astronomy or History, or who knows what, which would make the passage of time just a little bit more bearable. What do you think?"

"You're the boss," I said.

He really was the boss, too. He had made such a financial success of Athena that his corporate superiors allowed him to be completely autonomous. They had contracted with the State to take care of prisoners for only 2 thirds as much money per capita as the State had spent when it owned the place. That was about as much as it would have cost to send a convict to medical school or Tarkington. By importing cheap, young, short-term, nonunion labor, and by getting supplies from the lowest bidders rather than from the Mafia and so on, Hiroshi Matsumoto had cut the per capita cost to less than half of what it used to be.

He didn't miss a trick. When I went to work for him, he had just bought a state-of-the-art crematorium for the prison. Before that, a Mafia-owned crematorium on the outskirts of Rochester, in back of the Meadowdale Cinema Complex, across the highway from the National Guard Armory, had had a monopoly on cremating Athena's un-claimed bodies.

After the Japanese bought Athena, though, the Mob dou-bled their prices, using the AIDS epidemic as an excuse. They had to take extra precautions, they said. They wanted double even if the prison provided a doctor's certificate guaranteeing that a body was AIDS-free, and the cause of death, as anybody could see, was some sort of knife or gar-rote or blunt instrument.

There wasn't a Japanese manufacturer of crematoria, so Warden Matsumoto bought one from A. J. Topf und Sohn in Essen, Germany. This was the same outfit that had made the ovens for Auschwitz in its heyday.

The postwar Topf models all had state-of-the-art smoke scrubbers on their smokestacks, so people in Scipio, unlike the people living near Auschwitz, never knew that they had a busy corpse carbonizer in the neighborhood.

We could have been gassing and incinerating convicts over there around the clock, and who would know?

Who would care?

A while back I mentioned that Lowell Chung's mother died of tetanus. I want to say before I forget that tetanus might have a real future in astronautics, since it becomes an extremely rugged spore when life becomes intolerable.

I haven't nominated AIDS viruses as promising inter-galactic rock jockeys, since, at their present state of develop-ment, they can't survive for long outside a living human body.

Concerted efforts to kill them with new poisons, though, if only partially successful, could change all that.

229

The Mafia crematorium behind the Meadowdale Cinema Complex has all this valley's prison business again. Some of the convicts who stayed in or near Athena after the great escape, rather than attack Scipio across the ice, felt that at least they could bust up the A. J. Topf und Sohn crematorium.

The Meadowdale Cinema Complex itself has gone belly up, since so few people can afford to own an automobile anymore.

Same thing with the shopping malls.

One thing interesting to me, although I don't know quite what to make of it, is that the Mafia never sells anything to foreigners. While everybody else who has inherited or built a real business can't wait to sell out and take early retirement, the Mafia holds on to everything. Thus does the paving business, for example, remain a strictly American enterprise.

Same thing with wholesale meat and napkins and table-cloths for restaurants.

I told the Warden right up front that I had been canned by Tarkington. I explained that the charges against me for sexual irregularities were a smokescreen. The Trustees were really angry about my having wobbled the students' faith in the intelligence and decency of their country's leadership by telling them the truth about the Vietnam War.

"Nobody on this side of the lake believes there is such a thing in this miserable country," he said.

"Such a thing as what, sir?" I said.

And he said, "Leadership." As for my sexual irregularities, he said, they seemed to be uniformly heterosexual, and there were no women on his side of the lake. He himself was a bachelor, and members of his staff were not allowed to bring their wives with them, if they had them. "So over

230

here," he said, "you would truly be Don Juan in Hell. Do you think that you could stand that?"

I said I could, so he offered me a job on a trial basis. I would start work as soon as possible, offering general education mostly on the primary-school level, not all that different from what I had done at Tarkington. An immediate problem was housing. His staff lived in barracks in the shadows of the prison walls, and he himself had a renovated house down by the water and was the only inhabitant of the ghost town, a ghost hamlet, actually, after which the prison was named: Athena.

If I didn't work out for some reason, he said, he would still need a teacher on the property, who would surely not want to live in the barracks. So he was having another old house in the ghost town made livable, right next to his own. But it wouldn't be ready for occupancy until August. "Do you think the college will let you stay where you are until then, and meanwhile you could commute to work from over there? You have a car?"

"A Mercedes," I said.

"Excellent!" he said. "That will give you something in common with the inmates right away."

"How so?" I said.

"They're practically all former Mercedes owners," he said. This was only a slight exaggeration. He told the truth when he said, "We have one man in here who bought his first Mercedes when he was 15 years old." That was Alton Darwin, whose dying words on the skating rink after the prison break would be, "See the Nigger fly the airplane."

So the college did let us stay in the Scipio house over the summer. There was no summer session at Tarkington. Who would have come to one? And I commuted to the prison every day.

In the old days, before the Japanese took over Athena, the whole staff was commuters from Scipio and Rochester. They were unionized, and it was their unceasing demands for more and more pay and fringe benefits, including compensation for their travel to and from work, that made the State decide to sell the whole shebang to the Japanese.

My salary was what I had been paid by Tarkington. I could keep our Blue Cross–Blue Shield, since the corporation that owned the prison also owned Blue Cross–Blue Shield. No problem!
Cough.

That is another thing the prison break cost me: our Blue Cross–Blue Shield.

33

I T would work out well. When I moved Margaret and Mildred into our new home in the ghost town and pulled down the blinds, it was to them as though we had never left Scipio. There was a surprise present for me on our freshly sodded front lawn, a rowboat. The Warden had found an old boat that had been lying in the weeds behind the ruins of the old Athena Post Office since before I was born, quite possibly. He had had some of his guards fiberglass the outside of it, making it watertight again after all these years.

It looked a lot like the hide-covered Eskimo umiak that used to be in the rotunda outside the Dean of Women's Office here, with the outlines of the ribs showing through the fiberglass.

I know what happened to a lot of college property after the prison break, the GRIOT™ and so on, but I haven't a clue what became of that umiak.

If it hadn't been on display in the rotunda, I and hundreds of Tarkington students and their parents would have gone all the way through life without ever seeing a genuine Eskimo umiak.

I made love to Muriel Peck in that boat. I lay on the bottom, and she sat upright, holding my mother-in-law's fishing rod, pretending to be a perfect lady and all alone.

That was my idea. What a good sport she was!

I don't know what became of the man who claimed his name was John Donner, who wanted to teach shop at Athena, 8 years before the prison break. I do know that the Warden gave him very short shrift during his job interview, since the last things the prison needed inside its walls were chisels and screwdrivers and hacksaws and band saws and ball-peen hammers and so on.

I had to wait for Donner outside the Warden's Office. He was my ticket back to civilization, to my home and family and copy of *Black Garterbelt*. I didn't watch *Howdy Doody* on the little screen. I interested myself in another person, who was waiting to see the Warden. His color-coding alone would have told me that he was a convict, but he was also wearing leg irons and handcuffs, and was seated quietly on a bench facing mine across the corridor, with a masked and rubber-gloved guard on either side of him.

He was reading a cheap-looking booklet. Since he was literate, I thought he might be one of the people I was being hired to divert with knowledge. I was right. His name was Abdullah Akbahr. With my encouragement, he would write several interesting short stories. One, I remember, was supposedly the autobiography of a talking deer in the National Forest who has a terrible time finding anything to eat in winter and gets tangled in barbed wire during the summer months, trying to get at the delicious food on farms. He is shot by a hunter. As he dies he wonders why he was born in the first place. The final sentence of the story was the last thing the deer said on Earth. The hunter was close enough to hear it and was amazed. This was it: "What the blankety-blank was that supposed to be all about?"

The 3 violent crimes that had gotten Abdullah into Athena were murders in drug wars. He himself would be shot dead with buckshot and slugs after the prison break, while carrying a flag of truce, by Whitey VanArsdale, the mechanic, and Lyle Hooper, the Fire Chief.

"Excuse me," I said to him, "but may I ask what you are reading?"

He displayed the book's cover so I could read it for myself. The title was *The Protocols of the Elders of Zion.*

Cough.

Abdullah was summoned to the Warden's Office, incidentally, because he was 1 of several persons, guards as well as convicts, who claimed to have seen a castle flying over the prison. The Warden wanted to find out if some new hallucinatory drug had been smuggled in, or whether the whole place was finally going insane, or what on Earth was happening.

The Protocols of the Elders of Zion was an anti-Semitic work first published in Russia about 100 years ago. It purported to be the minutes of a secret meeting of Jews from many countries who planned to cooperate internationally so as to cause wars and revolutions and financial busts and so on, which would leave them owning everything. Its title was parodied by the author of the story in *Black Garterbelt,* and its paranoia, too.

The great American inventor and industrialist Henry Ford thought it was a genuine document. He had it published in this country back when my father was a boy. Now here was a black convict in irons, who had the gift of literacy, who was taking it seriously. It would turn out that there were 100s of copies circulating in the prison, printed in Libya and passed out by the ruling gang at Athena, the Black Brothers of Islam.

That summer I would start a literacy program in the prison, using people like Abdullah Akbahr as proselytizers for reading and writing, going from cell to cell and offering lessons. Thanks to me, 1,000s of former illiterates would be able to read *The Protocols of the Elders of Zion* by the time of the prison break.

I denounced that book, but couldn't keep it from circulating. Who was I to oppose the Black Brothers, who regularly exercised what the State would not, which was the death penalty.

Abdullah Akbahr rattled and clinked his fetters. "This any way to treat a veteran?" he said.

He had been a Marine in Vietnam, so he never had to listen to one of my pep talks. I was strictly Army. I asked him if he had ever heard of an Army officer they called "The Preacher," who was me, of course. I was curious as to how far my fame had spread.

"No," he said. But as I've said, there were other veterans there who had heard of me and knew, among other things, that I had pitched a grenade into the mouth of a tunnel one time, and killed a woman, her mother, and her baby hiding from helicopter gunships which had strafed her village right before we got there.

Unforgettable.

You know who was the Ruling Class that time? Eugene Debs Hartke was the Ruling Class.

Down with the Ruling Class!

John Donner was unhappy on our trip back to Scipio from the prison. I had landed a job, and he hadn't. His son's bicycle had been stolen in the prison parking lot.

The Mexicans have a favorite dish they call "twice-fried beans." Thanks to me, although Donner never found out, that bicycle was now a twice-stolen bicycle. One week later, Donner and the boy dematerialized from this valley as mysteriously as they had materialized, leaving no forwarding address.

Somebody or something must have been catching up with them.

I pitied that boy. But if he is still alive, he, like me, is a grownup now.

Somebody was catching up with me, too, but ever so slowly. I am talking about my illegitimate son out in Dubuque, Iowa. He was only 15 then. He didn't even know my name yet. He had yet to do as much detective work to discover the name and location of his father as I have done to identify the murderer of Letitia Smiley, Tarkington College's 1922 Lilac Queen.

I made the acquaintance of his mother while sitting alone at a bar in Manila, soon after the excrement hit the air-conditioning in Vietnam. I didn't want to talk to anybody of either sex. I was fed up with the human race. I wanted nothing more than to be left strictly alone with my thoughts.

Add those to my growing collection of Famous Last Words.

This reasonably pretty but shopworn woman sat down on a stool next to mine. "Forgive my intrusion on your thoughts," she said, "but somebody told me that you are the man they call 'The Preacher.' " She pointed out a Master Sergeant in a booth with 2 prostitutes who could not have been much over 15 years of age.

"I don't know him," I said.

"He didn't say he knew you," she said. "He's heard you speak. So have a lot of other soldiers I've talked to."

"Somebody had to speak," I said, "or we couldn't have had a war."

"Is that why they call you 'The Preacher'?" she said.

"Who knows," I said, "in a world as full of baloney as this 1 is?" I had been called that as far back as West Point because I never used profanity. During my first 2 years in Vietnam, when the only troops I gave pep talks to were those who served under me, I was called "The Preacher" because it sounded sinister, as though I were a puritanical angel of death. Which I was, I was.

"Would you rather I went away?" she said.

"No," I said, "because I think there is every chance we could wind up in bed together tonight. You look intelligent, so you must be as blue as I am about our nation's great unvictory. I worry about you. I'd like to cheer you up."

What the heck.

It worked.

If it ain't broke, don't fix it.

34

I was reasonably happy teaching at the prison. I raised the level of literacy by about 20 percent, with each newly literate person teaching yet another one. I wasn't always happy with what they chose to read afterward.

One man told me that literacy made it a lot more fun for him to masturbate.

I did not loaf. I like to teach.

I dared some of the more intelligent prisoners to prove to me that the World was round, to tell me the difference between noise and music, to tell me how physical traits were inherited, to tell me how to determine the height of a guard tower without climbing it, to tell me what was ridiculous about the Greek legend which said that a boy carried a calf around a barn every day, and pretty soon he was a man who could carry a bull around the barn every day, and so on.

I showed them a chart a fundamentalist preacher from downtown Scipio had passed out to Tarkington students at the Pavilion one afternoon. I asked them to examine it for examples of facts tailored to fit a thesis.

Across the top the chart named the leaders of warring nations during the Finale Rack, during World War II. Then, under each name was the leader's birthdate and how many years he lived and when he took office and how many years he served, and then the total of all those numbers, which in each case turned out to be 3,888.

It looked like this:

	CHURCHILL	HITLER	ROOSEVELT	IL DUCE	STALIN	TOJO
BORN	1874	1889	1882	1883	1879	1884
AGE	70	55	62	61	65	60
TOOK OFFICE	1940	1933	1933	1922	1924	1941
YEARS IN OFFICE	4	11	11	22	20	3

As I say, every column adds up to 3,888.

Whoever invented the chart then pointed out that half that number was 1944, the year the war ended, and that the first letters of the names of the war's leaders spelled the name of the Supreme Ruler of the Universe.

The dumber ones, like the dumber ones at Tarkington, used me as an ambulatory *Guinness Book of World Records*, asking me who the oldest person in the world was, the richest one, the woman who had had the most babies, and so on. By the time of the prison break, I think, 98 percent of the inmates at Athena knew that the greatest age ever attained by a human being whose birthdate was well documented was about 121 years, and that this incomparable survivor, like the Warden and the guards, had been Japanese. Actually, he had fallen 128 days short of reaching 121. His record was a natural foundation for all sorts of jokes at Athena, since so many of the inmates were serving life sentences, or even 2 or 3 life sentences either superimposed or laid end to end.

They knew that the richest man in the world was also Japanese and that, about a century before the college and the prison were founded across the lake from each other, a woman in Russia was giving birth to the last of her 69 children.

240

The Russian woman who had more babies than anyone gave birth to 16 pairs of twins, 7 sets of triplets, and 4 sets of quadruplets. They all survived, which is more than you can say for the Donner Party.

Hiroshi Matsumoto was the only member of the prison staff with a college education. He did not socialize with the others, and he took his off-duty meals alone and hiked alone and fished alone and sailed alone. Neither did he avail himself of the Japanese clubs in Rochester and Buffalo, or of the lavish rest-and-recuperation facilities maintained in Manhattan by the Japanese Army of Occupation in Business Suits. He had made so much money for his corporation in Louisville and then Athena, and was so brilliant in his understanding of American business psychology, that I am sure he could have asked for and gotten an executive job in the home office. He may have known more about American black people than anybody else in Japan, thanks to Athena, and more and more of the businesses his corporation was buying here were dependent on black labor or at least the goodwill of black neighborhoods. Again thanks to Athena, he probably knew more than any other Japanese about the largest industry by far in this country, which was the procurement and distribution of chemicals that, when introduced into the bloodstream in one way or another, gave anybody who could afford them undeserved feelings of purpose and accomplishment.

Only 1 of these chemicals was legal, of course, and was the basis of the fortune of the family that gave Tarkington its band uniforms, and the water tower atop Musket Mountain, and an endowed chair in Business Law, and I don't know what all else.

That mind-bender was alcohol.

In the 8 years we lived next door to him in the ghost town down by the lake, he never once indicated that he longed to be back in his homeland. The closest he came to doing that was when he told me 1 night that the ruins of the locks at the head of the lake, with huge timbers and boulders tumbled this way and that, might have been the creation of a great Japanese gardener.

In the Japanese Army of Occupation he was a high-ranking officer, the civilian peer of a Brigadier, maybe, or even a Major General. But he reminded me of several old Master Sergeants I had known in Vietnam. They would say worse things about the Army and the war and the Vietnamese than anybody. But I would go away for a couple of years, and then come back, and they were all still there, crabbing away. They wouldn't leave until the Vietnamese either killed them or kicked them out of there.

How they hated home. They were more afraid of home than of the enemy.

Hiroshi Matsumoto called this valley a "hellhole" and the "anus of the Universe." But he didn't leave it until he was kicked out of here.

I wonder if the Mohiga Valley hadn't become the only home he ever knew after the bombing of Hiroshima. He lives in retirement now in his reconstructed native city, having lost both feet to frostbite after the prison break. Is it possible that he is thinking now what I have thought so often: "What is this place and who are these people, and what am I doing here?"

The last time I saw him was on the night of the prison break. We had been awakened by the racket of the Jamaicans' assault on the prison. We both came running out onto the street in front of our houses barefoot and in our nightclothes, although the temperature must have been minus 10 degrees centigrade.

The name of our main street in the ghost town was Clinton Street, the name of the main street in Scipio. Can you imagine that: two communities so close geographically, and yet in olden times so separate socially and economically that, with all the street names they might have chosen, they both named their main street Clinton Street?

The Warden tried to reach the prison on a cordless telephone. He got no answer. His 3 house servants were looking out at us from upstairs windows. They were convicts over 70 years old, serving life sentences without hope of parole, long forgotten by the outside world, and coked to the gills on Thorazine.

My mother-in-law came out on our porch. She called to me, "Tell him about the fish I caught! Tell him about that fish I caught!"

The Warden said to me that a boiler up at the prison must have blown, or maybe the crematorium. It sounded to me like military weaponry, whose voices he had never heard. He hadn't even heard the atomic bomb go off. He had only felt the hot whoosh afterward.

And then all the lights on our side of the lake went off. And then we heard the strains of "The Star-Spangled Banner" floating down from the blacked-out penitentiary.

There was no way that the Warden and I, even with massive doses of LSD, could have imagined what was going on up there. We were faulted afterward for not having alerted Scipio. As far as that goes, Scipio, hearing the explosion and "The Star-Spangled Banner" and all the rest of it across the frozen lake, might have been expected to take some defensive action. But it did not.

Survivors over there I talked to afterward said they had just pulled the covers over their heads and gone to sleep again. What could be more human?

What was happening up there, as I've already said, was a stunningly successful attack on the prison by Jamaicans wearing National Guard uniforms and waving American flags. They had a public-address system mounted atop an armored personnel carrier and were playing the National Anthem. Most of them probably weren't even American citizens!

But what Japanese farm boy, serving a 6-month tour of duty on a dark continent, would be crazy enough to open fire on seeming natives in full battle dress, who were waving flags and playing their hellish music?

No such boy existed. Not that night.

If the Japanese had started shooting, they would have lost their lives like the defenders of the Alamo. And for what?

For Sony?

Hiroshi Matsumoto threw on some clothes! He drove up the hill in his Isuzu jeep!

He was fired upon by the Jamaicans!

He bailed out of his Isuzu! He ran into the National Forest!

He got lost in the pitch blackness. He was wearing sandals and no socks.

It took him 2 days to find his way back out of the forest, which was almost as dark in the daytime as it was at night.

Yes. And gangrene was feasting on his frostbitten feet.

I myself stayed down by the lake.

I sent Mildred and Margaret back to bed.

I heard what must have been the Jamaicans' shots at the Isuzu. Those were their parting shots. After that came silence.

My brain came up with this scenario: An attempted escape had been thwarted, possibly with some loss of life. The explosion at the beginning had been a bomb made by the convicts from nail parings or playing cards or who knows what?

They could make bombs and alcohol out of anything, usually in a toilet.

I misread the silence as good news.

I dreaded a continuation of the shooting, which would have meant to me that the Japanese farm boys had developed a taste for killing with guns, which can suddenly become, for the uninitiated, easy and fun.

I envisioned convicts, in or out of their cells, becoming ducks in a shooting gallery.

I imagined, now that there was silence, that order had been restored, and that an English-speaking Japanese was notifying the Scipio Police Department and the State Police and the County Sheriff about the squashed escape attempt, and probably asking for doctors and ambulances.

Whereas the Japanese had been bamboozled and overwhelmed so quickly that their telephone lines were cut and their radio was smashed before they could get in touch with anyone.

There was a full moon that night, but its rays could not reach the floor of the National Forest.

The Japanese were not hurt. The Jamaicans disarmed them and sent them up the moonlit road to the head of the lake. They told them not to stop running until they got all the way back to Tokyo.

Most of them had never seen Tokyo.

And they did not arrive at the head of the lake hollering bloody murder and flagging down passing cars. They hid up there. If the United States was against them, who could be for them?

I had no gun.

If a few convicts had broken out and were still at large, I thought, and they came down into our ghost town, they would know me and think well of me. I would give them whatever they wanted, food, money, bandages, clothes, the Mercedes.

No matter what I gave them, I thought, since they were color-coded, they would never escape from this valley, from this lily-white cul-de-sac.

There was nothing but White people all the way to Rochester's city-limits sign.

I went to my rowboat, which I had turned upside down for the wintertime. I sat down astride its slick and glossy bow, which was aimed at the old barge terminal of Scipio.

They still had lights over in Scipio, which was a nice boost for my complacency.

There wasn't any excitement over there, despite the noise at the prison. The lights in several houses went off. None went on. Only 1 car was moving. It was going slowly down Clinton Street. It stopped and turned off its lights in the parking lot behind the Black Cat Café.

The little red light atop the water tower on the summit of Musket Mountain winked off and on, off and on. It became a sort of mantra for me, so that I sank even deeper into thoughtless meditation, as though scuba diving in lukewarm bouillon.

Off and on that little light winked, off and on, off and on.

How long did it give me rapture from so far away? Three minutes? Ten minutes? Hard to say.

I was brought back to full wakefulness by a strange transformation in the appearance of the frozen lake to the north of me. It had come alive somehow, but noiselessly.

And then I realized that I was watching 100s of men

engaged in a sort of project which I myself had planned and led many times in Vietnam, which was a surprise attack.

It was I who broke the silence. A name tore itself from my lips before I could stop it.

The name? "Muriel!"

35

MURIEL Peck wasn't a barmaid anymore. She was a Full Professor of English at Tarkington, making good use of her Swarthmore education. She was asleep at the time of the surprise attack, all alone in faculty housing, a vine-covered cottage at the top of Clinton Street. Like me, she had sent her 2 kids to expensive boarding schools.

I asked her one time if she ever thought of marrying again. She said, "Didn't you notice? I married you."

She wouldn't have gotten a job at Tarkington if the Trustees hadn't fired me. An English teacher named Dwight Casey hated the head of his department so much that he asked for my old job just to get away from him. So that created a vacancy for Muriel.

If they hadn't fired me, she probably would have left this valley, and would be alive today.

If they hadn't fired me, I would probably be lying where she is, next to the stable, in the shadow of Musket Mountain when the Sun goes down.

Dwight Casey is still alive, I think. His wife came into a great deal of money soon after he replaced me. He quit at the end of the academic year and moved to the south of France.

His wife's family was big in the Mafia. She could have taught but didn't. She had a Master's Degree in Political Science from Rutgers. All he had was a BS in Hotel Management from Cornell.

The Battle of Scipio lasted 5 days. It lasted 2 days longer than the Battle of Gettysburg, at which Elias Tarkington was shot by a Confederate soldier who mistook him for Abraham Lincoln.

On the night of the prison break, I was as helpless a voyeur, once the attack had begun, as Robert E. Lee at Gettysburg or Napoleon Bonaparte at Waterloo.

There was 1 shot fired by someone in Scipio. I will never know who did it. It was some night owl with a loaded gun in easy reach. Whoever did it must have been killed soon afterward, otherwise he would have bragged about what he had done so early in the game.

Those were good soldiers who crossed the ice. Several of them had been in Vietnam, and so, like me, had had lessons in Military Science on full scholarships from the Government. Others had had plenty of experience with shooting and being shot at, often from early childhood on, and so found a single shot unremarkable. They saved their ammunition until they could see clearly what they were shooting at.

When those seasoned troops went ashore, that was when they commenced firing. They were stingy with their bullets. There would be a *bang,* and then silence for several minutes, and then, when another target appeared, maybe a bleary-eyed householder coming out his front door or peering out a window, with or without a weapon, there would be another *bang* or 2 or 3 *bang*s, and then silence again. The escaped convicts, or Freedom Fighters as they would soon call themselves, had to assume, after all, that many if not most households had firearms, and that their owners had long daydreamed of using them with deadly effect should precisely what was happening happen. The Freedom Fighters had no choice. I would have done the same thing, had I been in their situation.

Bang. Somebody else would jerk backward and downward, like a professional actor on a TV show.

The biggest flurry of shots came from what I guessed from afar to be the parking lot in back of the Black Cat Café, where the prostitutes parked their vans. The men who visited the vans that late at night had handguns with them, just in case. Better safe than sorry.

And then I could tell from the sporadic firing that the Freedom Fighters had begun to climb the hill to this college, which was brightly lit all night every night to discourage anybody who might be tempted to do harm up here. From my point of view across the lake, Tarkington might have been mistaken for an emerald-studded Oz or City of God or Camelot.

You can bet I did not go back to sleep that night. I listened and listened for sirens, for helicopters, for the rumble of armored vehicles, for proofs that the forces of law and order would soon put a stop to the violence in the valley with even greater violence. At dawn the valley was as quiet as ever, and the red light on top of the water tower on the summit of Musket Mountain, as though nothing remarkable had happened over there, winked off and on, off and on.

I went next door to the Warden's house. I woke up his 3 servants. They had gone back to bed after the Warden charged up the hill in his Isuzu. These were old, old men, sentenced to life in prison without hope of parole, back when I was a little boy in Midland City. I hadn't even

250

learned to read and write, probably, when they ruined some lives, or were accused of doing so, and were forced to lead lives not worth living as a consequence.

That would certainly teach them a lesson.

At least they hadn't been put into that great invention by a dentist, the electric chair.

"Where there is life there is hope." So says John Gay in the Atheist's Bible. What a starry-eyed optimist!

These 3 old geezers hadn't had a visitor or a phone call or a letter for decades. Under the circumstances, they had no vivid ideas of what they would like to do next, so they were glad to take orders from almost anybody. Other people's ideas of what to do next were like brain transplants. All of a sudden they were full of pep.

So I had them drink a lot of black coffee. Since I was worried about what might have happened to the Warden, they acted worried, too. Otherwise, they wouldn't have. I did not tell them that there had been a mass prison break and that Scipio had been overrun by criminals. Such information would have been useless to them, would have been like more TV. They were supposed to stay where they had been put, no matter what in the real world might be going on.

Those 3 were what psychologists call "other-directed."

I took them over to my house and ordered them to keep the wood fire in the fireplace going, and to feed Margaret and Mildred when they got hungry. There were plenty of canned goods. I didn't have to worry about the perishables in the refrigerator, since the air in the kitchen was already so cold. The stove itself ran on bottled propane, and there was a month's supply of that science fiction miracle.

Imagine that: bottled energy!

251

Margaret and Mildred, thank goodness, felt neutral about the Warden's zombies, the same way they felt about me. They didn't like them, but they didn't dislike them, either. So everything was falling into place. They would still have a life-support system, even if I went away for several days or got wounded or killed.

I didn't expect to get wounded or killed, except by accident. All the combatants in Scipio would regard me as unthreatening, the Whites because of my color-coding and the Blacks because they knew and liked me.

The issues were clear. They were Black and White.

All the Yellow people had run away.

I had hoped to get away from the house while Margaret and Mildred were fast asleep. But as I passed my boat on my way to the ice, an upstairs window flew open. There my poor old wife was, a scrawny, addled hag. She sensed that something important was happening, I think. Otherwise she wouldn't have exposed herself to the cold and daylight. Her voice, moreover, which had been rasping and bawdy for years, was liquid and sweet, just as it had been on our Honeymoon. And she called me by name. That was another thing she hadn't done for a long, long time. This was disorienting.

"Gene—" she said.

So I stopped. "Yes, Margaret," I said.

"Where are you going, Gene?" she said.

"I'm going for a walk, Margaret, to get some fresh air," I said.

"You're going to see some woman, aren't you?" she said.

"No, Margaret. Word of Honor I'm not," I said.

"That's all right. I understand," she said.

It was so pathetic! I was so overwhelmed by the pathos, by the beautiful voice I hadn't heard for so long, by the young

Margaret inside the witch! I cried out in all sincerity, "Oh, Margaret, I love you, I love you!"

Those were the last words she would ever hear me say, for I would never come back.

She made no reply. She shut the window and pulled down the opaque black roller blind.

I have not seen her since.

After that side of the lake was recaptured by the 82nd Airborne, she and her mother were put in a steel box on the back of one of the prison vans and delivered to the insane asylum in Batavia. They will be fine as long as they have each other. They might be fine even if they didn't have each other. Who knows, until somebody or something performs that particular experiment?

I have not been on that side of the lake since that morning, and may never go there again, as close as it is. So I will probably never find out what became of my old footlocker, the coffin containing the soldier I used to be, and my very rare copy of *Black Garterbelt*.

I crossed the lake that morning, as it happens, never to return, to deliver a particular message to the escaped convicts, with the idea of saving lives and property. I knew that the students were on vacation. That left nothing but social nobodies, in which category I surely include the college faculty, members of the Servant Class.

To me this low-grade social mix was ominous. In Vietnam, and then in later show-biz attacks on Tripoli and Panama City and so on, it had been perfectly ordinary for our Air Force to blow communities of nobodies, no matter whose side they were on, to Kingdom Come.

It seemed likely to me, should the Government decide to bomb Scipio, that it would be sensible to bomb the prison, too.

And everything would be taken care of, and no argument. Next problem?

How many Americans knew or cared anyway where or what the Mohiga Valley was, or Laos or Cambodia or Tripoli? Thanks to our great educational system and TV, half of them couldn't even find their own country on a map of the world.

Three-quarters of them couldn't put the cap back on a bottle of whiskey without crossing the threads.

As I expected, I was treated by Scipio's conquerors as a harmless old fool with wisdom. The criminals called me "The Preacher" or "The Professor," just as they had on the other side.

I saw that many of them had tied ribbons around their upper arms as a sort of uniform. So when I came across a man who wasn't wearing a ribbon, I asked him jokingly, "Where's your uniform, Soldier?"

"Preacher," he said, referring to his skin, "I was born in a uniform."

Alton Darwin had set himself up in Tex Johnson's office in Samoza Hall as President of a new nation. He had been drinking. I do not mean to present any of these escapees as rational or capable of redemption. They did not care if they lived or died. Alton Darwin was glad to see me. Then again, he was glad about everything.

I had to advise him, nonetheless, that he could expect to be bombed unless he and the rest of them got out of town right away. I said their best chance to survive was to go back to the prison and fly white flags everywhere. If they did that right away, they might claim that they had nothing to do with all the killings here. The number of people the es-

254

capees killed in Scipio, incidentally, was 5 less than the number I myself had killed single-handedly in the war in Vietnam.

So the Battle of Scipio was nothing but a "tempest in a teapot," an expression the Atheist's Bible tells us is proverbial.

I told Alton Darwin that if he and his people didn't want to be bombed and didn't want to return to the prison, they should take whatever food they could find and disperse to the north or west. I told him one thing he already knew, that the floor of the National Forest to the south and east was so dark and lifeless that anyone going in there would probably starve to death or go mad before he found his way back out of there. I told him another thing he already knew, that there would soon be all these white people to the west and north, having the times of their lives hunting escaped convicts instead of deer.

My second point, in fact, was something the convicts had taught me. They all believed that the White people who insisted that it was their Constitutional right to keep military weapons in their homes all looked forward to the day when they could shoot Americans who didn't have what they had, who didn't look like their friends and relatives, in a sort of open-air shooting gallery we used to call in Vietnam a "Free Fire Zone." You could shoot anything that moved, for the good of the greater society, which was always someplace far away, like Paradise.

Alton Darwin heard me out. And then he told me that he thought I was right, that the prison probably would be bombed. But he guaranteed that Scipio would not be bombed, and that it would not be attacked on the ground, either, that the Government would have to keep its distance and respect the demands he meant to put to it.

"What makes you think that?" I said.

"We have captured a TV celebrity," he said. "They won't let anything happen to him. Too many people will be watching."

"Who?" I said.

And he said, "Jason Wilder."

That was the first I heard that they had taken hostage not only Wilder but the whole Board of Trustees of Tarkington College. I now realize, too, that Alton Darwin would not have known that Wilder was a TV celebrity if old tapes of Wilder's talk show hadn't been run again and again at the prison across the lake. Poor people of any race on the outside never would have watched his show for long, since its basic message was that it was poor people who were making the lives of the rest of us so frightening.

36

"STAR Wars," said Alton Darwin.

He was alluding to Ronald Reagan's dream of having scientists build an invisible dome over this country, with electronics and lasers and so on, which no enemy plane or projectile could ever penetrate. Darwin believed that the social standing of his hostages was an invisible dome over Scipio.

I think he was right, although I have not been able to discover how seriously the Government considered bombing the whole valley back to the Stone Age. Years ago, I might have found out through the Freedom of Information Act. But the Supreme Court closed that peephole.

Darwin and his troops knew the lives of the hostages were valued highly by the Government. They didn't know why, and I am not sure that I do, either. I think that the number of people with money and power had shrunk to the point where it felt like a family. For all the escaped convicts knew about them, they might as well have been aardvarks, or some other improbable animal they had never seen before.

Darwin regretted that I, too, was going to have to stay in Scipio. He couldn't let me go, he said, because I knew too much about his defenses. There were none as far as I could see, but he sounded as though there were trenches and tank traps and mine fields all around us.

Even more hallucinatory was his vision of the future. He was going to restore this valley to its former economic vitality. It would become an all-Black Utopia. All Whites would be resettled elsewhere.

He was going to put glass back into the windows of the factories, and make their roofs weather-tight again. He would get the money to do this and so many other wonderful things by selling the precious hardwoods of the National Forest to the Japanese.

That much of his dream is actually coming true now. The National Forest is now being logged by Mexican laborers using Japanese tools, under the direction of Swedes. The proceeds are expected to pay half of day-before-yesterday's interest on the National Debt.

That last is a joke of mine. I have no idea if any money for the forest will go toward the National Debt, which, the last I heard, was greater than the value of all property in the Western Hemisphere, thanks to compound interest.

Alton Darwin looked me up and down, and then he said with typical sociopathic impulsiveness, "Professor, I can't let you go because I need you."

"What for?" I said. I was scared to death that he was going to make me a General.

"To help with the plans," he said.

"For what?" I said.

"For the glorious future," he said. He told me to go to this library and write out detailed plans for making this valley into the envy of the World.

So that, in fact, is what I mainly did during most of the Battle of Scipio.

It was too dangerous to go outside anyway, with all the bullets flying around.

My best Utopian invention for the ideal Black Republic was "Freedom Fighter Beer." They would get the old brewery going again, supposedly, and make beer pretty much like any other beer, except that it would be called Freedom Fighter Beer. If I say so myself, that is a magical name for beer. I envisioned a time when, all over the world, the bored and downtrodden and weary would be bucking themselves up at least a little bit with Freedom Fighter Beer.

Beer, of course, is actually a depressant. But poor people will never stop hoping otherwise.

Alton Darwin was dead before I could complete my long-range plan. His dying words, as I've said, were, "See the Nigger fly the airplane." But I showed it to the hostages.

"What is this supposed to mean?" said Jason Wilder.

"I want you to see what they've had me doing," I said. "You keep talking as though I could turn you loose, if I wanted. I'm as much a prisoner as you are."

He studied the prospectus, and then he said, "They actually expect to get away with this?"

"No," I said. "They know this is their Alamo."

He arched his famous eyebrows in clownish disbelief. He has always looked to me a lot like the incomparable comedian Stanley Laurel. "It would never have occurred to me to compare the rabid chimpanzees who hold us in durance vile with Davy Crockett and James Bowie and Tex Johnson's great-great-grandfather," he said.

"I was just talking about hopeless situations," I said.

"I certainly hope so," he said.

I might have added, but didn't, that the martyrs at the Alamo had died for the right to own Black slaves. They didn't want to be a part of Mexico anymore because it was against the law in that country to own slaves of any kind.

I don't think Wilder knew that. Not many people in this

country do. I certainly never heard that at the Academy. I wouldn't have known that slavery was what the Alamo was all about if Professor Stern the unicyclist hadn't told me so.

No wonder there were so few Black tourists at the Alamo!

Units of the 82nd Airborne, fresh from the South Bronx, had by then retaken the other side of the lake and herded the prisoners back inside the walls. A big problem over there was that almost every toilet in the prison had been smashed. Who knows why?

What was to be done with the huge quantities of excrement produced hour after hour, day after day, by all these burdens on Society?

We still had plenty of toilets on this side of the lake, which is why this place was made an auxiliary prison almost immediately. Time was of the essence, as the lawyers say.

Imagine the same sort of thing happening on a huge rocket ship bound for Betelgeuse.

37

On the last afternoon of the siege, National Guard units relieved the Airborne troops across the lake. That night, undetected, the paratroops took up positions behind Musket Mountain. Two hours before the next dawn, they came quietly around either side of the mountain, captured the stable, freed the hostages, and then took possession of all of Scipio. They had to kill only 1 person, who was the guard dozing outside the stable. They strangled him with a standard piece of equipment. I had used one just like it in Vietnam. It was a meter of piano wire with a wooden handle at either end.

So that was that.

The defenders were out of ammunition. There were hardly any defenders left anyway. Maybe 10.

Again, I don't believe there would have been such delicate microsurgery by the best ground troops available, if it hadn't been for the social prominence of the Trustees.

They were helicoptered to Rochester, where they were shown on TV. They thanked God and the Army. They said they had never lost hope. They said they were tired but happy, and just wanted to get a hot bath and then sleep in a nice clean bed.

All National Guardsmen who had been south of the Meadowdale Cinema Complex during the siege got Combat Infantryman's Badges. They were so pleased.

The paratroops already had theirs. When they dressed up for the victory parade, they wore campaign ribbons from Costa Rica and Bimini and El Paso and on and on, and from the Battle of the South Bronx, of course. That battle had had to keep on going without their help.

Several nobodies tried to get onto a helicopter with the Trustees. There was room. But the only people allowed aboard were on a list which had come all the way from the White House. I saw the list. Tex and Zuzu Johnson were the only locals named.

I watched the helicopters take off, the happy ending. I was up in the belfry, checking on the damage. I hadn't dared to go up there earlier. Somebody might have taken a shot at me, and it could have been a beautiful shot.

And as the helicopters became specks to the north, I was startled to hear a woman speak. She was right behind me. She was small and was shod in white sneakers and had come up ever so quietly. I wasn't expecting company.

She said, "I wondered what it was like up here. Sure is a mess, but the view is nice, if you like water and soldiers." She sounded tired. We all did.

I turned to look at her. She was Black. I don't mean she was so-called Black. Her skin was very dark. She may not have had any white blood whatsoever. If she had been a man at Athena, skin that color would have put her in the lowest social caste.

She was so small and looked so young I mistook her for a Tarkington student, maybe the dyslexic daughter of some overthrown Caribbean or African dictator who had absquatulated to the USA with his starving nation's treasury.

Wrong again!

If the college GRIOT™ had still been working, I am sure it couldn't have guessed what she was and what she was doing there. She had lived outside all the statistics on which GRIOT™ based its spookily canny guesses. When GRIOT™ was stumped by somebody who had given statistical expectations as wide a berth as she had, it just sat there and hummed. A little red light came on.

Her name was Helen Dole. She was 26. She was unmarried. She was born in South Korea, and had grown up in what was then West Berlin. She held a Doctorate in Physics from the University of Berlin. Her father had been a Master Sergeant in the Quartermaster Corps of the Regular Army, serving in Korea and then in our Army of Occupation in Berlin. When her father retired after 30 years, to a nice enough little house in a nice enough little neighborhood in Cincinnati, and she saw the horrible squalor and hopelessness into which most black people were born there, she went back to what had become just plain Berlin and earned her Doctorate.

She was as badly treated by many people over there as she would have been over here, but at least she didn't have to think every day about some nearby black ghetto where life expectancy was worse than that in what was said to be the poorest country on the planet, which was Bangladesh.

This Dr. Helen Dole had come to Scipio only the day before the prison break, to be interviewed by Tex and the Trustees for, of all things, my old job teaching Physics. She had seen the opening advertised in *The New York Times*. She had talked to Tex on the telephone before she came. She wanted to make sure he knew she was Black. Tex said that was fine, no problem. He said that the fact that she was both female and black, and held a Doctorate besides, was absolutely beautiful.

If she had landed the job and signed a contract before

Tarkington ceased to be, that would have made her the last of a long succession of Tarkington Physics teachers, which included me.

But Dr. Dole had blown up at the Board of Trustees instead. They asked her to promise that she would never, whether in class or on social occasions, discuss politics or history or economics or sociology with students. She was to leave those subjects to the college's experts in those fields.

"I plain blew up," she said to me.

"All they asked of me," she said, "was that I not be a human being."

"I hope you gave it to them good," I said.

"I did," she said. "I called them a bunch of European planters."

Lowell Chung's mother was no longer on the Board, so all the faces Dr. Dole saw were indeed of European ancestry.

She asserted that Europeans like them were robbers with guns who went all over the world stealing other people's land, which they then called their plantations. And they made the people they robbed their slaves. She was taking a long view of history, of course. Tarkington's Trustees certainly hadn't roamed the world on ships, armed to the teeth and looking for lightly defended real estate. Her point was that they were heirs to the property of such robbers, and to their mode of thinking, even if they had been born poor and had only recently dismantled an essential industry, or cleaned out a savings bank, or earned big commissions by facilitating the sale of beloved American institutions or landmarks to foreigners.

She told the Trustees, who had surely vacationed in the Caribbean, about the Carib Indian chief who was about to be burned at the stake by Spaniards. His crime was his failure to see the beauty of his people's becoming slaves in their own country.

264

This chief was offered a cross to kiss before a professional soldier or maybe a priest set fire to the kindling and logs piled up above his kneecaps. He asked why he should kiss it, and he was told that the kiss would get him into Paradise, where he would meet God and so on.

He asked if there were more people like the Spaniards up there.

He was told that of course there were.

In that case, he said, he would leave the cross unkissed. He said he didn't want to go to yet another place where people were so cruel.

She told them about Indonesian women who threw their jewelry to Dutch sailors coming ashore with firearms, in the hopes that they would be satisfied by such easily won wealth and go away again.

But the Dutch wanted their land and labor, too.

And they got them, which they called a plantation.

I had heard about that from Damon Stern.

"Now," she said to them, "you are selling this plantation because the soil is exhausted, and the natives are getting sicker and hungrier every day, begging for food and medicine and shelter, all of which are very expensive. The water mains are breaking. The bridges are falling down. So you are taking all your money and getting out of here."

One Trustee, she didn't know which, except that it wasn't Wilder, said that he intended to spend the rest of his life in the United States.

"Even if you stay," she said, "you and your money and your soul are getting out of here."

So she and I, working independently, had noticed the same thing: That even our natives, if they had reached the top or been born at the top, regarded Americans as foreigners. That seems to have been true, too, of people at the top in what used to be the Soviet Union: to them their own ordinary people weren't the kinds of people they understood and liked very much.

"What did Jason Wilder say to that?" I asked her. On TV he was always so quick to snatch any idea tossed his way, cover it with spit, so to speak, and throw it back with a crazy spin which made it uncatchable.

"He just let it lie there for a while," she said.

I could see how he might have been flummoxed by this little black woman who spoke many more languages than he did, who knew 1,000 times more science than he did, and at least as much history and literature and music and art. He had never had anybody like that on his talk show. He may never have had to debate with a person whose destiny GRIOT™ would have described as unpredictable.

He said at last, "I am an American, not a European."

And she said to him, "Then why don't you act like one?"

38

YES, and now the Japanese are pulling out. Their Army of Occupation in Business Suits is going home. The prison break at Athena was the straw that broke the camel's back, I think, but they were already abandoning properties, simply walking away from them, before that expensive catastrophe.

Why they ever wanted to own a country in such an advanced state of physical and spiritual and intellectual dilapidation is a mystery. Maybe they thought that would be a good way to get revenge for our having dropped not 1 but 2 atomic bombs on them.

So that makes two groups so far who have given up on owning this country of their own free will, mainly, I think, because so many unhappy and increasingly lawless people of all races, who don't own anything, turn out to come along with the properties.

It looks like they will keep Oahu as a sort of memento of their empire's high-water mark, just as the British have kept Bermuda.

Speaking of unhappy poor people of all races, I have often wondered how the Tarkington Board of Trustees would have been treated if Athena had been a White prison instead of a Black one. I think Hispanic convicts would have regarded them as the Blacks did, as aardvarks, as exotic creatures who had nothing to do with life as they had experienced it.

It seems to me that White convicts, though, might have wanted to kill them or at least beat them up for not caring what became of them any more than they cared what became of Blacks and Hispanics.

Dr. Dole went back to Berlin. At least that is where she said she was going.

I asked her where she had hidden during the siege. She said she had crawled into the firebox under an old boiler in the basement of this library. It hadn't been used since before I taught here, but it would have cost a lot of money to move. The school hated to spend money on improvements that didn't show.

So during the siege she was only a few meters away from me while I sat up here and engaged in the wonderful new science of Futurology.

Dr. Dole sure didn't think much of her own country. She ranted on about its sky-high rates of murder and suicide and drug addiction and infant mortality, its low rate of literacy, the fact that it had a higher percentage of its citizens in prison than any other country except for Haiti and South Africa, and didn't know how to manufacture anything anymore, and put less money into research and primary education than Japan or Korea or any country in East or West Europe, and on and on.

"At least we still have freedom of speech," I said.

And she said, "That isn't something somebody else gives you. That's something you have to give yourself."

Before I forget: During her job interview, she asked Jason Wilder where he had gone to college.

He said, "Yale."

"You know what they ought to call that place?" she said.

"No," he said.

And she said, "Plantation Owners' Tech."

When she was living in Berlin, she told me, she had been appalled by how ignorant so many American tourists and soldiers were of geography and history, and the languages and customs of other countries. She asked me, "What makes so many Americans proud of their ignorance? They act as though their ignorance somehow made them charming."

I had been asked the same general question by Alton Darwin when I was working at Athena. A World War II movie was being shown on all the TVs over there. Frank Sinatra had been captured by the Germans, and he was being interrogated by an SS Major who spoke English at least as well as Sinatra, and who played the cello and painted watercolors in his spare time, and who told Sinatra how much he looked forward to getting back, when the war was over, to his first love, which was lepidopterology.

Sinatra didn't know what lepidopterology was. It is the study of moths and butterflies. That had to be explained to him.

And Alton Darwin asked me, "How come in all these movies the Germans and the Japanese are always the smart ones, and the Americans are the dumb ones, and still the Americans win the war?"

Darwin didn't feel personally involved. The American combat soldiers in the movie were all White. That wasn't just White propaganda. That happened to be historically accurate. During the Finale Rack, American military units

269

were segregated according to race. The feeling back then was that Whites would feel like garbage if they had to share quarters and dining facilities and so on with Blacks. That went for civilian life, too. The Black people had their own schools, and they were excluded from most hotels and restaurants and places of entertainment, except onstage, and polling booths.

They were also strung up or burned alive or whatever from time to time, as reminders that their place was at the very bottom of Society. They were thought, when they were given soldier suits, to be lacking in determination and initiative in battle. So they were employed mostly as common laborers or truck drivers behind the Duke Waynes and Frank Sinatras, who did the fearless stuff.

There was one all-Black fighter squadron. To the surprise of many it did quite well.

See the Nigger fly the airplane?

To get back to Alton Darwin's question about why Frank Sinatra deserved to win even though he didn't know anything: I said, "I think he deserves to win because he is like Davy Crockett at the Alamo." The Walt Disney movie about Davy Crockett had been shown over and over again at the prison, so all the convicts knew who Davy Crockett was. And one thing it might be good to bring out at my trial is that I never told the convicts the Mexican General who besieged the Alamo was trying and failing to do what Abraham Lincoln would later do successfully, which was to hold his country together and outlaw slavery.

"How is Sinatra like Davy Crockett?" Alton Darwin asked me.

And I said, "His heart is pure."

Yes, and there is more of my story to tell. But I have just received a piece of news from my lawyer that has knocked the wind out of me. After Vietnam, I thought there was nothing that could ever hit me that hard again. I thought I was used to dead bodies, no matter whose.

Wrong again.

Ah me!

If I tell now who it is that died, and how that person died, died only yesterday, that will seem to complete my story. From a reader's point of view, there would be nothing more to say but this:

THE END

But there is more I want to tell. So I will carry on as though I hadn't heard the news, albeit doggedly. And I write this:

The Lieutenant Colonel who led the assault on Scipio and then kept locals off the helicopters was also a graduate of the Academy, but maybe 2 score and 7 years younger than myself. When I told him my name and he saw my class ring, he realized who I was and what I used to be. He exclaimed, "My Lord, it's the Preacher!"

If it hadn't been for him, I don't know what would have become of me. I guess I would have done what most of the other valley people did, which was to go to Rochester or Buffalo or beyond, looking for any kind of work, minimum wage for sure. The whole area south of the Meadowdale Cinema Complex was and still is under Martial Law.

His name was Harley Wheelock III. He told me he and his wife were infertile, so they adopted twin girl orphans from Peru, South America, not Peru, Indiana. They were cute little Inca girls. But he hardly ever got home anymore, his Division was so busy. He was all set to go home on leave from the South Bronx when he was ordered here to put down the prison break and rescue the hostages.

His father Harley Wheelock II was 3 years ahead of me at the Academy, and died, I already knew, in some kind of accident in Germany, and so never served in Vietnam. I asked Harley III how exactly Harley II had died. He told me his father drowned while trying to rescue a Swedish woman who committed suicide by opening the windows of her Volvo and driving it off a dock and into the Ruhr River at Essen, home, as it happens, of that premier manufacturer of crematoria, A. J. Topf und Sohn.

Small World.

Now Harley III said to me, "You know anything about this excrement hole?" Of course, he himself didn't say "excrement." He had never heard of the Mohiga Valley before he was ordered here. Like most people, he had heard of Athena and Tarkington but had no clear idea where they were.

I replied that the excrement hole was home to me, although I had been born in Delaware and raised in Ohio, and that I expected 1 day to be buried here.

"Where's the Mayor?" he said.

"Dead," I said, "and all the policemen, too, including the campus cops. And the Fire Chief."

"So there isn't any Government?" he said.

"I'd say you're the Government," I said.

He used the Name of Our Savior as an explosive expletive, and then added, "Wherever I go, all of a sudden I am the Government. I'm already the Government in the South Bronx, and I've got to get back there as quick as I can. So I hereby declare you the Mayor of this excrement hole." This time he actually said, "excrement hole," echoing me. "Go down to the City Hall, wherever that is, and start governing."

He was so decisive! He was so loud!

As though the conversation weren't weird enough, he was wearing one of those coal-scuttle helmets the Army started issuing after we lost the Vietnam War, maybe to change our luck.

Make Blacks, Jews, and everybody else look like Nazis, and see how that worked out.

"I can't govern," I protested. "Nobody would pay any attention to me. I would be a joke."

"Good point!" he cried. So loud!

He got the Governor's Office in Albany on the radio. The Governor himself was on his way to Rochester by helicopter, in order to go on TV with the freed hostages. The Governor's Office managed to patch through Harley III's call to the Governor up in the sky. Harley III told the Governor who I was and what the situation was in Scipio.

It didn't take long.

And then Harley III turned to me and said, "Congratulations! You are now a Brigadier General in the National Guard!"

"I've got a family on the other side of the lake," I said. "I've got to go find out how they are."

He was able to tell me how they were. He personally, the day before, had seen Margaret and Mildred loaded into the steel box on the back of a prison van, consigned to the Laughing Academy in Batavia.

"They're fine!" he said. "Your country needs you more than they do now, so, General Hartke, strut your stuff!"

He was so full of energy! It was almost as though his coal-scuttle helmet contained a thunderstorm.

Never an idle moment! No sooner had he persuaded the Governor to make me a Brigadier than he was off to the stable, where captured Freedom Fighters were being forced to dig graves for all the bodies. The weary diggers had every reason to believe that they were digging their own graves. They had seen plenty of movies about the Finale Rack, in which soldiers in coal-scuttle helmets stood around while people in rags dug their own final resting places.

I heard Harley III barking orders at the diggers, telling

them to dig deeper and make the sides straighter and so on.
I had seen leadership of such a high order exercised in Vietnam, and I myself had exhibited it from time to time, so I
am quite certain that Harley III had taken some sort of
amphetamine.

There wasn't much for me to govern at first. This place,
which had been the sole remaining business of any size in
the valley, stood vacant and seemed likely to remain so.
Most locals had managed to run away after the prison break.
When they came back, though, there was no way to make
a living. Those who owned houses or places of business
couldn't find anybody to sell them to. They were wiped out.

So most of the civilians I might have governed had soon
packed the best of their belongings into cars and trailers,
and paid small fortunes to black marketeers for enough gasoline to get them the heck out of here.

I had no troops of my own. Those on my side of the lake
were on loan from the commander of the National Guard
Division, the 42nd Division, the "Rainbow Division," Lucas
Florio. He had his headquarters in Hiroshi Matsumoto's old
office at the prison. He wasn't a graduate of West Point, and
he was too young to have fought in Vietnam, and his home
was in Schenectady, so we had never met before. His troops
were all White, with Orientals classified as Honorary White
People. The same was true of the 82nd Airborne. There
were also Black and Hispanic units somewhere, the theory
being, as with the prisons, that people were always more
comfortable with those of their own race.

This resegregation, although I never heard any public
figure say so, also made the Armed Forces more like a set of
golf clubs. You could use this battalion or that one, depend-
ing on what color people they were supposed to fight.

The Soviet Union, of course, with its citizenry, including

every sort of a human being but a Black or Hispanic, found out the hard way that soldiers wouldn't fight hard at all against people who looked and thought and talked like them.

The Rainbow Division itself began during World War I, as an experiment integrating unlike Americans who weren't Army Regulars. Reserve Divisions activated back then were all identified with specific parts of the country. Then somebody got the idea of putting together a Division composed of draftees and volunteers from all different parts of the country, to prove how well they could get along.

Harmony between White people thought not to like each other very much was what the rainbow represented then. The Rainbow Division did in fact fight about as well as any other one during the War to End Wars, the prelude to the Finale Rack.

Afterward, the experiment complete, the 42nd Division became merely one more National Guard outfit, arbitrarily handed over with its battle ribbons to New York State.

But the symbol of the rainbow lives on in its shoulder patch.

Before I was arrested for insurrection, I myself was a wearer of that rainbow, along with the star of a Brigadier!

39

URING my first 2 weeks as Military Com-
mander of the Scipio District, all the way to the head of the
lake and all the way down to the National Forest, the best
thing I did, I think, was to make some of the soldiers firemen.
A few had been firemen in civilian life, so I got them to
familiarize themselves with the town's firefighting apparatus, which hadn't been hurt during the siege. One real
stroke of luck: the fire trucks all had full tanks of gasoline.
You would have thought, in a society where everybody from
top to bottom was stealing everything that wasn't nailed
down, that somebody would have siphoned off that priceless
gasoline.

Every so often, in the midst of chaos, you come across an
amazing, inexplicable instance of civic responsibility. Maybe
the last shred of faith people have is in their firemen.

I also supervised the exhumation of the bodies next to the
stable. They had been buried for only a few days, but then
the Government, personified by a Coroner and the Medical
Examiner from the State Police who knew so much about
crucifixions, ordered us to dig them up again. The Government had to fingerprint and photograph them, and describe
their dental work, if any, and their obvious wounds, if any,

and so on. We didn't have to dig up the Shultzes again, who had already been dug up once, to make room for the Pavilion.

And we hadn't found the young woman's skull yet. The digging hadn't gone deep enough yet to find out what had become of the head of the missing Lilac Queen.

The Government, just those 2 guys from out of town, said we had to bury the bodies much deeper when they were through with them. That was the law.

"We wouldn't want to break the law," I said.

The Coroner was black. I wouldn't have known he was Black if he hadn't told me.

I asked him if he couldn't arrange for the County or the State or somebody to take possession of the bodies until the next-of-kin, if any, could decide what was to be done with them. I hoped they would be taken to Rochester, where they could be embalmed or refrigerated or cremated, or at least buried in decent containers of some kind. They had been buried here in nothing but their clothing.

He said he would look into it, but that I shouldn't get my hopes up. He said the County was broke and the State was broke and the Country was broke and that he was broke. He had lost what little he had in Microsecond Arbitrage.

After the Government left, I faced the problem of what the best way would be to dig much deeper graves. I was reluctant to ask National Guardsmen to do it with shovels. They had been resentful when I had them dig up the bodies and were growing more sullen in any case as it became more and more apparent, even that early in the game, that they might never be allowed to return to civilian life. The glamour of their Combat Infantryman's Badges was wearing thin.

I couldn't use convict labor from across the lake. That, too, was the law. And then I remembered that the college had a backhoe which ran on diesel fuel, which wasn't a hot item on the black market. So if somebody could find the backhoe, there might still be some fuel in its tank.

A soldier found it, and the tank was full!

Miracle!

Again I ask the question: "How much longer can I go on being an Atheist?"

The tank was full because there was only one diesel automobile in Scipio when the diaspora began. It was a Cadillac General Motors put on the market about the time we got kicked out of Vietnam. It is still here. It was such a lemon that you might as well have tried to go on a Sunday spin in an Egyptian pyramid.

It used to belong to a Tarkington parent. He was coming to his daughter's graduation when it broke down in front of the Black Cat Café. It had already stopped of its own accord many times between here and New York City. So he went to the hardware store and bought yellow paint and a brush and painted big lemons all over it, and sold it to Lyle Hooper for a dollar.

This was a man who was on the Board of Directors of General Motors!

During the brief time the bodies were all aboveground again, a person showed up with a Toyota hearse and an undertaker from Rochester to claim 1. That was Dr. Charlton Hooper, who had been invited to try out for the New York Knickerbockers basketball team but had chosen to become a Physicist instead. As I've said, he was 2 meters tall.

That's tall!

I asked the undertaker where he had found the gasoline for the trip.

He wouldn't tell me at first, but I kept after him. He finally said, "Try the crematorium in back of the Meadowdale Cinema Complex. Ask for Guido."

278

I asked Charlton if he had come all the way from Waxahachie, Texas. The last I'd heard, he was running experiments with the enormous atom-smasher, the Supercollider, down there. He said the funds for the Supercollider had dried up, so he had moved to Geneva, New York, not that far away. He was teaching Freshman Physics at Hobart College.

I asked him if there was any way the Supercollider could be turned into a prison.

He said he guessed they could put a bunch of bad guys in there, and throw the switch, and make their hair stand on end and raise their temperatures a couple of degrees centigrade.

About a week after Charlton took his father's body away and we reburied all the others to a legal depth with the backhoe, I was awakened 1 afternoon by a terrible uproar in what had been such a peaceful town. I was living down in the Town Hall back then, and often took naps in the afternoon.

The noise was coming from up here. Chain saws were snarling. There was hammering. It sounded like an army. As far as I knew, there were supposed to be only 4 Guardsmen up here, keeping a fire watch.

The soldier who was stationed in my reception room, to wake me up in case there was something important for me to do, had vanished. He had gone up the hill to discover what on Earth was happening. There had been no warning of any special activity.

So I trudged up Clinton Street all alone. I was wearing civilian shoes and a camouflage suit General Florio had given me, along with 1 of his own stars on each shoulder. That was all I had for a uniform.

When I got to the top of Clinton Street, I found General Florio directing soldiers brought over from his side of the lake. They were turning the Quadrangle into a city of tents. Others constructed a barbed-wire fence around it.

I did not have to ask the meaning of all this. It was obvious that Tarkington College, which had stayed small as the prison across the lake had grown and grown, was itself a prison now.

General Florio turned to me and smiled. "Hello, Warden Hartke," he said.

Once all those 10-man tents, which were brought down from the Armory across the highway from the Meadowdale Cinema Complex, were set up on the Quadrangle as though on a checkerboard, it seemed so logical. The surrounding buildings, Samoza Hall, this library, the bookstore, the Pavilion, and so on, with machine-gunners at various windows and doorways, and with barbed wire between them and the tents, served well enough as prison walls.

General Florio said to me, "Company's coming."

I remember a lecture Damon Stern gave about his visit with several Tarkington students to Auschwitz, the infamous Nazi extermination camp in Poland during the Finale Rack. Stern used to make extra money taking trips to Europe with students whose parents or guardians didn't want to see them over Christmas or during the summertime. He caught a lot of heck for taking some to Auschwitz. He did it impulsively and without asking permission from anyone. It wasn't on the schedule, and some of the students were very upset afterward.

He said in his lecture that if the fences and gallows and gas chambers were removed from the tidy, tidy checkerboard of streets and old stucco two-story shotgun buildings, it might have made a nice enough junior college for low-income or underachieving people in the area. The buildings had been put up years before World War I, he said, as a

280

comfortable outpost for soldiers of the Austro-Hungarian Empire. Among the many titles of that Emperor, he said, was Duke of Auschwitz.

What General Florio was after on our side of the lake was our sanitary facilities. The prisoners were to use buckets in their tents for toilets, but then these could be emptied into toilets in the surrounding buildings and flushed from there into Scipio's state-of-the-art sewage-disposal plant. Across the lake they were having to bury everything.

And no showers.

We had plenty of showers.

One touching rather than horrible thing about the siege, surely, was how little damage the escaped convicts did to this campus. It was as though they really believed that it was going to be theirs for generations.

This brings to mind another of Damon Stern's lectures, which was about how the brutalized and starving poor people of Petrograd in Russia behaved after they broke into the palace of the Czars in 1917. They got to see for the first time all the treasures inside the palace, and they were so outraged they wanted to wreck them.

But then one man got their attention by firing a gun at the ceiling, and he said, "Comrades! Comrades! This is all ours now! Don't hurt anything!"

They renamed Petrograd "Leningrad." Now it's Petrograd again.

In a way, the escaped convicts were like a neutron bomb. They had no compassion for living things, but they did surprisingly little damage to property.

Damon Stern the unicyclist, on the other hand, laid down his life for living things. They weren't even human beings. They were horses. They weren't even his horses.

His wife and kids got away, and, last I heard, were living in Lackawanna, where they have relatives. That's nice when people have relatives they can run away to.

But Damon Stern is buried deep and close to where he fell, next to the stable, in the shadow of Musket Mountain when the Sun goes down.

His wife Wanda June came back here after the siege in a pickup truck she said belonged to her half brother. She paid a fortune for enough gas to get here from Lackawanna. I asked her what she was doing for money, and she said she and Damon had put away a lot of Yen in their freezer in a box marked "Brussels sprouts."

Damon woke her up in the middle of the night and told her to get into the Volkswagen with the kids and take off for Rochester with the headlights off. He had heard the explosion across the lake, and seen the silent army crossing the ice to Scipio. The last thing he ever did with Wanda June was hand her the box marked "Brussels sprouts."

Damon himself, over his wife's objections, stayed behind to spread the alarm. He said he would be along later, by hitching a ride in somebody else's car, or by walking all the way to Rochester on back roads he knew, if he had to. It isn't clear what happened after that. He probably called the local police, although none of them lived to say so. He woke up a lot of people in the immediate neighborhood.

The best conjecture is that he heard gunfire inside the stable and unwisely went to investigate. A Freedom Fighter with an AK-47 was gut-shooting horses for the fun of it. He didn't shoot them in the head.

Damon must have asked him to stop, so the Freedom Fighter shot him, too.

His wife didn't want his body. She said the happiest years of his life had been spent here, so he should stay buried here.

282

She found all 4 of the family unicycles. That was easy. The soldiers were taking turns trying to ride them. Before that, several of the convicts had also tried to ride them, so far as I know with no success.

So I went back down Clinton Street to the Town Hall, to ponder this latest change in my career, that I was next to be a Warden.

There was a Rolls-Royce Corniche, a convertible coupe, parked out front. Whoever had a car like that had enough Yen or Marks or some other stable currency to buy himself or herself enough black-market gas for a trip from anywhere to anywhere.

My guess was that it was the chariot of some Tarkington student or parent who hoped to recover property left in a dorm suite at the start of the vacation period, a vacation which now, obviously, might never end.

The soldier who was supposed to be my receptionist was back on duty. He had returned to his post after General Florio told him to stop standing around with his thumb in his anus and start stringing barbed wire or erecting tents. He was waiting for me at the front door, and he told me I had a visitor.

So I asked him, "Who is the visitor?"

He said, "It's your son, sir."

I was thunderstruck. "Eugene is here?" I said. Eugene Jr. had told me that he never wanted to see me again as long as he lived. How is that for a life sentence? And he was driving a Rolls-Royce now? Eugene?

"No, sir," he said. "Not Eugene."

"Eugene is the only son I have," I said. "What did he say his name was?"

"He told me, sir," he said, "that he was your son Rob Roy."

That was all the proof I needed that a son of mine did indeed await me in my office: that name, "Rob Roy." "Rob" and "Roy," and I was back in the Philippine Islands again, having just been kicked out of Vietnam. I was back in bed with a voluptuous female war correspondent from *The Des Moines Register,* whose lips were like sofa pillows, telling her that, if I had been a fighter plane, I would have had little pictures of people painted all over me.

I calculated how old he was. He was 23, making him the youngest of my children. He was the baby of the family.

He was in the reception room outside my office. He stood up when I came in. He was exactly as tall as myself. His hair was the same color and texture as mine. He needed a shave, and his potential beard was as black and thick as mine. His eyes were the same color as mine. All 4 of our eyes were greenish amber. We had the same big nose, my father's nose. He was nervous and polite. He was expensively dressed in leisure clothes. If he had been learning-disabled or merely stupid, which he wasn't, he might have had a happy 4 years at Tarkington, especially with that car of his.

I was giddy. I had taken off my overcoat on the way in, so that he could see my General's stars. That was something, anyway. How many boys had a father who was a General?

"How can I help you?" I said.

"I hardly know how to begin," he said.

"I think you've already begun by telling the guard that you were a son of mine," I said. "Was that a joke?"

"Do you think it was a joke?" he asked.

"I don't pretend I was a Saint when I was young and away from home so much," I said. "But I never made love using an alias. I was always easy to find afterward, if somebody wanted to find me badly enough. So, if I did father a child out of wedlock somewhere along the line, that comes as a complete surprise to me. I would have thought the mother, the minute she found out she was pregnant, would have gotten in touch with me."

"I know 1 mother who didn't," he said.

Before I could reply, he blurted words he must have rehearsed en route. "This is going to be a very brief visit," he said. "I am going to be in and out of here before you know it. I'm on my way to Italy, and I never want to see this country ever again, and especially Dubuque."

It would turn out that he had been through an ordeal that lasted much, much longer than the siege of Scipio, and was probably harder on him than Vietnam had been on me. He had been tried for child molestation in Dubuque, Iowa, where he had founded and run a free child-care center at his own expense.

He wasn't married, a strike against him in the eyes of most juries, a character flaw like having served in the Vietnam War.

"I grew up in Dubuque," he would tell me, "and the money I inherited was made in Dubuque." It was a meat-packing fortune.

"I wanted to give something back to Dubuque. With so many single parents raising children on minimum wage, and with so many married couples both working to make enough to feed and clothe their children halfway decently, I thought what Dubuque needed most was a child-care center that was nice and didn't cost anything."

Two weeks after he opened the center, he was arrested for child molestation because several of the children came home with inflamed genitalia.

He was later to prove in court, after smears were taken from the children's lesions, that a fungus was to blame. The fungus was closely related to jock itch, and may actually have been a new strain of jock which had learned how to rise above all the standard remedies for that affliction.

By then, though, he had been held in jail without bail for 3 months, and had to be protected from a lynch mob by the National Guard. Luckily for him, Dubuque, like so many communities, had backed up its police with Armor and Infantry.

After he was acquitted, he had to be transported out of town and deep into Illinois in a buttoned-up tank, or somebody would have killed him.

The judge who acquitted him was killed. He was of Italian ancestry. Somebody sent him a pipe bomb concealed in a huge salami.

But that son of mine did not tell me about any of that until just before he said, "It's time to say, 'Good-bye.'" He prefaced the tale of how he had suffered so with these words: "I hope you understand, the last thing I wanted to do was make any demands on your emotions."

"Try me," I said.

Thinking about our meeting now fills me with a sort of sweetness. He had liked me enough, found me warm enough, to use me as though I were a really good father, if only for a little while.

In the beginning, when we were feeling each other out very gingerly, and I hadn't yet admitted that he was my son, I asked him if "Rob Roy" was the name on his birth certificate, or whether that was a nickname his mother had hung on him.

He said it was the name on his birth certificate.

"And the father on the birth certificate?" I asked.

"It was the name of a soldier who died in Vietnam," he said.

"Do you remember what it was?" I said.

Here came a surprise. It was the name of my brother-in-law, Jack Patton, whom his mother had never met, I'm sure. I must have told her about Jack in Manila, and she'd remembered his name, and that he was unmarried and had died for his country.

I thought to myself, "Good old Jack, wherever you are, it's time to laugh like hell again."

"So what makes you think I'm your father instead of him?" I said. "Your mother finally told you?"

"She wrote me a letter," he said.

"She didn't tell you face to face?" I said.

"She couldn't," he said. "She died of cancer of the pancreas when I was 4 years old."

That was a shock. She sure hadn't lasted long after I made love to her. I've always enjoyed thinking of the women I have made love to as living on and on. I had imagined his mother, game and smart and sporty and funny, with lips like sofa pillows, living on and on.

"She wrote me a letter on her deathbed," he continued, "which was put into the hands of a law firm in Dubuque, not to be opened until after the death of the good man who had married her and adopted me. He died only a year ago."

"Did the letter say why you were named Rob Roy?" I inquired.

"No," he said. "I assumed it must be because she liked the novel by that name by Sir Walter Scott."

"That sounds right," I said. What good would it do him or anybody else to know that he was named for 2 shots of Scotch, 1 shot of sweet vermouth, cracked ice, and a twist of lemon peel?

"How did you find me?" I said.

"At first I didn't think I wanted to find you," he said. "But

287

then 2 weeks ago I thought that we were entitled to see each other once, at least. So I called West Point."

"I haven't had any contact with them for years," I said.

"That's what they told me," he said. "But just before I called they got a call from the Governor of New York, who said he had just made you a Brigadier General. He wanted to make sure he hadn't been made a fool of. He wanted to make sure you were what you were claimed to be."

"Well," I said, and we were still standing in the reception room, "I don't think we need to wait for blood tests to find out whether you are really my son or not. You are the spit and image of me when I was your age.

"You should know that I really loved your mother," I went on.

"That was in her letter, how much in love you were," he said.

"You will have to take my word for it," I said, "that if I had known she was pregnant, I would have behaved honorably. I'm not quite sure what we would have done. We would have worked something out."

I led the way into my office. "Come on in. There are a couple of easy chairs in here. We can close the door."

"No, no, no," he said. "I'm on my way. I just thought we should see each other just one time. We've done that now. It's no big thing."

"I like life to be simple," I said, "but if you went away without another word, that would be much too simple for me, and for you, too, I hope."

So I got him into my office and closed the door, and got us settled in facing easy chairs. We hadn't touched. We never would touch.

"I would offer you coffee," I said, "but nobody in this valley has coffee."

"I've got some in my car," he said.

"I'm sure," I said. "But don't go get it. Never mind, never mind." I cleared my throat. "If you'll pardon my saying so, you seem to be what I have heard called 'fabulously well-to-do.'"

He said that, yes, he was fortunate financially. The Dubuque meat packer who married his mother and adopted him had sold his business to the Shah of Bratpuhr shortly before he died, and had been paid in gold bricks deposited in a bank in Switzerland.

The meat packer's name was Lowell Fenstermaker, so my son's full name was Rob Roy Fenstermaker. Rob Roy said he certainly wasn't going to change his last name to Hartke, that he felt like Fenstermaker and not Hartke.

His stepfather had been very good to him. Rob Roy said that the only thing he didn't like about him was the way he raised calves for veal. The baby animals, scarcely out of the womb, were put in cages so cramped that they could hardly move, to make their muscles nice and tender. When they were big enough their throats were cut, and they had never run or jumped or made friends, or done anything that might have made life a worthwhile experience.

What was their crime?

Rob Roy said that his inherited wealth was at first an embarrassment. He said that until very recently he never would have considered buying a car like the 1 parked outside, or wearing a cashmere jacket and lizard-skin shoes made in Italy. That was what he was wearing in my office. "When nobody else in Dubuque could afford black-market coffee and gasoline, I, too, did without. I used to walk everywhere."

"What happened very recently?" I said.

"I was arrested for molesting little children," he said.

I itched all over with a sudden attack of psychosomatic hives.

He told me the whole story.

I said to him, "I thank you for sharing that with me."

The hives went away as quickly as they had come.

I felt wonderful, very happy to have him look me over and think what he would. I had seldom been happy to have my legitimate children look me over and think what they would.

What made the difference? I hate to say so, because my answer is so paltry. But here it is: I had always wanted to be a General, and there I was wearing General's stars.

How embarrassing to be human.

There was this, too: I was no longer encumbered by my wife and mother-in-law. Why did I keep them at home so long, even though it was plain that they were making the lives of my children unbearable?

It could be, I suppose, because somewhere in the back of my mind I believed that there might really be a big book in which all things were written, and that I wanted some impressive proof that I could be compassionate recorded there.

I asked Rob Roy where he had gone to college.

"Yale," he said.

I told him what Helen Dole said about Yale, that it ought to be called "Plantation Owners' Tech."

"I don't get it," he said.

"I had to ask her to explain it myself," I said. "She said Yale was where plantation owners learned how to get the natives to kill each other instead of them."

"That's a bit strong," he said. And then he asked me if my first wife was still alive.

"I've only had 1," I said. "She's still alive."

"There was a lot about her in Mother's letter," he said.

"Really?" I said. "Like what?"

"About how she was hit by a car the day before you were going to take her to the senior prom. About how she was paralyzed from the waist down, but you still married her, even though she would have to spend the rest of her life in a wheelchair."

If that was in the letter, I must have told his mother that.

"And your father, is he still alive?" he said.

"No," I said. "The ceiling of a gift shop fell on him at Niagara Falls."

"Did he ever regain his eyesight?" he said.

"Regain his what?" I said. And then I realized that his question was based on some other lie I had told his mother.

"His eyesight," he said.

"No," I said. "Never did."

"I think it's so beautiful," he said, "how he came home from the war blind, and you used to read Shakespeare to him."

"He sure loved Shakespeare," I said.

"So," he said, "I am descended not just from 1 war hero, but 2."

"War hero?" I said.

"I know you would never call yourself that," he said. "But that's what Mother said you were. And you can certainly call your father that. How many Americans shot down 28 German planes in World War II?"

"We could go up to the library and look it up," I said. "They have a very good library here. You can find out anything, if you really try."

"Where is my Uncle Bob buried?" he said.

"Your what?" I said.

"Your brother Bob, my Uncle Bob," he said.

I had never had a brother of any kind. I took a wild guess. "We threw his ashes out of an airplane," I said.

"You have certainly had some bad luck," he said. "Your father comes home blind from the war. Your childhood sweetheart is hit by a car right before the senior prom. Your brother dies of spinal meningitis right after he is invited to try out for the New York Yankees."

"Yes, well, all you can do is play the cards they deal you," I said.

"Have you still got his glove?" he said.

"No," I said. What kind of glove could I have told his mother about when we were both sozzled on Sweet Rob Roys in Manila 24 years ago?

"You carried it all the way through the war, but now it's gone?" he said.

He had to be talking about the nonexistent baseball glove of my nonexistent brother. "Somebody stole it from me after I got home," I said, "thinking it was just another baseball glove, I'm sure. Whoever stole it had no idea how much it meant to me."

He stood. "I really must be going now."

I stood, too.

I shook my head sadly. "It isn't going to be as easy as you think to give up on the country of your birth."

"That's about as meaningful as my astrological sign," he said.

"What is?" I said.

"The country of my birth," he said.

"You might be surprised," I said.

"Well, Dad," he said, "it certainly won't be the first time."

"Can you tell me who in this valley might have gasoline?" he said. "I'll pay anything."

"Do you have enough gas to make it back to Rochester?" I said.

"Yes," he said.

"Well," I said, "head back the way you came. That's the only way you can get back, so you can't get lost. Right at the Rochester city limits you will see the Meadowdale Cinema Complex. Behind that is a crematorium. Don't look for smoke. It's smokeless."

"A crematorium?" he said.

"That's right, a crematorium," I said. "You drive up to the crematorium, and you ask for Guido. From what I hear, if you've got the money, he's got the gasoline."

"And chocolate bars, do you think?" he said.

"I don't know," I said. "Won't hurt to ask."

40

NOT that there is any shortage of real child-molesters, child-shooters, child-starvers, child-bombers, child-drowners, child-whippers, child-burners, and child-defenestrators on this happy planet. Turn on the TV. By the luck of the draw, though, my son Rob Roy Fenstermaker does not happen to be one of them.

OK. My story is almost ended.

And here is the news that knocked the wind out of me so recently. When I heard it from my lawyer, I actually said, "Ooof!"

Hiroshi Matsumoto was dead by his own hand in his hometown of Hiroshima! But why would I care so much?

He did it in the wee hours of the morning, Japanese time, of course, while sitting in his motor-driven wheelchair at the base of the monument marking the point of impact of the atomic bomb that was dropped on Hiroshima when we were little boys.

He didn't use a gun or poison. He committed hara-kiri with a knife, disemboweling himself in a ritual of self-loathing once practiced by humiliated members of the ancient caste of professional soldiers, the samurai.

And yet, so far as I am able to determine, he never shirked his duty, never stole anything, and never killed or wounded anyone.

Still waters run deep. R.I.P.

If there really is a big book somewhere, in which all things are written, and which is to be read line by line, omitting nothing, on Judgment Day, let it be recorded that I, when Warden of this place, moved the convicted felons out of the tents on the Quadrangle and into the surrounding buildings. They no longer had to excrete in buckets or, in the middle of the night, have their homes blown down. The buildings, except for this 1, were divided into cement-block cells intended for 2 men, but most holding 5.

The War on Drugs goes on.

I caused 2 more fences to be erected, 1 within the other, enclosing the back of the inner buildings, and with antipersonnel mines sown in between. The machine-gun nests were reinstalled in windows and doorways of the next ring of buildings, Norman Rockwell Hall, the Pahlavi Pavilion, and so on.

It was during my administration that the troops here were Federalized, a step I had recommended. That meant that they were no longer civilians in soldier suits. That meant that they were full-time soldiers, serving at the pleasure of the President. Nobody could say how much longer the War on Drugs might last. Nobody could say when they could go home again.

General Florio himself, accompanied by six MPs with clubs and sidearms, congratulated me on all I had done. He then took back the two stars he had loaned me, and told me that I was under arrest for the crime of insurrection. I had come to like him, and I think he had come to like me. He was simply following orders.

I asked him, as 1 comrade to another, "Does this make any sense to you? Why is this happening?"

It is a question I have asked myself many times since, maybe 5 times today between coughing fits.

His answer to it, the first answer I ever got to it, is probably the best answer I will ever get to it.

"Some ambitious young Prosecutor," he said, "thinks you'll make good TV."

Hiroshi Matsumoto's suicide has hit me so hard, I think, because he was innocent of even the littlest misdemeanors. I doubt that he ever double-parked, even, or ran a red light when nobody else was around. And yet he executed himself in a manner that the most terrible criminal who ever lived would not deserve!

He had no feet anymore, which must have been depressing. But having no feet is no reason for a man to disembowel himself.

It had to have been the atom bomb that was dropped on him during his formative years, and not the absence of feet, that made him feel that life was a crock of doo-doo.

As I have said, he did not tell me that he had been atom-bombed until we had known each other for 2 years or more. He might never have told me about it, in my opinion, if a documentary about the Japanese "Rape of Nanking" hadn't been shown on the prison TVs the day before. This was a program chosen at random from the prison library. A guard who did the choosing couldn't read English well enough to know what the convicts would see next. So there was no censorship.

The Warden had a small TV monitor on his desk, and I knew he watched it from time to time, since he often remarked to me about the inanity of this or that old show, and especially *I Love Lucy.*

The Rape of Nanking was just one more instance of soldiers slaughtering prisoners and unarmed civilians, but it became famous because it was among the first to be well photographed. There were evidently movie cameras everywhere, run by gosh knows whom, and the footage wasn't confiscated afterward.

I had seen some of the footage when I was a cadet, but not as a part of a well-edited documentary, with a baritone voice-over and appropriate music underneath.

The orgy of butchery followed a virtually unopposed attack by the Japanese Army on the Chinese city of Nanking in 1937, long before this country became part of the Finale Rack. Hiroshi Matsumoto had just been born. Prisoners were tied to stakes and used for bayonet practice. Several people in a pit were buried alive. You could see their expressions as the dirt hit their faces.

Their faces disappeared, but the dirt on top kept moving as though there were some sort of burrowing animal, a woodchuck maybe, making a home below.

Unforgettable!

How was that for racism?

The documentary was a big hit in the prison. Alton Darwin said to me, I remember, "If somebody is going to do it, I am going to watch it."

This was 7 years before the prison break.

I didn't know if Hiroshi had seen the show on his monitor or not. I wasn't about to ask. We were not pals.

I was willing to be a pal, if that was part of the job. I believe he moved me in next door to him with the idea that it was time he had a pal. My guess is that he never had had a pal. No sooner had I become his neighbor, I think, than he decided he didn't want a pal after all. That didn't have anything to do with what I was or how I acted. To him, I think, a pal was like a piece of merchandise heavily promoted at Christmas, say. Why junk up his life with such a cumbersome contraption and all its accessories merely because it was advertised?

So he went on hiking alone and boating alone and eating alone, which was OK with me. I had a rich social life across the lake.

But the day after the documentary was shown, late in the afternoon, about suppertime, I was rowing for shore in my fiberglass umiak, headed for the mud beach in front of our 2 houses in the ghost town. I had been fishing. I hadn't been to Scipio. My own 2 great pals over there, Muriel Peck and Damon Stern, were on vacation. They wouldn't be back until Freshman Orientation Week, before the start of the fall semester.

The Warden was waiting for me on the beach, looking out at me in my crazy boat like a mother who had been worried to death about where her little boy had gone. Had I failed to keep a date with him? No. We had never had a date. My best supposition was that Mildred or Margaret had tried to burn 1 of our houses down.

But he said to me as I disembarked, "There is something you should know about me."

There was no pressing reason why I should know anything about him. We didn't work as a team up at the prison. He didn't care what or how I taught up there.

"I was in Hiroshima when it was bombed," he said.

I am sure there was an implied equation there: The bombing of Hiroshima was as unforgivable and as typically human as the Rape of Nanking.

So I heard about his going into a ditch after a ball when he was a schoolboy, about his straightening up to find that nobody was alive but him.

And on and on.

When he was through with that story he said to me, "I thought you should know."

I said earlier that I had a sudden attack of psychosomatic hives when Rob Roy Fenstermaker told me that he had been busted for molesting children. That wasn't my first such attack. The first was when Hiroshi told me about being atom-bombed. I suddenly itched all over, and scratching wouldn't help.

And I said to Hiroshi what I would say to Rob Roy: "I thank you for sharing that with me."

This was an expression, if I am not mistaken, which originated in California.

I was tempted to show Hiroshi "The Protocols of the Elders of Tralfamadore." I'm glad I didn't. I might now be feeling a little bit responsible for his suicide. He might have left a note saying: "The Elders of Tralfamadore win again!"

Only I and the author of that story, if he is still alive, would have known what he meant by that.

The most troubling part of his tale about the vaporization of all he knew and loved had to do with the edge of the area of the blast. There were all these people dying in agony. And he was only a little boy, remember.

That must have been for him like walking down the Appian Way back in 71 B.C., when 6,000 nobodies had just been crucified there. Some little kid or maybe a lot of little kids may have walked down that road back then. What could a little kid say on such an occasion? "Daddy, I think I have to go to the bathroom"?

It so happens that my lawyer is on a first-name basis with our Ambassador to Japan, former Senator Randolph Nakayama of California. They are of different generations, but my lawyer was a roommate of the Senator's son at Reed College out in Portland, Oregon, the town where Tex bought his trusty rifle.

My lawyer told me that both sets of the Senator's racially Japanese grandparents, one set immigrants, the other set native Californians, were put into a concentration camp when this country got into the Finale Rack. The camp, incidentally, was only a few kilometers west of the Donner Pass, named in honor of White cannibals. The feeling back then was that anybody with Japanese genes inside our borders was probably less loyal to the United States Constitution than to Hirohito, the Emperor of Japan.

The Senator's father, however, served in an infantry battalion composed entirely of young Americans of Japanese extraction, which became our most decorated unit taking part in the Italian Campaign during, again, the Finale Rack.

So I asked my lawyer to find out from the Ambassador if Hiroshi had left a note, and if there had been an autopsy performed to determine whether or not the deceased had ingested some foreign substance that might have made hara-kiri easier. I don't know whether to call this friendship or morbid curiosity.

The answer came back that there was no note, and that there had been no autopsy, since the cause of death was so horribly obvious. There was this detail: A little girl who didn't know him was the first person of any age or sex to see what he had chosen to do to himself.

She ran and told her mama.

Back when we were neighbors, I asked the Warden why he never left this valley, why he didn't get away from the prison and me and the ignorant young guards and the bells across the lake and all the rest of it. He had years of leave time he had never used.

He said, "I would only meet more people."

"You don't like any kind of people?" I said. We were talking in a sort of joshing mode, so I could ask him that.

"I wish I had been born a bird instead," he said. "I wish we had all been born birds instead."

He never killed anybody and had the sex life of a calf kept alive for its veal alone.

I have lived more vividly, and I promised to tell at the end of this book the number I would like engraved on my tombstone, a number that represents both my 100-percent-legal military kills and my adulteries.

If people hear of the number at the end and its double significance, some will turn to the end to learn the number in order to decide that it is too small or too big or just about right or whatever without reading the book. But I have devised a lock to thwart them. I have concealed its oddly shaped key in a problem that only those who have read the whole book will have no trouble solving.

So:

Take the year Eugene Debs died.

Subtract the title of the science fiction movie based on a novel by Arthur C. Clarke which I saw twice in Vietnam. Do not panic. This will give you a negative number, but Arabs in olden times taught us how to deal with such.

Add the year of Hitler's birth. There! Everything is nice and positive again. If you have done everything right so far, you should have the year in which Napoleon was banished to Elba and the metronome was invented, neither event, however, discussed in this book.

Add the gestation period of an opossum expressed in days. That isn't in the book, either, so I make you a gift of it. The number is 12. That will bring you to the year in which Thomas Jefferson, the former slave owner, died and James Fenimore Cooper published *The Last of the Mohicans,* which wasn't set in this valley but might as well have been.

Divide by the square root of 4.

Subtract 100 times 9.

Add the greatest number of children known to have come from the womb of just 1 woman, and there you are, by gosh.

Just because some of us can read and write and do a little math, that doesn't mean we deserve to conquer the Universe.

THE END

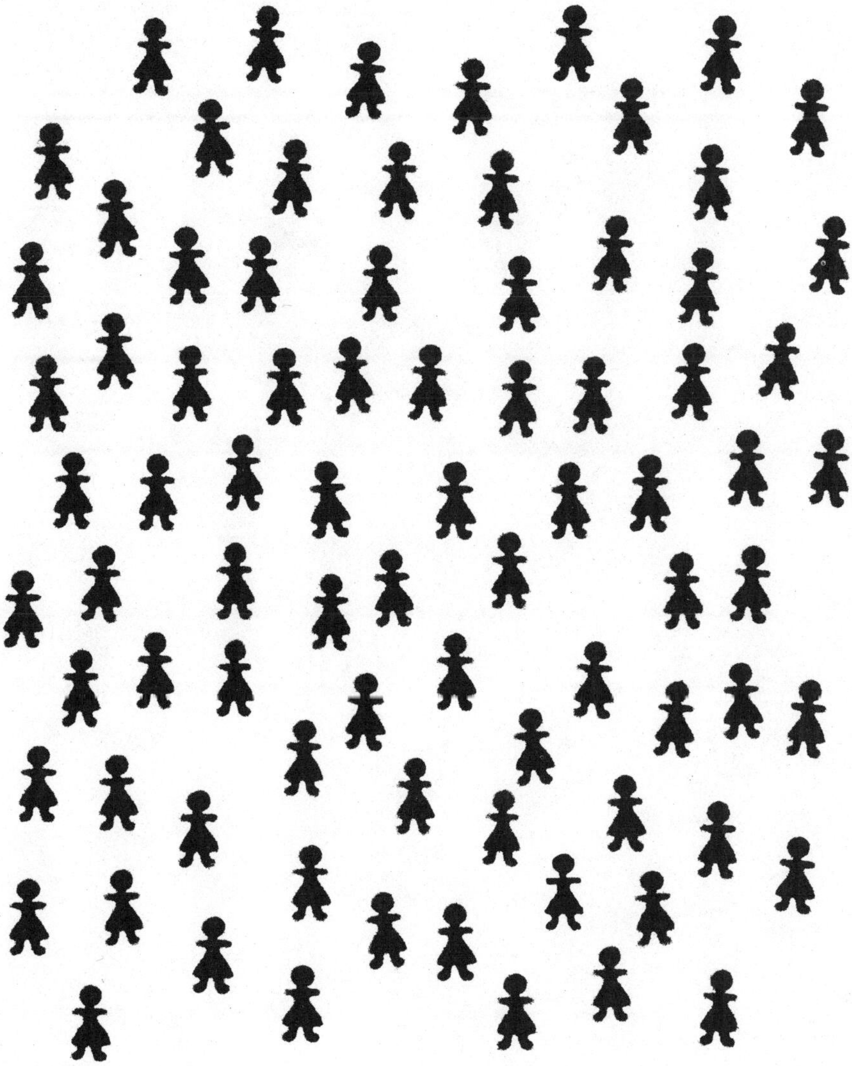